MAN-KZIN WARS XIV

MAN-KZIN WARS XIV

HAL COLEBATCH
◆
JESSICA Q. FOX
◆
MATTHEW JOSEPH HARRINGTON
◆
ALEX HERNANDEZ

CREATED BY
LARRY NIVEN

MAN-KZIN WARS XIV

A Baen Books Original

Baen Publishing Enterprises
P.O. Box 1403
Riverdale, NY 10471
www.baen.com

ISBN: 978-1-4516-3938-4

Cover art by Steve Hickman

First printing, December 2013

Distributed by Simon & Schuster
1230 Avenue of the Americas
New York, NY 10020

Library of Congress Cataloging-in-Publication Data

Man-Kzin wars XIV / edited by Larry Niven ; with Hal Colebatch, Jessica Q.
Fox, Matthew Joseph Harrington, Alex Hernandez.
     pages cm
ISBN 978-1-4516-3938-4 (pbk.)
1. Kzin (Imaginary place)--Fiction. 2. Space warfare--Fiction. I. Niven, Larry
editor of compilation. II. Colebatch, Hal, 1945- III. Title: Man-Kzin wars 14.
IV. Title: Man-Kzin wars fourteen.
 PS648.S3M3758 2014
 813'.0876208--dc23
                              2013033171

Printed in the United States of America

10 9 8 7 6 5 4 3 2 1

❧ CONTENTS ❧

A Man Named Saul
Hal Colebatch and Jessica Q. Fox
1

Heritage
Matthew Joseph Harrington
99

The Marmalade Problem
Hal Colebatch
131

Leftovers
Matthew Joseph Harrington
143

The White Column
Hal Colebatch
167

**Deadly Knowledge:
A Story of the Man-Kzin Wars**
Hal Colebatch
173

Lions on the Beach
Alex Hernandez
195

A MAN NAMED SAUL

by Hal Colebatch and Jessica Q. Fox

❧ A MAN NAMED SAUL ❧

Wunderland, East of the Höhe Kalkstein, 2437 AD

"HEY, JUDGE, there's a kzin outside the stockade!" The man was excited, with some reason. "He's lying down spread out, on his face, like he's already been shot."

The kzin could have jumped the stockade, at least got his claws high enough to fight his way over. It hadn't been built to keep out kzin. The judge had persuaded them to put it up because the lesslocks had become more than just a thieving nuisance, and their numbers had increased in recent years. What had puzzled everyone who had made it was how much bigger it was than seemed necessary; higher, and leaving a wide space between the village and the wall. But the judge had insisted they think for the future, and he was a persuasive man. So they'd gone along with him, as they usually did.

"I'd better come—and you men, don't shoot unless he attacks. Which is very unlikely, I'd say. The submission posture isn't something they take lightly." The old man struggled to his feet. He walked with a stick these days.

The gate was opened cautiously, and a lot of guns were held ready. They were not likely to be as effective as the owners thought, the judge knew. A kzin took a lot of killing, and a homemade musket firing homemade gunpowder wasn't even going to slow one down if he went into attack mode.

"Greetings, Hero," the judge spoke in the Heroes' Tongue, or at least the slaves' patois approximation to it. He was rusty, but it came back.

The kzin raised its head and looked at him. "No Hero, I," he answered bleakly. "I come to beg, human."

"What for, kzin warrior?" the judge asked. This was unprecedented in his experience.

"Not for myself, human," the kzin answered. "Medicine, for my kzinrett and my kits. Sooner would I die than humble myself so. I shame myself beyond measure. But if I do not, my kzinrett and her kits will die. My male kit is a good son, and I have a duty . . ."

The judge wondered. "Stand up, kzin warrior. There is no shame in what you do. It takes courage beyond measure to face down shame beyond measure."

The kzin rose to its feet. Its fur was patchy and matted, but it still looked imposing and dangerous as it looked down at the human. "What must I do, human?" it asked.

"Bring your family here. All of them. We will need to know what medicines we have which might be useful. We have little, but we will share them."

"It will shame me even more that I have to be given them by you," the kzin rumbled. "Better to take them by force, but I know not what to take."

"No, better to trade," the judge told him. The Heroes' Tongue—or at least the closest human approximation of the slave's patois—was coming back to him more easily now. But it was too easy to make an unintentional insult. In the days of the Occupation, any slave who attempted to mangle the Heroes' Tongue would have lost his own tongue and shortly afterward his life for the defilement. Fortunately, the slave's patois was relatively easy to speak and tolerated. "We help you and you help us. That way we both gain."

"Trade?" the kzin asked, mystified by the alien word. "What would you do, enslave me?"

"No, nothing like that. I don't know what you might have for us, but we can worry about that later. It will be a small debt of honor until then. And when you pay it off, we'll be even. And who knows? Maybe we can find something else to trade. There is usually employment for a warrior." There was no word that he knew for *profit* in the Heroes'

Tongue, in fact few words for any ideas about economics at all. Slave economies didn't need them. Teaching catallactics to kzin could be a long job. But the prize, oh yes, the prize!

The kzin was baffled, but not given to patience. "I will go and return with my brood. I will be a day." The huge beast turned and marched off without a word of thanks. There wasn't a word for that, either. Not between Heroes and food.

"What was all that about, Judge?" one of the men asked.

"The kzin wanted medicine for his mate and children," the judge explained. "He'll be bringing them tomorrow, probably in bad shape. I want them in the hospital for a spell." If there had been a dialectitian listening carefully, he might have picked the judge's rustic accent as assumed or at least lately acquired, but he would have had to be good.

"You're gonna let that monster into the stockade?" The man was aghast. Another spoke up: "An' your goin' t' give it our medicine? You're crazy, Judge."

"Crazy like a fox, Ben. Think about it. Suppose we can get some trade going with this one. Maybe others later. They'll have some value to us. That one could sure help take out a whole lot of those damned lesslocks if he figured he owed us something. Would you rather have them fighting for us or against us?"

One of the men scratched his head absently. "I guess if there are ratcats around, we sure don't want them as enemies."

"A good point," said the judge. "However, if anyone uses the term 'ratcat' again, they will regret it. I am not talking political correctness now, I am talking survival."

Another man grumbled. "But, Judge, that damned monster is a natural killer. You're not gonna let it wander around inside the stockade, for Chrissake?"

"For Christ's sake, that's exactly what I'm going to do," the judge said calmly. "What's the best way to totally destroy your enemy?"

They didn't know.

"You turn him into a friend," the judge told them. "It's there in the good book. You need to have a closer look, Hans, Ben."

"That doesn't sound very easy."

"Sorry, I don't recall anyone saying anything about 'easy.'"

The judge had won the argument. He was good at that. So when the next day, the kzin returned, supporting his kzinrett and with a kitten on each shoulder, he was let into the stockade and taken to the hospital, which was a slightly bigger shack than most there. All four looked at their last gasp. The nurse and doctor, just one woman, took one look at them and demanded that they bathe and all be put to bed, which was a bit impractical, because first, no bed was remotely big enough and second, because kzin didn't use them anyway. Also the adults wouldn't fit into any bath. Bathing the kits had been trying, but they, too, were too weak to effectively protest. The adult female was obviously close to dying, and had running sores on bald patches. The judge thought of the hunting technique of the Komodo dragons of Earth, to bite and scratch prey perhaps far larger than itself and then to follow it remorselessly until infection weakened it and brought it down.

When Nurse-Doctor Wendy Cantor had seen the damage, she sent out for the whisky. Partly to drink, but mostly as a disinfectant. There was a lot of whisky around the village. The female winced at the touch of it, and choked and spluttered. The kits howled. The kzin himself affected indifference when he finally got his turn for treatment, simply remarking that he was a Hero when the judge inquired after his feelings. The judge, who had had a lot to do with kzin once, was aware that they expected effective medical treatment to be painful. The judge had had to be summoned to translate the interrogation of Nurse-Doctor Cantor.

"What's wrong with them, Wendy?"

"Infections from the scratches mostly, I think. And poor diet. They only eat meat, don't they? Like cats? If they've been living off the wabbitohs and a few lesslocks, they won't be getting much vitamin D, and if their metabolism is much like ours, they need it. Worth pushing some fish-liver juice into them. Don't have the old pills left, but we have enough fish from the river. If we had some proper antibiotics I could get them healthy in three days, but we don't. The supply from the monastery was small, and we haven't had anyone go there for months, and no way of paying for it except whisky. They've got lots of that. Soon as we get something to pay with and someone to go, they should go with an order."

"I knew the abbott once. He was old and I don't know if he's still alive, but if the present one is anything like the man I knew, they will help us without payment. Or I could give them a few hours' work on their machinery. They've still got a lot of rebuilding to do. The kzin took most of their equipment."

"Would they want gunpowder?"

"They can make better than we can. They've got dogwood trees there—makes the best charcoal. I've heard they are trying to breed Jotok. They'll need ponds for that."

"You know a lot of things, Judge."

"Knowing things was my business."

"Say, Judge, sometimes, when you forget yourself, you don't talk like one of us back-country hicks. I've noticed it before."

"I see . . . have you ever talked about that to the others?"

"We're Wunderlanders, Judge. We're *live* Wunderlanders. We didn't come through the occupation alive by letting our mouths flap. Unless there's good reason we keep our lips closed . . . but our ears open, maybe. But you never told us what you were . . . before . . ."

"No, I never did, did I. Well, I'm a live Wunderlander, too. But just remember this: we are getting ourselves a kzin with a debt of honor to us."

Treating the kzin was at least not going to use much of what precious little resources they had, the judge realized. If it worked, he could easily defend the expense.

It worked. It took two weeks, but it worked. And in that time, someone had noticed the kits were playing with some pretty stones, a couple of chunks of gold, an uncut diamond and two sapphires. The kzin also liked gold as an ornament, and on some planets used it as currency, and, of course, it would have had many uses if they had anything left of a technology. The kzin remarked, as mildly as he was able, that the kits might not like to give the shiny nuggets up.

"Not these; wrestling your kits for them could cause some bad feeling, not to mention loss of body parts. But if you could show us where you got them, it will more than pay for the medicine and the treatment," the judge had explained.

"You want a kit's toys?" the kzin asked in disbelief.

The judge nearly grinned, but stopped himself in time.

"That's the way it goes, kzin warrior. What means little to you means a lot to us and the other way around. That's why trade is a good idea. We both gain. Dumb people think it's zero-sum, but it ain't. Not unless the government gets involved, and here, I'm the government, *and* the law, and a lot of other things besides, and I come pretty cheap, I can tell you."

"I can get you as much as a man can carry," with a shrugging motion, the kzin conveyed the impression that it did not believe a man's carrying abilities were great, which, compared to its own, was true enough. "If you come with me, I will show you. Which sort do you want?"

"We can use all of them, they'll all fetch something. But the gold is the best bet. That we can trade easily."

The kzin was bewildered. "You are mad creatures, human," he said. "What do you do with them?" Then, more thoughtfully, as though answering his own question. "These things are for Nobles' palaces."

"You wouldn't believe me if I told you," the judge told him. "But rich people will pay a lot for pretty stones. The manretti like to wear them, and the men buy them to impress the manretti."

"Something to do with your mating rituals?" the kzin hazarded.

"Yep, I guess so," the judge admitted. "There's other stuff too, but when you come down to the jewelry uses, I guess it amounts to getting a gal by giving her something other gals would like to have too. Pretty dumb when you think about it. But people are."

"Then we go tomorrow, Judge human," the kzin said. He had picked up the *Judge* part by hearing what other people called him. It was not clear if it was a name or a rank. But these human beings gave everyone a name, as if it meant nothing. Truly they were astonishing. Nothing to look at, but they had defeated the might of all the kzin on *Ka'ashi*. Not merely in space. The kzin remembered the last days of infantry combat on the ground.

"You can leave the kzinrett and the kits here," the judge said casually.

"But our base is in the cave," the kzin objected. "I must take them back. And my mate cannot care for the kits yet on her own."

"And in the cave you will run into trouble with the lesslocks all over again. It was partly those scratches that made you all sick. Why not live in the village? There's a house here that's empty. Too small for you, but we'll show you how to build it up. Our manrett is a skilled healer. Much experienced."

"I sometimes forget your manretti are sentient," the kzin admitted, "though I should not. My first sergeant warned me: 'Those manretti can be trouble,' he said. Next day one fetched the meat for the sergeant's mess. There was a bomb inside it. But indeed the lesslock vermin are getting worse. They get worse every year. We have moved to higher caves, but they find a way in. They appear to have an ability to learn from experience. But if I come here, I will have an honor debt to you. The home you speak of. And I do not know if there is much prey around."

"Any time you want to pay us, a few of those pretty stones, particularly the ones with soft yellow metal in, that will get you plenty. And there are wild deerylopes and boaries in the woods, as well as a herd of gagrumpers. Kill more than you can eat, bring some back and trade them for anything you might want."

It sounded very, very strange to the kzin. This trade idea was unnatural, surely. There was some trade between Heroes, mainly on long-settled planets, but between Heroes and slaves it was a different matter. Heroes generally took what they wanted, though they sometimes gave token payments to pets or as rewards to old retainers. He had known a trooper, long dead, whose sire on Kzin had sold medicines that the healers prescribed, but he had been honorably crippled. Things were different on Kzin. There were even organizations in which an economic historian might have seen the rudiments of guilds. But these still had as long a way to go.

"You mean I give you this gold, you give it to a man far away, he gives it to a man even farther away who makes it into a manrett toy, and in exchange gives some medicine to the man not so far away, who gives it to you. Why does everbody do this?"

"It's a little more complicated than that; you see, we have the stuff called *money,* which . . . Oh, never mind, you'll pick up the idea gradually. And we need a name for you."

"I have no Name," the Kzin said, with a doleful stare at the ground.

"Then I shall give you one. From now on, you are *Ruat,*" the judge told him calmly.

The kzin pondered. Truly this Judge human must be important if he could give names. And was a human-conferred name legitimate? It might as well be.

"Rrhouarrghrrt," he pronounced it doubtfully.

"Yep. That'll do fine. And I know you aren't much inclined to socialize with other kzin, but if you know of others in the same condition as you were, bring them in. We'll take care of them until they are healthy, and if they want to stay with us, well, we'll just have to learn to get along."

The judge and Ruat were making a patrol of the village just inside the perimeter the next evening. The judge felt a little tense. Something in the air, but not just that. Andersen, the community's chief woodworker and bowyer, had gone searching for some exotic red wood and had been away a long time. The judge had ideas that, now that the hyperdrive was making communication with Sol System a matter of weeks, most of them spent in accelerating and decelerating, rather than a one-way voyage of decades, a market might exist there for some of the more exotic Wunderland timber products, and Anderson had been building up a stock of the beautiful red and orange woods. There might even be a market among the kzin, many of whom were fanatical chess-players and prized ornate sets. The judge knew of Andersen's enthusiasm for his craft. Still, he should not have lingered out until this hour. Indeed, it was unlike him.

"The kits are growing stronger," Ruat said. "I shall have to make them new quarters. Male and female cannot grow up together."

The judge realized he had a point. Female kzinti, as far as he knew, were of very low intelligence. Why this was so, nobody knew, but there were theories that it was the result of some intervention long ago at the dawn of kzinti science. During the years of Occupation the human population of the Alpha Centauri System had had more pressing matters to think about.

"I suppose," Ruat went on, "I will have to be thinking of a nursery-name at least for my son."

"Think carefully," said the judge. "It may be that he will grow into a major historical figure."

"How so?"

"Who is to stop him?"

The lesslocks attacked with howls and screams. They carried bushes, which they used as scaling ladders. The human watch had grown slack after months of quiet. Had they been silent, a good number might have scrambled over the wall unobserved.

The judge had a double-barreled percussion-cap pistol. Men and women, wielding a variety of weapons, poured from the huts. The rush of the lesslocks overwhelmed the first humans. The judge realized with horror that they were outnumbered several times over. The armory contained most of their precious supply of percussion caps and most of what few modern combat weapons they possessed. Their hunting muskets had limited stopping power against the heavily-muscled anthropoids.

He fired his pistol as Ruat roared the kzin battle-cry, "I lead my Heroes!" the blade of his *wtsai* flashing, and tore into the thickest press of the lesslocks. The lesslocks clumped round him, allowing the humans to get to the armory. The human shots were telling now. It had been wearisome and time-consuming to beat out percussion caps from sheets of copper, but it paid off now in rapidity of fire and reliability. Someone threw a grenade. It was a homemade contraption, but the blast was effective in scattering the creatures. For a moment, before they closed in again, the judge saw Ruat standing in a heap of bodies, his roars drowning out the lesslocks' screams.

There was the sizzling roar of a modern strakkaker, its blizzard of glass-and-Teflon needles turning lesslocks into instant anatomist's diagrams. (The judge thought again with the detached part of his mind how human their structure was. Perhaps one day someone would find out why. Convergent evolution, he guessed. Maybe their remote ancestors had lived in trees.)

The lesslocks were armed with stones and weighted sticks. Whatever they had expected, it had not been that the defense would be led by a kzin. Ruat hurled himself into the thickest press of them. If they had anything like a chief or leader, he would be there. Between the flashes of the muskets, the judge had an impression of body parts flying. Like a streak of orange lightning, Ruat's male kit shot into the fray. He was already the size of a leopard. Whether he had been taught or whether his warrior instincts were enough, he was effective. He swiped and snapped at the throat of one of the lesslocks, swiped at a second, and was onto another before the first hit the ground. The second blundered past, howling in agony, entrails spilling. There was a third the kit had swiped, staggering blindly, a tier of white ribs showing.

The lesslocks were retreating. Outnumbered though they were, the humans were now keeping up a disciplined fire, one file loading as the other covered it. Fresh ammunition supplies were being brought up and passed out methodically.

The lesslocks found getting out of the stockade considerably more difficult than getting into it. Not many survived to get over the wall and back to the tree cover.

Ruat was bleeding from numerous new bites and scratches, but his eyes were shining. He walked back to the humans with the kit on his shoulder and a positive swagger in his step. He contemplated his ear-ring, imagining how it would look adorned with many new ears. There would be an ear-ring for his son too. The judge would have slapped him on the back, but remembered in time never to touch an adult male kzin without permission. Still, there were plenty of cheers for him. It was hard to estimate exactly how many lesslocks had died, but it seemed unlikely that they would attack again for a long time. Wendy Cantor produced some fish-flavored ice cream that she had been secretly preparing as a treat for the kits. They purred and preened against her, already knowing enough not to press so hard as to knock her down.

"I was an infantry trooper once," Ruat said. "I never thought it would fall to my lot to be the one to give our battle-cry—and lead."

"You are truly a Hero now," the judge told him. "But I think you will have the chance to lead us in battle again. That was a coordinated attack. I do not think it will be the last . . . We must heighten the wall, and make sure there are always sentries posted. The degree of organization behind the attack concerns me."

"Thinking of those days," said Ruat, "I remember the Surrender Day."

"So do I," said the judge. There was suddenly something very bleak in his voice. Then he laughed to cover it, but the laugh sounded forced and artificial to him.

"Our officer gave me a kzinrett from his own harem and told me I was not permitted to die nobly in battle. He said I was to make for the forest and do what I could to keep our species alive. You say you remember those days? A bad time."

"My Hero, you do not know how bad. I was once Captain Jorg von Thoma, of the Patriarch's human auxiliary police," said the judge. "A kzin saved my life at the risk of his own, that day. That secret puts my life in your hands."

"Why do you tell me this, then?"

"To seal the trust between us."

A month later there were four kzin families living in the village and Wendy had treated them successfully with antibiotics, which they now had in large quantities for both human and kzin. One single kzin had come in, had been made healthy as far as his body was concerned, and had subsequently killed a man who had laughed at him. Ruat had broken his neck with contemptuous ease: Darwin was working on the kzinti, too. The judge approved Ruat for maintaining Law and Order, and gave him a job as a policeman—the first the village had ever had. Some of the humans had grumbled at the appointment, but a larger number felt safer. Previously there hadn't been much by way of crime beyond the odd drunken fight, but afterwards there wasn't any.

Wunderland, Southern Continent, 2438 AD

"HEY, WHAT'S THAT?" Sarah pointed across the waves, high and roiling in Wunderland's light gravity.

Greg focused his binoculars on the object. "Looks a bit like a monster fin, doesn't it?"

Sarah shivered in her parka. The Southland was always cold, and with Wunderland between A and B, the biggest components of the Alpha Centauri triple star system, the planet was as far from A as it ever got. Winter on Wunderland was determined by the orbit, because the planetary axis inclination was small. And B sucked the aphelion out and made it precess. Coming here for a honeymoon was even more eccentric than the orbit.

"It's rolling a bit. Hold on, it's coming more upright. There's some letters on it," Greg turned his head sideways to read them. "It says 'UN' something . . . You look at it, and tell me I haven't lost my marbles."

Sarah took the binoculars and adjusted them. "I think you're right. Can we get closer?"

"If it's what it might be, we need to take the flyer over it. We can record it for the television studios. Hey, we might get enough to pay for the whole honeymoon! Come on, let's get back inside. It will be warmer, too."

They trudged through flurries of snow back to the flyer. Half an hour later, Sarah had gone back to T-shirt and shorts and was poised with the videocamera ready as Greg took them out to sea.

"Low tide, or we wouldn't have seen anything, but look, there's a lot of it underwater. It's a spaceship, or more than half of one. And it doesn't look like one of ours."

Wunderland ships had evolved their own design architecture around enclosed globes and spaces. The kzin favored wedge-and-ovoid shapes. Sol ships, however, came in many varieties.

"Must be one of the blockade runners from Sol System, one that nearly made it. Must have been here for at least since the end of the war."

"Why haven't the satellites picked it up, then?"

"Not many pass 'round here. The stationary ones look north, and the others look up for kzin warships, not down. Besides, a lot of the kzin satellites as well as nearly all the pre-war ones were destroyed."

Southland had never had too much interest to anybody. No minerals worth extracting, a lousy climate for crops or humans. There had been some kzin bases, of course, but they got a pasting at Liberation. Greg and Sarah had chosen it as an unusual honeymoon spot because it was practically pristine. Also, it lacked the dangerous life-forms of little Southland—or so they hoped. So far, they had seen nothing that a modern vehicle couldn't easily keep out.

Wunderland's biology was by no means fully classified yet. Now that the war was over, on the surface of the planet at least, and scientific research was resuming, professional and amateur scientists and collectors could still hope for major discoveries. Meanwhile, military craft and dedicated satellites guarded the skies, ceaselessly alert for anything that might be the radiation signature of a kzin ship that was unaware of, or disregarded, the still fragile cease-fire on the planet.

"Now, try not to interrupt, I'm starting to record." Sarah pointed the camera down as Greg obligingly tilted the flyer.

"This is Sarah and Greg Rankin reporting from just half a kilometer into the not particularly great Southern Ocean, off Southland, and less than a hundred meters up from the water," Sarah narrated.

"We're looking down at what appears to be a spaceship, sunken and hard to detect. It has quite a lot of marine growth on it. We saw the fin by chance, and came for a closer look. You can see that it has a UNSN insignia, so it must have been here for a couple of years. We think it's the wreck of a blockade runner." She looked straight at the camera and blinked.

"It's a very sad discovery to make on our honeymoon. Brave men and women died in that ship, and to no good purpose. They got so close, but crashed when they'd nearly made it. It would be worth finding out what it was that stopped them from bringing arms and other supplies to us, and perhaps to commemorate their efforts. Bravery should be recognized." No point in speculating too much. Every spacer knew the phrase "*The many deaths of space.*" She went on: "Maybe the kzin shot them down. But we don't know what brought them to Southland."

She turned off the recorder. "I'll send a copy to my parents to show them that coming here wasn't as stupid as they reckoned, and another to the government. And I'll ask the television news channels if they are willing to pay for the video before I send anything. Once they've got it, goodbye to our getting another cent for it. But if we can build up a bidding war, we might just pay for the rent on the flier at least."

"Go for it, girl. Who is that current affairs guy? Stan Adler? Try him, and tell your parents not to part with their copy. And instead of the government, try the Guthlacs. If it goes straight into the bureaucracy, nobody will ever hear anything more about it."

"You mean you don't trust the government?" She pronounced it "gummint" as a term of mockery. "But all those warm, loving politicians and bureaucrats exist only to look after us and protect us." Sarah grinned at him. Greg would either explode or start a rant. Either would be entertaining, and she had an instant cure for both. All she had to do was lean forward seductively and say: "Ooh, Greg, you are *so* clever," and he'd start laughing.

"There is one thing, though," she said before he could get started. "It was generally kzin tactical doctrine, after they got the measure of us in the early days, to travel in the largest possible fleets. This ship doesn't look as it it was hit by a fleet."

"Well, that's very interesting, but what has it got to do with me?"

Vaemar asked the two humans. Their breathing indicated they were nervous, but confronting a predator with more than twice their combined bodyweight would tend to have that effect. Vaemar was used to it, and went out of his way to underplay the fangs. Yawning was definitely out, and watching a videotape of a downed spacecraft isn't particularly stimulating, so concentration was needed.

"Well, we were all set to sell the video to a news channel. We'd agreed to a huge price, and everything looked grand. But then Sarah thought of something."

Sarah explained: "You see, I figured it was probably shot down by a kzin warcraft. I mean it's the easy explanation, isn't it? And that might stir up old resentments. If you think it would cause interspecies trouble, we wouldn't go through with it. I mean, we could do with the money, but money isn't everything, and it was just luck that we saw the fin. So it's not as if we did anything to earn any. We don't really deserve it." She would have smiled, but knew better. The circumstances in which humans showed their teeth to kzin were very restricted.

Vaemar looked at her thoughtfully. A sense of honor in a female human. He'd known it before, of course; he had several manrett friends, but it was not altogether common, and rather refreshing. "But why me?"

"We talked to Abbot Boniface first, and he said you were the one to see. He said you are effectively leader of the kzin, and it was time you got into politics," Sarah told him innocently.

Vaemar sighed, a kzin noise like treacle going down a drain. He was already getting into politics, and he hated every single politic he'd gotten into. But he liked these people. The male was ginger-haired and had orange spots all over his face. Freckles, he thought they were called. The female was a nice chocolate color, which looked much healthier, and she had crinkly black hair, which looked like spun wire. When he moved, the sun flashed on the metal of his ear-ring. After the adventure in the caves with Rarrgh, he had the beginnings of a respectable collection of human and kzinti ears hanging from his belt. The kzin—yes, call it *"surrender"*—on Wunderland, while the war went on in space, had been inevitable, and he was overwhelmingly glad of it for many reasons, but it did make life complex sometimes.

"It might, of course, have been downed by a kzin warcraft," his deep voice half-purred. "But a spacecraft is unlikely. Most of the ships from Earth that tried to run the blockade were detected and intercepted when still in deep space. Getting this close would have been difficult. An approach well out of the ecliptic might have been tried, but there were detecting satellites out there, too. If it had got as far as low orbit of *Ka'ashi*—I beg your pardon, of *Wunderland*—there would be little defense except aircraft and a few satellites. If it had run into the fleet or one of its prides, there would have been nothing left of it.

"I shall have records searched to see if there is any mention of the kzin shooting down a craft that got very close. They may not exist— much was destroyed at . . ." He couldn't quite bring himself to say either "*Liberation*" or "*surrender*" easily, and the humans noticed it—"at the signing of the truce with Man, but it would be interesting to see if there is anything left. Hroth, who was staff-officer, is writing an account."

Not a pleasant job for a kzin to undertake, thought Sarah. *Still, it may be an interesting document. And humans will enjoy buying it to read heroic things about themselves.*

The young kzin looked at them both. "But that is of historical interest. The question is, should you suppress your finding in the interests of kzin-man relations. The answer is 'no,' you must not. Sell it to your television station. Only complete honesty and openness between our species can help us forge the trust we both need. This is history, it is our task to make the future, we must not let the past dictate to us. And now, please join my mate and me for afternoon tea. I hope you like cucumber and tomato sandwiches, Karan is rather proud of her sandwiches. She has even tried eating some of them . . . I must confess my own vices include a taste for cake. My Sire took me when I was a very young kit to his secretary's children's party. She gave me cake and a large ball of fiber to leap upon. I sometimes wondered where she got that idea—until I found out." His ears lifted in the kzin equivalent of a smile.

"I trust you were not offended," Sarah said nervously.

"On the contrary, I have had some made for my own kits."

Senator von Hohenheim was busy. He was always busy. So when the little sharp-faced man knocked on his door and came in without being asked, the senator switched on a scowl that would have astonished his electorate. The senator was a bulky man, and on television could have passed for a bald Santa Claus out of uniform, but just at the moment his glare would have smashed mirrors and broken camera lenses. "What the hell do you want, you grubby little runt? I'm busy. I've got a committee to chair in ten minutes."

Alois Grün was apologetic. "I'm sorry, Senator, but it's important. The evening news will have some footage of a spaceship from Earth that crashed into the Great Southern Ocean some years ago. Nobody knew of it until now, apparently. Well, hardly anybody." He looked meaningfully at the senator.

"Why should it be of the slightest interest to me, for G—Oh." There was a pause which, if not in fact pregnant, had definitely been going into overdrive on the chocolate biscuits.

"Oh. You don't think . . ."

"Well, Senator," Grün was still deferential, but there was more than a faint hint of something a great deal less gentle. Skinny little Smeagol of a creature the man might be, but, Senator von Höhenheim reminded himself, he had survived the Occupation, where perhaps eight Wunderlanders in every ten had not. Darwin had operated ruthlessly among the humans of Wunderland for more than sixty years. There was cunning there, and even more importantly, ruthless determination. "It is hard to explain otherwise, is it not? I mean, your orders were obeyed instantly. I was there to see the missiles launched in accordance with your instruction. Obviously I didn't see the actual strike, but there must have been one, must there not? And since the ship was never found, well, this might well be it, don't you think?"

The senator looked at him and considered. "Is it too late to damp the story down? Can we prevent it going out?"

"I have read Earth history. I was a schoolteacher once, a long time ago, before the invasion." A not-so-subtle reminder that he had been one of the fortunate or cunning few who had retained access to geriatric drugs. And that he knew a lot. "The Marconi scandals, Watergate, the climate change falsifications. In each case the cover-up was worse than the original wrongdoing. To cover up now would surely cause an even bigger storm than the video itself. It would prove there was something to hide. I cannot recommend that approach, Senator." The little man rubbed his hands together. It didn't show in any *too* obvious way, but he was enjoying this, just as he enjoyed lecturing the senator on subjects he would know nothing about.

"Of course, it goes without saying that should an unfortunate accident befall me, I have left a record that would be published. Killing my attorney, banker, or other obvious trustees would be an inadequate means of suppression. It is not in an obvious or vulnerable place, and indeed, there may be more than one copy."

The senator looked at him narrowly. "Well, it surely is inconsequential. After all, it's been eighteen years. The thing has been in the sea and must surely be corroded. There will be nothing to show what brought it down. And one hole must look much like another. Everyone will take it for granted that it was some kzin attack that destroyed it."

"Forensic science is very advanced, Senator. And some modern materials resist corrosion. Spaceship hull alloys, for instance."

"Most of the police stations and laboratories were destroyed at Liberation."

"Only 'most.' Some records survived. As did a few of the police—the lucky ones. You know how collaborators were dealt with . . . Except for those smart enough to keep a foot in each camp," Grün said. "The Kzin got most of those early, with telepath sweeps." He went on: "Meanwhile, ARM has been bringing in new up-to-date detection equipment. To say nothing of the rumors we hear that they've got kzin telepaths working for them on interrogations. Kzin torturers, too, some say."

"I refuse to believe that, even of ARM. If the population found out . . ."

"I could not be at all sure that there won't be some that tell the truth," Grün said. "And if that got out, well, you would be in serious trouble, Senator. Hanged as a traitor, very likely. You've seen plenty of hangings, and worse. You know what they entail. Certainly the story of how you only pretended to join the collaborators to spy on them would be . . . difficult . . . to sustain. At best, it would be the end of your career. Even if you escaped the noose or the axe, I doubt you would find eking out a living as a laborer in some back-block farm very appealing. And don't forget there are still plenty of people who wouldn't let an acquittal by a court inhibit them."

"But there cannot be many of the KzinDiener left alive. Who could tell that the order was mine?"

"Well, I was there, of course, and I saw you give the order. Oh, not that *I* would say anything, *of course*." The little man rubbed his hands together again. "But there might well have been other survivors. The abbot at Circle Bay Monastery tried to protect von Thoma, and maybe ... some others. Naturally, they would not be anxious to draw attention to themselves at this stage of things, but they might seek amnesty in exchange for testifying against you. I don't say this is inevitable or even likely, but are you prepared to completely rule it out?" He looked with his head tilted to the side, at his master. His master pursed his lips and looked back.

Stan Adler was in fine form. His current affairs program always beat the competition in the audience ratings. He spoke into the camera with his trademark lopsided half-grin. "Tonight, the Appropriations Committee Chairman, Senator von Höhenheim, has again objected to funding a proper investigation of the downing of the spaceship *Valiant* in the Southern Ocean. Our news investigators, following the initial sighting of the wreck by honeymooners Sarah and Greg Rankin in the Southern Ocean," the screen cut to a wedding picture of the happy pair, "have gone diving in difficult storm-tossed waters to find the wreck and have positively identified her.

"It is known that she was bringing military and medical supplies, which might have saved many lives had they arrived and been transferred to the Resistance. Perhaps even shortened the final phase. Tell me, Senator, why exactly do you object to a properly equipped government investigation of this tragedy?"

The camera facing the senator showed a green light, and he looked into its lens rather than at his interrogator. "Well, Stan, you know that I am only the chairman, I don't make these decisions all on my own." The senator was genial.

Stan the Man smiled in the way that, his admirers had suggested, would make a kzin warrior nervous. He wore a casual shirt with his monogram, a small stylized eagle in black, over the pocket holding his phone. Cell phones had been back in the city for less than six months, so it was something of a status symbol.

"But I hear that your voice was the strongest in opposition to it. In fact, it was taken for granted that it would go through unopposed. It was only at the last moment that your supporters came out against it. And you got the casting vote. That was the first passage. And things aren't very different now you have it back from the lower house."

"You have to understand, Stan, that we cannot spend the taxpayers' money just the way we would like. It is a matter of priorities. Of course we would all like to know exactly what happened, and someday we shall. But it is hardly urgent. The wreck has been there for many years, a few more will hardly make much difference."

"But you funded the building of a new Arts Complex costing over ten million dollars. Many people could give you long lists of things they would say were needed more urgently. From orphanages to prostheses to pharmaceutical factories. Not many on Wunderland are interested in arts today. Poetry and painting were not really survival skills. Dancing a ballet for a hungry kzin would be like playing a lure for a hungry fish. Not to mention rebuilding our space navy instead of relying on Sol forces. And what about the very controversial plan to drain much of Grossgeister Swamp at a much bigger cost? Even if one accepts that both of these are worthwhile projects, which I don't, they are hardly more urgent. The longer the wreck is underwater, the less information we shall be able to recover. I can hardly take it that that is what you want, Senator?"

"On the subject of the Arts Complex . . ." von Höhenheim began.

"Perhaps it would be better if we remained with the subject at hand at the moment, Senator. The question was, why do you want to delay getting any information about what downed the *Valiant*?"

"I want nothing of the kind. After all, what mystery is there? We are certain to discover that a kzin warship crippled it somewhere in space, as happened to countless others," said von Höhenheim.

"Not according to the kzin leader, Vaemar, who is in the process of getting a couple of doctoral degrees in mathematics and history, and who had a look at the kzin records."

"A kzin!" The senator's scorn was virtually palpable.

"A kzin, may I remind you, Senator, who has proved his loyalty to the ideal of kzin-human cooperation on more than one occasion. You will recall that it is only a few years since he saved an entire expedition into Grossgeister Swamp, *and* was instrumental in obtaining our first live specimens of Jotok. Before that, he helped thwart a plan by former collaborators to kidnap him and use him against humanity. ARM, which is not renowned for being over-trustful, has allowed him to accept a commission in the Reserve Officer Training Corps at Munchen University. He works with Nils and Leonie Rykermann, not only two of the most heroic leaders of the Resistance, but also two of the most respected leaders on Wunderland today. He is a friend of Dimity Carmody."

"Quite a paragon of felinoid virtue, in fact!" *The sneer would play well with a big part of the audience*, the senator thought. "Perhaps you'd like to remind your audience of his family connections, also! And the humans his sire sent to the public hunts!"

Stan the Man's body language projected confidence and relaxation. It was a tool of his trade that he he'd worked on for a long time, and modern fabrics dealt with the sweat. "Yes, it is true that Chuut-Riit was his sire. Personally, I don't think that that should be held against him in this context. Quite the reverse, if anything: the values of the high kzin nobility may differ from ours in many ways, but their sense of honor is almost physically real. Unless there is a very strong reason for supposing otherwise, I think it likely that he is telling the truth."

"High nobility . . . Assuming what you say is true, the kzin still fighting us in space—and many of those who have grudgingly accepted a peace with us here on Wunderland—regard him as a quisling."

"Sometimes it takes courage to accept the name of quisling. Vaemar has mixed with humans—on equal terms—since he was a kit . . . But tell me, Senator, why are you so hostile to Vaemar-Ritt?"

"Apart from the fact that the idea of quislings—of any species— disgusts me, I am hostile to all kzin—I suppose it is no longer politically correct to call them *ratcats*. It you want a reason, doesn't my record in the Resistance speak for itself? Of my guerrilla group, only I and one other survived to see the Liberation. I am a lawmaker and a law-abiding citizen, but I don't mind telling you and the people of Wunderland that I have some sympathy for the exterminationist position. Wipe them out while we still have a chance! Before they get the hyperdrive!" *Careful*, he thought, *don't go overboard here*. "Or so many say." He caught himself up quickly. "I'm not saying that is exactly how I feel, I appreciate the necessity for peace, but I do understand how the exterminationists feel."

Stan fired back. "But if we attack the surrendered kzinti here, the war in space will have no chance of a settlement. Surely it would mean a fight to the finish, with one race or the other annihilated—and they might very well be the ones doing the annhilating. The Kzin Empire is big. We don't even know its full size. There is no guarantee we would win, hyperdrive or not."

"Exactly, Stan. That is why I have used my influence, when I can, to try to restrain the exterminationists as a movement. We must have peace with the kzin of this planet at least, but let it be a firm and watchful peace. Anyway," he continued, "although I am opposed to this expedition, if I should be overridden by the lower house, I intend to accompany it personally. I will pay my own expenses, and will be able to ensure that there is no more wastage than necessary."

"Don't you have to be invited?" Stan asked quizzically.

"Professor Rykerman and his wife will no doubt be organizing it, and they are old colleagues of mine, both politically since Liberation, albeit on opposing sides, and before that in the Resistance, though we were in different groups. I shall have no trouble arranging it with them."

Senator von Höhenheim was thinking he had diverted the interview satisfactorily, when Stan the Man returned to the attack like a barracuda.

"And now, we come back to Vaemar-Riit. I talked to him earlier today, and here is what he said."

Stan the Man turned to a screen, which took up most of a wall, and still showed Vaemar at reduced size. The young kzin was standing in the garden of his palace, and Stan, seen from the back, held up a microphone.

"Lord Vaemar, I gather you have seen the video we showed last week of the wreck of the *Valiant*?"

"Yes, I saw it nearly two weeks ago." The kzin was a long way from the microphone, but his voice was unmistakably clear.

"How come you saw it before we broadcast it?" Stan appeared miffed.

"The two humans who took it came to see me and showed it to me."

"Why did they show it to you?"

To those who knew how to tell, Vaemar looked slightly uncomfortable. "They wanted to know if I thought it should be made public out of fear that it might damage man-kzin relations."

"And what did you say?" Stan asked.

"I told them that complete openness between us is the only basis for the trust both species need if we are to live together on this world,"

Vaemar told him reluctantly. *It was true enough,* he told himself, *but it sounded too good and virtuous.* Kzin didn't like feeling virtuous. It tended to go with self-deception, a very bad habit for a warrior.

"So, you told them to go ahead and give it to the media?" Stan asked.

"I take it that they would want to sell it to the highest bidder, not give it," Vaemar explained. Stan changed the subject hurriedly.

"It was obviously important for us to know about this tragedy, and the kids deserved some sort of reward for their enterprise. And did you think it was likely that the *Valiant* was shot down by a kzin warship?"

"It was the simplest explanation, of course, but it was a little puzzling that it had got so close. Most of the Earth ships trying to run the blockade were detected way out in space. There were few kzin resources so close to the planet beyond aircraft and satellite defense. But I now know that it was not a kzin satellite or aircraft. I have had the surviving records checked, and they show no sign of any strike from space defenses at a spacecraft at that time."

"Then what could it have been that brought it down?"

Vaemar looked thoughtful. "The most likely explanation is that it was wounded but not destroyed out in space. Since we do not know exactly when the *Valiant* crashed, we cannot say with confidence that this did not happen. A kzin commander might have thought he had destroyed a vessel that he had only injured. However, that particular error seems to have been more common in human than in kzin record-keeping. But there were not many blockade runners at around that time. A close examination of the ship and its log would go some way to resolving the matter. There would be records of when it left Sol System, but they would only give an estimated time of arrival. It might have slowed or been diverted for some reason.

"There were countless minor skirmishes in space of which no records were kept. One of my earliest memories is of my Honored Sire's rage when the *Man's Bone-Shredder* disappeared. There were many such. Our capital ships travelled in squadrons—'prides'—as we called them, or fleets, but there were a variety of smaller ships travelling alone on innumerable tasks. Perhaps one met the *Valiant,* though I think that is unlikely."

"Why, sir?"

"Space is too big to make chance encounters likely. Especially with modern detection technology."

"Indeed. Yet they have happened. Especially near planets. And what other possibilities are there?"

"There is always the possibility of a freak accident. Even a meteor impact, for instance. Although that would seem most improbable given modern meteor-defenses. But the Wunderland System is cluttered with junk, of course. And again, an examination of the wreck might provide evidence on this point."

"You are a qualified space pilot. Is there any other explanation that you can think of?"

Vaemar thought hard, but he couldn't see any way to avoid this.

"There is the possibility that the KzinDiener fired missiles at it. There was a group of very enthusiastic collaborators who had some weaponry. They were not under very strict control; they had been passed as loyal by telepaths. Eventually their armaments would have had to be replaced, and the kzin commander would have found out that missiles had been launched. The missiles would have been numbered, of course, but if this happened just before the truce, then it might have been overlooked. It would not have had a high priority by then."

"You mean it might have been attacked by human beings working for the kzin?" Stan sounded aghast at the thought. Today more or less the entire human population claimed to have been in the Resistance at one level or another. Known collaborators, at least the prominent ones, were either dead or hunted outlaws. Officially there was a general amnesty and reconciliation, but a number of people had commited suicide in some very strange ways, sometimes stabbing themselves in the back on dark nights, or shooting themselves in the head several times. Stan, who had been a genuine member of the Resistance, although not at any high level, had congratulated (on prime time television) the corpses who had recognized the error of their ways and atoned for their treachery to humanity with such remarkable dedication and persistence. Sniffing out collaborators and naming them was good television. Unlike kzin, most human beings enjoy feeling virtuous.

"It is not something I can rule out," Vaemar told him politely. Although he felt more comfortable with humans than many kzin did, he did not enjoy television interviews. However, some kzin was going to have to do it, and anybody else might make an even worse mess of it than he would. Besides, actually answering the questions, and doing so truthfully, seemed to cause the interviewers such consternation and surprise that it had its entertaining side. Perhaps the custom would spread to human 'politicians.' There were some kzin on Wunderland who would lose no opportunity in their considerable repertoire of psychological tricks to discomfort humans. Vaemar, who genuinely desired peace between the two species and got on well with his human friends, was not like that, but even he found it impossible to pass up the temptation to tweak the monkeys' tails at times.

"Thank you, Lord Vaemar, I'm very grateful for the kzin perspective." Stan had finished. He had cut the bit where Vaemar had explained that he wasn't a Lord exactly, and that as far as kzin were concerned, they weren't so extensively equipped with herd genes as human beings, so there would always be in any group of kzin at least as many opinions as there were kzinti. Sometimes more than twice as many.

The screen blanked out and Stan turned back to the Senator who was projecting a slightly bored indifference. Over the years von Höhenheim had worked as hard on his mannerisms as Stan had on his.

"Comments, Senator?"

"I don't see anything much there. You would expect the kzin to try to shift the blame onto humans. Oh, he was subtle, I'll give Vaemar that. He didn't offer it as his first guess, it was his third, but he left the inference there for your viewers."

"Crap, Senator. I had to drag it out of him. And if he'd wanted to exonerate the kzin, why did he tell the kids to publish and be damned?"

"Because he knew it would get out sooner or later. Better to try to establish that he was in favor of it being made public than that he had tried to suppress it." The senator looked smug.

"Then why were *you* trying to suppress it? Not the video, that's out there, but the examination to see what *did* down the *Valiant*?"

The senator sighed. "Nothing of the kind. I have said that we need to know the truth and we will find it. I give you my word on that. I think, though, that this is ancient history. The government is always anxious to pursue the truth. But what difference could it make these days? The old bad days of private revenge are over anyway, even if, to take the most implausible case, human deviants were involved. And I simply cannot believe that many human beings would have aided the enemy in this fashion. Oh, some did, no doubt, some malcontents, traitors. And any who still live must surely be ashamed of themselves." Von Höhenheim put on his stateman's face.

"The utter shame and disgrace of collaborating is now obvious to everyone. I am sure your viewers feel that as strongly as you or I do," he went on smoothly. "But we need to move on, to strive for reconciliation with all. Some may well have collaborated to protect their families. Some may have believed, in a twisted way, that they were doing humanity a service—that they or their children might eventually rise to positions of authority or influence within the Patriarchy."

"But they would have seen what happened to the Jotok—a once proud and civilized species, reduced to the kzins' slaves and food animals," Stan objected.

"I did not say that I agreed with such an attitude, or that it was plausible, only that it may have existed. We are reconciled with our *quondam* conquerors, as you have shown by interviewing a kzin tonight. We have forgiven them. We are striving to extend the hand of friendship even to these ferocious aliens. And we should extend it also to those lost souls who strayed under the occupation and gave aid to the enemy."

"It's not the hand of friendship I'll be extending if I find a human traitor who shot down a human ship to cozy up to the kzin rulers," Stan told him. "It would be a quite different hand, believe me. That wasn't just shameful or disgraceful, though it was that too. Not exactly on the order of some wretch in the *Ordungspolitzei* issuing a traffic violation notice on behalf of the collabo Government! Treason to humanity is a bit closer, don't you think?"

Without waiting for an answer, Stan turned to the camera and started his closing spiel. "This is Stan the Man, Stan Adler here, on the topic of who shot down the *Valiant*. Was it a legitimate kzin strike, a part of the war, or something much worse? Was it an act of treachery by human collaborators trying to ingratiate themselves with their overlords? Tonight you've seen one of the kzin, a student, not an overlord, and only born towards the end of the war, who has shown himself friendly to man. We of Wunderland also know that, however cruel and merciless they may be, the kzin despise liars and seldom if ever lie themselves. And you've seen Senator von Höhenheim, who doesn't want us to find the truth any time soon. You make up your own minds as to which of them you'd rather have on your side in a fight, which one you'd trust. Good night."

"That bastard knows something. He'd not have dared speak to me that way if he didn't." The senator was white with rage. Alois Grün sat down without permission. They were alone in the senator's office, a suitably large room with a rich carpet and wood panelling enriched by gold and crimson swirls, in a suite of rooms high above the streets of Munchen, spread out like a plan below. Low gravity encouraged high building, but the war had flattened much. Lights moved at the park near the spaceport, where acres of hulked kzin warships were gradually being demolished. It was night, but the sky was lit by the vast jewel of Alpha Centauri B, and the sliding points of light that were natural and artificial satellites.

"He can hardly *know* anything," Grün said carefully. "I agree he seems to have some definite suspicions. His closing remarks were tantamount to an accusation, but he was not as explicit as he would surely have been did he have any hard evidence. Oh, I don't blame you," said Grün. "I remember what we were promised: estates and slaves of our own on Earth or Wunderland if we cooperated, dinner in the officers' mess if we didn't. It wasn't a difficult choice. Oh yes, we should have been good scouts and defied Ktrodni-Stkaa! Ktrodni-Stkaa, whom even other kzin were terrified of!"

Von Höhenheim glared. His mind was working hard.

Abbot Boniface walked in the abbey grounds with Vaemar. It was night, and the stars glittered above them in eternal silence. The orange exhaust flame of a chemical rocket vanished skyward. Somewhere, far beyond the range of visual sight, human and kzin fleets might be locked in battle. Splashes from the fenced-off Jotok ponds suggested the young amphibians were busy.

"Yes, I did tell that nice couple that you should go into politics. I don't for a moment suppose you want to. Anybody who *does* want to go into politics shouldn't be allowed to. But you are needed. It's your duty, in my view."

Vaemar made a noise in the back of his throat that could almost have been a growl. Kzin have a clear grasp of the concept of duty; in Vaemar's view, this was a dirty card to play.

"You will have to convince me of that. I have a duty to put my mind to use in mathematics also. That is ultimately much more important than politics."

"More important, yes, I grant you that. Mathematics is one of the bases for our civilization and has been since Euclid, and making a contribution to it is certainly important. But not as *urgent* as making a contribution to good government. Ignore the political environment and you will find that your mathematical work is unfinished because of the meddling of the ignorant. Things like that have happened in the history of both our species, as you know. Didn't the kzin equivalent of universities start because kzin with a bent for mathematical thought were forced to flee into the wilderness to escape the incessant challenges to death-duels? As our Archimedes was killed by a conquering soldier at the fall of his city. Wernher von Braun nearly died at the bombing of Peenemunde. If that had happened, we would hardly be talking together today."

"No. My Sire would have had vast estates on Earth."

"And you would have had eights of ambitious elder brothers between you and the throne, as you yourself have observed. You are an eccentric, Vaemar, a misfit like your friend Dimity. Like Karan, for that matter. And you know what happens to misfits in the Patriarchy."

Vaemar knew very well. He would have had difficulty surviving, even with his illustrious family to protect him.

The abbot pressed his point. "Your work might even be destroyed, labelled as *kzin* mathematics and consequently not real, proper *human* mathematics at all, since your arithmetic is on base eight or for some other rationalization." The abbot put his hand up. "No, you don't have to tell me that the idea is insane, I know that, but there are some insane people about. And there have been such arguments before. Einstein's theories were banned in Nazi Germany as Jewish physics. In fact, you could say that the whole idea of government is to keep fools, knaves and lunatics from disturbing their neighbors. And if no intelligent being will contribute to government because other things are more fun, and, in the long run we may never have, more important, then those who *do* take power will be all fools, knaves or lunatics. It has happened in the past."

"But I shouldn't be any good at it," Vaemar protested. "I know what is required, I have seen enough human politicians to know. Compromise and lies. Those are the foundations of politics. And I cannot lie. My honor does not permit me." Vaemar made that noise in his throat that the abbot correctly translated as intense distaste. "I speak not only of human politics. I was too young to be aware of the intrigues that filled my Sire's palace, but I have learned much since— our Heroes sent out on wars of conquest for glory, yes, and for land and slaves, and to expand our Empire up the spiral arm, but also simply to keep them out of the way. A warrior doctrine whose purpose was to have rival claimants to the throne kill each other off! The mass-production of dead Heroes who are so much less inconvenient than live ones. And even that was more honorable than what a politician has to do in a democracy."

Abbot Boniface smiled to himself. A human who spoke of his honor would have rung alarm bells, but for a kzin it was perfectly natural. "But you can compromise. You can accept the good without rejecting it in favor of unattainable perfection. You, perhaps you alone, have enough insight into both kzin and man to see another point of view. And the fact that you cannot lie is a great strength. Oh yes," Boniface said wryly, "I know that the main method of politicians has usually been to let everyone think that you are on their side. Shading the truth at best, downright misleading lies at worst. Trying vainly to be all things to all men. But both man and kzin have a respect for those who tell the truth as they believe it to be. Our best statesmen in the past have usually been like that. They have told the truth and argued honestly for what they believed to be right, and the power of honest belief can accomplish much. I know. In my own small way I am a politician, you see.

"Sometimes. I have to guide and advise, I seldom command. And when I do, it is after much earnest reflection and prayer. It needs a good deal of faith in my own judgment, and I have a great talent for doubt."

"Look out! Get behind me!" Vaemar had dropped into a fighting crouch. His claws were extended and his *wtsai* had appeared like magic in his paw.

"Tigrepard!" The abbot could see nothing but a hint of something yellowish-red in the long grass of the garth. Vaemar screamed and leapt. In an instant the two great felinoids were locked in battle, flattening the plants. The abbot groped for his own weapon, but he could not use it for fear of hitting Vaemar.

It was over in an instant. The tigrepard was a big one, but Vaemar was bigger and quicker. He stood back, panting a little, as it died, then removed the ears.

"Your defenses are not all they should be, father," he remarked. "I noticed a patch of the west wall looked rather tumble-down."

"And you have reminded me what the price may be for relaxing eternal vigilance," said the abbot, holding his voice steady with an effort. "I would not have lasted long on my own. I shall have a repair party to the west wall tomorrow."

"No, father, not tomorrow, tonight. At this time of year tigrepards travel in prides. But sweep the grounds first of all."

"I am in no position to disregard your advice. You seem to know a lot about them."

"Of course. We are cats, too."

Vaemar watched the sweeping of the monastery grounds by parties of well-armed novices under the eyes of the monastery's hunters, and then turned back to the abbot. What had he been saying? Ah, yes, he'd talked of doubt.

"But how can you maintain your faith in the Bearded God if you are troubled by doubts? Don't you doubt His very existence?"

"Oh, lots of times. I think He wants me to. So I am not *troubled* by doubts; if God didn't want me to doubt, I wouldn't be able to. He wants me to pursue truth, and that inevitably requires doubt about everything. There was a time once when I suddenly realized that I was in danger of becoming an atheist for religious reasons. When I saw it in those terms, I laughed for a week, and felt the inner warmth that told me God was pleased that I had seen the joke. But we are getting off the subject, and although I would be very proud if I managed to convert you, I don't expect to do so any time soon. So we shall leave the theology for another time and return to the politics, if you will.

"We live in very interesting times, as the old Chinese curse had it. And hence very dangerous times. We need the very best brains to see the possibilities and to guide the people wisely. We need a kzin in our political system very badly, and no other is as well suited as you. That is why I think it is your duty."

Vaemar pondered. The abbot was a wise man, Vaemar could sense it. He was also a good man, a man of integrity and honor. A strange sort of honor; turning the other cheek when struck was something hard to even think about. Vaemar sensed that there was something deep about this, something even few human beings could fully grasp. To not fight back when you could, that was paradoxical, but maybe it was a very clever strategy. Perhaps it was something to do with destroying your enemy by turning him into a friend. He would think about this some time.

But was the abbot right? Was it truly urgent that he play a role in the political turmoil? His instincts were violently opposed to the very thought. And yet . . . Sometimes the instincts were wrong and had to be bridled. Human beings were good at doing that, often too good. Kzin didn't get a lot of practice. Maybe they weren't good enough. And it would certainly be needed if he were in politics. And he, Vaemar, was much better than any other kzin he knew at holding off the gut reaction and taking time for reflection. The cortico-thalamic pause, as an ancient Earth writer had called it. Vaemar's sire had seen this as one of the strengths of man, and one he wanted his people to acquire. Perhaps, Vaemar thought, he *was* the right kzin for the job.

"How is this done, this becoming a politician?" Vaemar asked cautiously.

"The local member of the bundestag, a conservative, died last week. Old age officially, exacerbated by the time under Occupation. We shall be having a by-election within a month. I would strongly support your candidature for the conservative party. There is a natural platform already made. The liberals are planning to drain part of Grossgeister Swamp, and we are mounting opposition. I take it that you are not in favor of draining the swamp?"

"It would be madness. We have a rich and wonderful ecology here, which would be devastated. What are they thinking of?"

"Building housing for the poor, who are more likely to vote for them, so as to change this electorate to give a majority who would support them. They know the locals oppose the idea, and are playing it as being kind to those who have to live in tumbledown slums in Munchen."

"Well, why not improve the housing in Munchen?"

"Needed for commercial purposes. So they say. I think it's because they have a huge majority in the city and want to take some of it away from where it is wasted and gain another electorate. This one is big in area but sparsely populated."

Vaemar thought hard. The abbot was a clever man. He knew what Vaemar would think about draining the swamp, and was putting his case for Vaemar fighting it officially. There might be good arguments in favor of draining the swamp, but if it was a political gambit then he, Vaemar, would fight it tooth and claw. Metaphorically only, of course. More prosaically, he'd be using words. But words, he knew, could be as powerful as teeth or claws or much heavier weapons. A kzin warrior training, at his level, required an understanding of how to motivate troops, of how to get the best out of them using words and body language.

These things had been neglected the first time the kzin found themselves in a serious war. Too many of their aristocrats and young officers desperate for Names had been unable to propose a plan in such a way that their staff dared to point out potential weaknesses. Rarrgh had told him: "I have seen many die from that mistake." This was, perhaps, not altogether different. Thinking of it as combat, using ideas and words as weapons, somehow made him feel a lot better about it. He would vanquish his opponents! Not as satisfying as physical combat, but more real and with more serious consequences than chess.

"Very well, my friend and adviser. If you truly believe it is my duty and that I am needed, then I will do it, though it will sadden me greatly to take time from mathematics and history. And I rather think that if I go down this path, I shall have little time for anything else. What exactly must I do?"

Boniface smiled, as much as anyone ever does when facing a kzin. His mouth turned up at the corners and his eyes crinkled. "Thank you, my friend and one-time student. I believe it is the best thing for all of us on Wunderland that you do this. I shall put your name forward to the committee. They will have several candidates, I daresay, and the selection committee will interview all of them. I shall have to explain rather a lot of things to you."

"So there is hope for me. The selection committee may reject me," Vaemar reflected out loud.

"They might be that stupid. I don't think so, but it is possible. It depends on the alternatives. You will, of course, do your best to get selected."

"Yes, of course," Vaemar said without any enthusiasm. And he would indeed have to do his best, any less would be dishonorable. Whatever doing his best might mean.

"What is it that makes this urgent?" Vaemar asked.

The abbot looked up at the silent stars. "Many small things. And just possibly one big thing. You know I have many sources of information, some not perhaps as reliable as others. And urgent is a word with many nuances."

"I do not understand you," Vaemar told him.

The abbot sighed. "There are some hints, some fragments which I have pieced together. I may be wrong. I hope I am."

"Go on."

"I have some reason to think there may be something out there. Further along the spiral arm. Something coming this way. You know, of the few sentient species in the galaxy that we have ever recorded, the thing I notice is how much we share. We can understand in some limited way what sort of things drive us. All men are brothers. Well, cousins at least, and we know this from genetics. But it goes deeper than that. You and I are very different in our genetics, but the universe has shaped us, and we have responded in ways which although different show striking similarities. We are both made up of star-stuff, both evolved in the Goldilocks Zone through similar sets of fantastic improbabilities. We both understand what truth and honor and justice mean, and they are important to both of us. You have your Fanged God, and we our Bearded God, but they might almost be two faces of the same entity. Both of them demand truth, honor and justice of us."

"But your Bearded God also demands that you love your enemy," the kzin rumbled softly. "And the Fanged God does not."

"True," Boniface admitted.

"Perhaps the Fanged God feared such a dreadful weapon being loosed in the universe."

The abbot's eyes lit. "Ah. You have seen that. Good. All the same, our response to the demands made upon us makes us almost brothers. And brothers, of course, fight and squabble with each other. But there may be something outside which is very different from all the species we know. Something terrible, something which threatens us all. And something which neither man nor kzin separately could face. It has been hinted to me that there is some sort of plan to forge a deeper alliance between our species, and perhaps others. Perhaps both our gods want that, and something acts for both of them. Perhaps because one day, perhaps a thousand years from now, we shall have to meet something so terrible that only a melding of the traditions of our people can hope to overcome it. The odds against our ships first encountering each other in the way they did were long indeed."

"How stupid our telepaths were then, to discover you had no weapons but kitchen knives, and to miss entirely that your chief religious symbol was an instrument of torture!"

The abbot nodded to concede the point and then went back to his own. "Who knows what lies in wait for us, further up the spiral arm? You know how we got the hyperdrive: a race that lives in deep space— a race we knew nothing of—contacted our colony at Jinx and sold the colonists a manual. You know the size of space. Beyond your ability to imagine, or mine. Can that have been blind chance? I have heard a theory—no, less than a theory, a fingertip feeling—that our wars have been made by others, in order to forge in that flame some power that may be needed one day to defend truth and honor and justice and perhaps, yes, even love, and save them from something which would smash them as meaningless baubles and scatter the dust into endless night."

There was a pause as man and kzin regarded each other calmly.

"One cannot make a life decision on mere speculation," Vaemar rumbled.

"Of course not. But we have played enough chess, you and I, for you to know that it is foolish to make a move for only one reason. Strategy and tactics both are involved in making a move. The tactical issues are much easier to think about. But in the end, the strategy may be what makes a move into a winning game. And I sense that Wunderland may be the world on which man and kzin achieve something jointly which neither could hope for alone. Let that be no more than a dream, still it is a dream worth dreaming, don't you think?

"There is another thing. Given that you are a reserve officer in our armed forces, and given that I have no hard facts to tell, I may tell you something else about this theory of mine: the telepaths have told us much that they never told you, their masters. Their range is short, but when one links to another, it is not so short. They cannot always correlate well, but when they do, the product is powerful. The telepaths have stores of secret knowledge. They do not, I think, know, but they have guessed—how, I know not—that something cataclysmic is happening in space.

"You know we offered Kzin a temporary truce so the kzinretti and kits on Wunderland left without . . . Heroes to care for them might be repatriated. It was . . . is . . . hoped that there might be more talks, leading to a permanent truce, though that may be but a dream. Still, our chief negotiator, McDonald, found out much—for the Patriarchy to talk to us at all is a huge step. It would never have happened if we had not gotten the hyperdrive and won the Liberation of this planet, along with Down and some other worlds. But we have discovered something you may find uncomfortable. The Patriarchy has found out about you, Vaemar."

"I suppose they were bound to find out about me sooner or later," Vaemar admitted.

"It was expected that their attitude would be berserk rage. But— forgive me if I use a monkey expression, for I do not mean to be insulting—it appears the Patriarch is no fool. In fact, his attitude appears to be something like 'Lurk in the long grass. Wait and see.' That must be our attitude too."

"You so often give me things to think about. And so seldom anything easy." Vaemar looked down at the little man who looked back at him with the hint of a smile on his lips. "You spoke of chess. Do I need to tell you, an Aspirant System Master, that you improve only by playing against better players?"

Dimity Carmody could see that Vaemar was unhappy with his decision. "I do understand, Vaemar," she told him. "You are not the only mathematician to get mugged by reality. Remember, Gauss was a senior bureaucrat, and Evariste Galois died in a duel for political reasons. I guess mathematics and science are what are called 'market failures'; most people are too dumb to see how important they are and don't value them as much as pursuing power. At least you don't fall into that set."

"Thank you for seeing my dilemma and for being so understanding, Dimity. I had thought you would be angry with me."

Dimity shook her head sadly. "Angry, yes, but not with you. With the dreadful fools we have to live among. And who can stay angry with them for long? After a short time it turns to pity, then a determination to have as little to do with them as possible. The trouble with politics started with Plato, who thought that our leaders should be selected from the best and brightest of the human race. Were he a bit more of a thinker and less of a literary man, he'd have realized that the best and brightest don't want the job. They pursue insight, not power. Power is an empty piece of nonsense no intelligent person would waste time on. But that leads to power going to fools who want it, and they can make our lives a misery. So every so often, the intelligent must take control, however little they like the idea. And now is one of those times, I suspect. If the abbot thinks so, he is likely right. He has a lovely, simple mind, does Boniface. In a better world, he'd have been a mathematician. He has that hunger for the transcendent which is the mark of the best scientists and mathematicians."

"Will I ever be able to go back to it, do you think?"

"Given that we can stop getting old in these times, I am sure you will, one day. As long as you stay playful, Vaemar. All the best work is play. And you may find enough in politics to stop you getting stodgy.

"The times constrain us, Vaemar, my love. How you put your mind to work is not a matter of personal preference. No man is an island, nor a kzin either. Mathematicians are ultimately the most practical of people; once you see things clearly there are no choices."

Vaemar considered. He recalled that she had once pulled his tail playfully. Very few other beings could have done that and lived. But she saw everything with a terrible clarity and she saw his mind. She saw him *as* a mind; the outer form was not important to Dimity, just something to be played with. What Dimity said was right. There were no choices.

"Thank you, Dimity. You have opened doors for me into strange and wonderful worlds. And now the abbot has opened another, and I must pass through. But I will not forget the other worlds. Nor the joy of exploring them."

"Come and see me when the need arises, Vaemar. When the squalor of engaging with mental and moral pygmies becomes too much to bear; when the pain of not being able to say what you think becomes intolerable, for fear of its effect on fools, I shall be here for you."

"Where does it all come from?"

"There's this little village, out in the boondocks. East of the range. Started off just after the kzin surrender, lots of people realized they'd starve to death without a government to organize bringing stuff into the city, and we hanged or shot most of the collabos. So some smart folk went out to do some farming and keep themselves in food. And some were already out there. Seems to have worked, there's a whole collection of villages out there now, and the land around gets farmed and hunted."

"But gold? And other stones?"

The trader shrugged. "There's other stuff besides farming land. There's a whole lot of country out there, some people just upped and grabbed their share of it. Like the Wild West in some of those old movies. Someone found the gold. There's big seams of the stuff in quartz sometimes. And there are things pushed up from the deeps by volcanoes, plenty of those around. The abbey's built on one."

"And this comes from the other side of the abbey?"

"So they tell me."

"Don't you want to go off and get yourself some of that there gold?" The man was hungry. You could see it in his eyes.

"Nope. There's other things out there besides gold. Like kzin hunters, who went out too, wanting to stay away from the conquerors, and with a mighty big grudge against humans, some of them. And other things, some of them as murderous as a kzin. The tigrepards and the lesslocks are bad enough, and the Morlocks, when they come out onto the surface at night, are worse. Me, I'm a city boy. Don't fancy getting ate."

"Still, if a bunch of guys, say a dozen of us with guns, was to go and find this place, we could get us our hands on some of the gold, maybe?"

"Maybe. And then again, maybe not. One of they kzin could take out a dozen men with his bare claws 'n' fangs afore they could work out where to point the guns. Believe me, I've seen it. Thirty of us jumped a kzin during the war. I got away."

"Can't be much kind of law out there, yet," the man argued. The trader could read him like a picture book, one with really dirty pictures. *Yes, and a dozen armed men could find that village and take all that gold without having to do much digging at all, at all. Some people couldn't abide work.* He shrugged. No point in telling them the village was well armed. He remembered a psychopath in the early days of the Occupation, maddened by everything, a really nasty piece of work, who had enjoyed killing orphaned children. A kzin had decided the children were the Patriarch's property. What had happened to the man had not been pleasant. This man, and his accomplices too, were the sort of people Wunderland would be better off without.

"I wouldn't know. Like I said, I don't want to get ate."

This wasn't quite true. The trader had spent some time yarning and exchanging gossip with the men and women and the odd kzin who had come in from the village. And he had heard of the judge. Judge Tom, the Law East of the Ranges. He sounded a tough cookie.

"Dimity Carmody says that you have a lovely, simple mind," Vaemar told the abbot. He nodded.

"Yes, I do have a simple mind," he admitted. "But it has taken me many years to get it that way. I think she was born with one, lucky girl."

"She said that in a better world, you might yourself have been a mathematician. She said you have the hunger for transcendence which is the mark."

"She would know. I have never seen myself that way. I feel myself to be too muddled, too confused. Still, it could be worse. I could be like so many people, who are so muddled and confused they haven't even *noticed* they are muddled and confused. I give thanks to God that He has shown me something of the extent of my muddle and confusion. Just enough to see it and not so much as to make me despair. And now you have some questions about politics, I think."

"Yes, some quite basic ones. For a start, why are there two political parties? What is special about two?" Vaemar was puzzled. He was stretched out before a roaring fire, polishing his ear-ring, while the abbot was sitting in a chair close by.

"I believe there was some mathematics developed about a century ago to consider that question, but it has puzzled others before you," the abbot told him. He went on and started to sing in an artificial deep voice:

"I often think it's comical, Fa la la, Fa la la,
"That every boy and every girl that's born into this world alive,

"*Is either a little liberal, or else a little conservative.*
"*Fa, la, la.*"

The abbot looked quizically at Vaemar, who was astonished by what seemed to be unusual frivolity, even by human standards, and explained:

"That was written in the last part of the nineteenth century, so you are hardly the first person to find it puzzling. Gilbert's guardsman did too. It has something to do with stability. You see, human beings have a good share of herd genes. Ninety-eight percent of our genes we have in common with chimpanzees, and about seventy percent we share with cows. And rather more with wolves. We have an impulse towards the collective. We also have an impulse towards hierarchical power structures, as do you kzin. We also have some who are individuals with a strong wish for freedom. These things are written inside us, and we all have something of them. In our various cultures, some of those impulses are expressed more freely than others, and get buttressed by memes.

"A political party is a coalition of memes, and these can change. For example, in Gilbert's time, conservatives were generally much more collectivist and hierarchical, and the liberals much more individualist. In our day it is nearly the other way around, the conservatives are more inclined to individualism, the liberals are more collectivist. Of course, a coalition of individualists can be formed, but they tend to argue with each other rather a lot, so they are underrepresented in the political system. The individualists in the present conservative party are perhaps less individual and more hierarchical than those who vote for them.

"Of course, the general population has all these dispositions to different degrees. In any society, individuals learn that they have to cooperate to stay alive, and collectivists learn they have to be able to be independent sometimes. But the collectivist impulse ensures that people gather together with those who think alike, that's the nature of collectivism. And those who need freedom stay away from them, disliking the mutual coercion the collectivists habitually use on each other. But the individualists, too, need the support of a collective. They tend to feel 'There is no such thing as society,' because they make relatively few concessions for the approval of their partners. They expect to have to fight for what they want. The collectivist impulse means that an individual who has it strongly virtually lives for the approval of other members of the collective. Both are survival strategies, and are seldom met in their pure forms, but the genes are there, and the memes to express them in any culture.

"In stable times, the collectivist impulse can lead to mass hysteria, with the preference for believing things not because they are true but because you want to, or because your friends all do. These are not stable times, and believing things just because you want to can easily get you killed in a hostile environment, so there has been a strong selection pressure to be realistic. So the liberal party is not yet as dominated by ideology as it has been in the past, or as it will be again. It's much more complicated than that, but it contains the essentials. So, there are two groups because human beings drift away from weaker collectives to more powerful ones. Not that two is always the necessary count of parties. Highly individualist cultures often have more, but then the groups themselves form coalitions. And fracture when the conflicting memes become too painfully apparent. People tend to vote as their parents do, sometimes seeing it as a matter of tribal loyalties rather than self-interest. There are other dimensions than the collectivism-individualism one of course, but that axis is important.

"Generally, in our culture, conservatives want justice and liberals want mercy. Conservatives expect to live with risk, liberals want security. Conservatives see the society as a delicate organism, to be altered with care. Liberals see it as a machine to be rejigged at will. Conservatives seek to minimize the size of the State, yet, because they are inclined to a more realistic view of life, they are more likely than liberals to see threats, so they are more inclined to large military expenditure and all the State intrusiveness that goes with it. These are, broadly, the things liberals and conservatives want. Obviously, everybody wants all of them, but when they conflict as they usually do, this is the way people tend to split. I don't pretend to understand it in any detail, it is a specialist subject. But parties can change, and do. I suppose I can tell you that during the war on Earth, before Dimity arrived with the hyperdrive, there were conservatives who seriously wanted to make peace—not in spite of the fact we were losing, mind you, but because of it. Every defeat and disaster led, as time went on, to more and more cries, growing louder and louder, to stop the space-war. They even had a slogan, 'Come home, Earth,' until

Vrissriv-Admiral's raid broke through the planetary defenses, levelled cities and spaceports and seized a couple of thousand slaves. Templemount had just taken over then. A pacifist delegation went to see him after that. He evidently decided that it was necessary to show he meant business and publically executed the lot of them. Of course, the fact that there was a kzin radio transceiver found in their party headquarters didn't exactly help their case."

"That sounds very odd thinking," Vaemar objected. "Defeat is no reason to surrender. Not before all is plainly lost. And not even then, unless it is necessary to preserve the species. We surrendered only because the alternative was annihilation, and Hroth, who was the senior surviving officer, ordered us to. It seems utterly perverted otherwise. Had these people not read even your own '*Battle of Maldon*'?"

"No, not then. Senechel was out of his depth. He did his best, and we owe him for what preparation there was, but he couldn't think in the appropriate way after centuries of ARM-enforced pacifism. Considering the conditioning he labored under, he did heroically. Finally Templemount took over. That fat old man, who had been in every party and who none of the political class trusted. He roused Earth and the Belt to fight to the bitter end. He sent out counterattacks to catch the kzin fleets while they were still outfitting. He even sent an expedition to find your homeworld. It was armed with *The Sabbath Goat*."

"What was that? I don't know of it."

"Believe me, it is better you don't. Anyway, they were never heard of again. Perhaps one of your patrols got them.

"Anyway, without Templemount we would have surrendered before the hyperdrive arrived. And those were conservatives who wanted it, more than the liberals, which tells you that parties can change, sometimes very quickly if there is a leader of principle like Templemount."

"Kzin politics seems much simpler," Vaemar remarked. "It's largely a matter of fighting to get to be in charge of the whole system. We don't have anything like political parties. I suppose we have clan loyalties, but there are lots of clans. They form alliances, but break them whenever it is convenient. Formal notice should be given in such cases. Perhaps in the Patriarch's palace things are a little different."

Vaemar tried to find common patterns between kzin and human culture, and decided he needed to study kzin history as well as human history. "Alright, shelve that for the present, as you human beings say. What exactly is a *policy*? Parties seem to have lots of them."

"If you are going to keep a party together, everyone has to agree on some things that are important and need doing. Once they've agreed, it gets written down and is called a 'policy.'"

"What if you don't agree?"

"Well, you have to vote in the approved way in the house, or the party may expel you. But you get a chance to determine what the collective policy will be when it's being debated in the party room. At least, that's how the conservatives do it."

"What do the liberals do?"

"They have a smaller group called a 'caucus', which decides what the policies will be. They used to have it open to every member of the party, not just politicians, but it was too unwieldy. Or maybe sometimes the party voted for things the leaders didn't want. There are all sorts of ways of getting your ideas imposed on other people. It's much easier to do this in a party of collectivists, where social disapproval is a serious threat. In a party of individualists you need compelling arguments. Sometimes, historically, both parties are very collectivist or hierarchical or both, and the individualists in the world at large get practically no say in what is decided. It's not quite that bad at present, but it could get that way."

"I don't think I'm a very collectivist being," Vaemar said slowly.

"Well, at least you'll be in the right party. You wouldn't last long in the liberal party," the abbot pointed out.

"This business of having to vote for something I might disagree with. What if someone asks me if I agree with a policy that I didn't vote for, and thought was wrong but was outvoted on? I shall just have to say that the rules are that I have to, and I follow the rules. And then they would ask why do I follow such stupid rules, and I can't think of any good answer," Vaemar complained.

"Happens all the time. The good answer is that if you want to get anything right done, you have to have a party, and that means you will sometimes have to put up with something stupid being done. I must admit that when politicians are asked a question like that, they usually answer a totally different question and hope nobody will notice."

"Does it work?"

"Not very often, except with the stupid."

"I'm glad, because I don't think I could do that. I should just answer the question truthfully."

The abbot's shoulders heaved as he manfully suppressed a laugh. "That would surprise everyone. And a good thing it would be, too."

"This interview committee I am seeing tomorrow. Are there right answers and wrong answers to the questions they will ask me? Is it like a mathematics *viva voce*? Or is it quite different? What are they trying to find out?"

"Different committee members will have different concerns. Some will want to be reassured that you aren't going to rip apart any member of the government who you happen to disagree with. Not that they'd mind if you did for themselves, but it would look bad. Others will want to be confident that you will toe the party line and not argue back. You won't keep those people happy whatever you say, so don't bother about them. Just be yourself and tell the truth as you always do; let them work out the probable consequences. I shall be on the committee, and they know you are my preferred candidate. I shan't be able to vote, of course, but I can present some arguments. I'm quite looking forward to it. I don't say you'll get the approval of a majority, but at least you won't be dull. Some of them will prefer dull, but there are some sensible people there who will see you as an opportunity."

Vaemar looked doleful. He had never much enjoyed examinations, but at least in mathematics, you knew where you were. And even in history, which was a bit trickier, if your facts were right and your arguments solid, you survived.

The villagers now had horses, and ploughing was a lot easier. Ruat watched them ride about in disbelief. The horses no longer panicked when he was upwind of them. He wondered if somewhere there was an animal *he* could ride. It would have to be a lot bigger than a horse, and he had never seen anything that might do, but the country was big, and who knew? He had never seen horses before the villagers had bought some with his gold. Not that it was his gold any longer, of course; he had traded it for other things. Medicine, and help in building . . . a . . . *home*. That was the word. Owning things was not an unfamiliar concept in principle, kzin nobles and officers owned things.

Names, and slaves, and homes. But for a low-grade kzin, it hardly ever made sense to own anything. But, Ruat reflected, now *he* did own things. Maybe that made him some sort of noble. It was a strange idea, but not without attraction.

Ruat paced along outside the stockade. He was on patrol. A silver five-pointed star hung from a silver chain around his neck. He even knew what the words embossed on the star meant. Sheriff. He could pronounce that word now, quite clearly. The judge was the Law East of the Ranges, and Ruat enforced the judge's law. That's what sheriffs did. Because his honor required it, he was going to do it well.

Of course, it was pretty easy.

"Tell me, Lord Vaemar, why exactly do you want to join the conservative party, and why in particular do you want to stand for the Grossgeister District?" The questioner was the chairman, actually a woman, with a thin, worried look and wispy hair, wearing a hat that looked like roadkill. She looked up at Vaemar nervously.

Vaemar responded promptly: "I want to join the conservative party because I want to conserve something, the Grossgeister Swamp. And I have long associations with the area, I know some of the people here, humans and kzin. They are fine people and I like nearly all of them. One of them, the old man known as Marshy, saved my life and my mate's life, as well as that of my . . . colleague . . . Swirl-Stripes and other humans. I have helped explore the swamp, and am well aware of the vast variety of life-forms there, many rare and . . ." it was a strange, difficult word to pronounce . . . "beautiful. Never will I forget watching the creatures of the swamp passing through the water by Marshy's window—the procession of bright creatures passing was one of the wonders of this world—or the bioluminescent life-forms at night. Further, there are the dolphins, your allies. And our sentient brothers, at least. For them it is hunting ground and nursery. There are land-dwelling animals on the bigger islands, and stretches of blue water. Future generations will thank us for preserving it."

"Didn't the kzin burn the heart out of it during the war?" someone asked.

"Assessing the damage was one of the purposes of my expedition," Vaemar replied. "Although other events overtook us, I am happy to report that it appears to be recovering rapidly. I believe in a few years no trace of damage will remain, if it is simply left untouched. And the expedition team I went on was good training for me in leading a mixed human-kzin team successfully."

"And you brought out specimens of value," piped up one old fellow, evidently trying to be helpful.

"Yes. Among other things, the only surviving specimens we know of unattached Jotok on this planet. They are being reared at the monastery." He had also brought out Karan, but she was not the business of these men.

"There are many other swamps," said someone. It was true. Frequent meteor strikes had left much of Wunderland's coast riddled with circular holes like a Swiss cheese. Nonetheless, Vaemar's words seemed to have moved the meeting. Further, they had forgotten the dolphins, and many felt guilty of their forgetfulness at Vaemar's reminder.

Vaemar could feel a current running against the interjector. It was not merely a subjective impression. Like all male kzin, he had a rudimentary ability to detect emotions, which with the telepaths was developed into a complete sense. Like most kzin he had felt rather embarrassed by this, precisely because of its connection with the despised telepath caste. Suddenly he realized what a useful political asset it might be.

"We kzin," he continued, "have at times destroyed species in our wars, but never willingly or wantonly. Even when the Chunquen fired missiles at us from their submerged sea-ships, we only boiled part of their seas."

"Very nice of you," someone muttered. Vaemar looked at the interjector, who seemed to suddenly shrink under his gaze. Vaemar was big, even for a kzin.

"But why should a kzin want to go into politics at all?" a heavily built man with a ginger beard sat next to the woman and scowled as he asked his question. The panel were seated around a table, and Vaemar stood before it, looming over them. When he had come into the room, the chairman had invited him to sit in the solitary chair facing the table, and then stopped in embarrassment. Kzin didn't normally use chairs, and few human chairs would have survived, this one clearly would not. Then he had been asked if he would care to lie down on the carpet, and had politely declined. Nobody argued the point.

"My species is sharing this world with yours. We have the vote, although I do not know of a kzin who has used it. So far we have been somewhat dismissive of the political process, but that must change in time. I am the first to consider standing for public office, but I will not be the last. When the kzin see that they have some measure of control over their own future by reasoned debate, they will start taking an interest. It is not in our traditions, this democracy. But not all human beings have been used to it either. Perhaps it is similar to the way in which Japan on your homeworld came to accept and even embrace what must have seemed a very alien way of doing things."

There was a stunned silence. Vaemar knew a lot more about human history than the committee did, and this was a little embarrassing. He recognized Nils and Leonie Rykermann, sitting towards the back of the room. That meant some support for him, at least. The sight of them brought back old memories.

"Hmmph. Well, be that as it may, what do you do in the Bundestag when a liberal front bencher smiles at you? Are you going to go into attack mode and rip his throat out?"

"Liberal members are not going to do much smiling at me. But in general, I agree that there is a problem. I am actually quite used to people smiling at me, and at each other in my presence. Nils and Leonie Rykermann tried not to, but they gradually forgot, and Dimity Carmody does it all the time these days. Yes, it triggers a reflex, but if you or any other human sees someone of the opposite sex who attracts you, you do not automatically commit rape. You have been socialized. It is harder for kzin, who do not socialize so readily, we are more impulsive, and it is harder for the older ones. I do not encourage human beings to show their teeth, but not because I cannot contain my reaction. It would go hard with them if they were to forget that not all kzin were socialized with human beings as much as I have been. This will gradually change as more kzin get used to the strange way you show an emotion which we express quite differently, and which we can misinterpret rather easily. But no. I shall not tear out any throats from the opposite side. Not unless they really irritate me."

That last was Vaemar's idea of a joke. It fell very flat. Nobody was quite sure what to do about it. He realized he had to tell them.

"That was a joke. Not a very funny one, perhaps. We kzin do not have the same sense of humor as you do, although we also react to the incongruous."

"I would advise against humor in general." The man with the beard looked as if it was a long time since he'd tried any.

There was a pause. The majority of the committee were obviously making up their minds that Vaemar was going to be more of a liability than an asset. As a filler question and an attempt to see if there was any prospect at all of anything positive coming out of the interview, a solidly built woman at the end asked her only question:"Do you think that kzin will more likely vote for one of their own?"

"The kzin will have no interest in the species of their representative. But once they decide to engage, almost all will vote conservative," Vaemar assured them calmly.

The panel brightened considerably. "Why is that?" the lady chairman enquired, looking almost lively.

Vaemar thought for some seconds. What was the best way to put this so it didn't sound terrifying? "The liberal party is very collectivist. Kzin are more individualistic. They can obey orders under a military rule, of course. But in a democracy where they are not so constrained, they will have little sympathy for a collectivist belief system." That sounded a lot better than telling them that from a kzin perspective, herd species looked like prey and the individualists more like predators, and the kzin weren't ever going to even consider joining the side of the prey. Besides, apart from those die-hards who regarded him as a quisling, the idea of voting against the son of Chuut-Riit and a grand-nephew of the Patriarch was literally unthinkable. Vaemar decided that this business of choosing words carefully so as to put things in a good light without telling lies was quite interesting.

"So once the kzin see that we are for genuine freedom, they will vote for us preferentially?" The man with the beard was incredulous. He hadn't expected the kzin to show such good sense.

"Only a few deranged kzin would consider voting for the liberal party as it is at present. The old parties—the Herrenmanner and the Progressive Democrats—are shadows of their former selves, and I think will take a long time to rebuild, if they do so at all. Too many humans blame them, perhaps unfairly, for the lackadaisical pace of the original rearmament effort. There is no reason for any kzin to be interested in them. Perhaps the odd telepath. Once they can see the merit of voting at all, kzinti will overwhelmingly vote for conservatives, just as I would not consider joining the liberals."

"And the kzinretti?"

"Those of low intelligence will either not vote or will vote as their masters direct them. The intelligent ones, the ones we call 'the secret others'—of whom my own mate is one—will vote as they please, and any attempt to influence them would be met with defensive hostility. But there are too few of those to make a great difference. Much less than one in an eight-cubed.

"It is not just that the liberals do not conserve," Vaemar continued. "It is not even that they are willing to destroy the ecology of the swamp as a foolish ploy to change the electorate so as to favor themselves. It is that they favor the herd against the individual. Self-respect is central to the kzin ethos. It is built into our genes. To speak candidly, all normal kzin would see liberals as perverted and disgusting and less than, well, human." And natural prey, but he didn't *have* to say that.

The bearded man brightened even more. That was pretty much how *he* felt about liberals.

Vaemar went on. "And if the conservative party shows the way to allowing the kzin to engage in the political life of the world, then they will change the balance here drastically." Vaemar sounded confident. He was. The knowledge that kzin did not lie was something the committee knew and were busily factoring into their calculations. There was an excited buzz as the panel discussed these interesting points with each other in an undertone. Vaemar thought that it wasn't necessary to point out that one of the longer-term effects would be to drive more human beings towards the liberals, and to make the liberals more individualistic and less collectivist, until one day some kzin would vote for them. *That* they could work out for themselves. Or not.

The rest of the questions were formal and nobody was very interested in the answers. The prospect of getting a fair number of new voters on the right side, their side, was absolutely irresistible.

"Thank you, Lord Vaemar, I think we have enough information to be able to come to a decision quite soon. You will be hearing from us within a day or two," the chairman told him. She even smiled at him until she remembered, but Vaemar didn't smile back. Nobody had bothered about the effect on human beings of a kzin smile, because when a kzin bared his teeth, it wasn't because he was amused by something, but because he was preparing to spring. But he didn't tear her throat out either, he just bowed politely and left.

😺 😺 😺

After Vaemar had gone there were still some worried voices.

"It's all very well to say that we'll win even in Munchen if we get the kzin vote. What if every human being votes against any kzin? 'Dirty ratcat-lovers.' They could hang that label on us."

"Who cares? Vaemar's exploits are well-known. Including the fact that he fought beside the Rykermanns, two of our most respected leaders"—he paused and bowed to them—"and is a friend of Dimity Carmody, or Lilly the Pink, as the old song calls her—'The savior of the 'uman race.' Anyway, it will be a long time before we have many more kzin candidates. Just one to show we want to engage with the kzin is all we need. If he does well, it will prove our foresight and wisdom. Also, the Jotok will get the vote when they grow to sentience. It was his expedition that found and saved them—as we will emphasize to them, if he is one of our party."

"If . . ."

"Hell, it doesn't matter if he doesn't even make it, and I can't see that happening. Not many folk around here will be voting for the liberals."

"He speaks quite well, don't you think? Sounds educated, of course. Might go down well in the Bundestag, those bloody libs posture around as if we're all a load of hicks. And he's a lord or something."

"Yeah, but can you see him on the hustings getting through to some of the old-timers who hate the kzin worse than poison? And for Pete's sake, can you see him kissing babies?"

There was a long silence as this picture went through their minds.

"I can't imagine many mothers offering their babies to be kissed," someone said. "They might be unsure of getting the whole baby back."

"Vaemar's teacher, Rarrgh who was Rarrgh-Sergeant, saved my life when I nearly drowned in a cave in the Hohe Kalkstein," said Leonie Rykermann. "He gave me artificial respiration, and, as you can see, he kept his claws sheathed."

The Rykermanns' words mattered. Almost the only figures to have fought in the Resistance from the first day to nearly the last, they were Heroes of virtually legendary stature in Wunderland's mythology.

Opinion was divided. "Perhaps we should ask Nils Rykermann's opinion?" the abbot suggested quietly. This looked to be an excellent idea, and the committee brightened again.

"Professor Rykermann, do you have any views on the candidacy of Lord Vaemar?" the bearded man asked.

"To reject Vaemar's candidacy will hardly improve man-kzin relations on this planet," Nils Rykermann told them. "There are kzin on Wunderland, on Tiamat, and in the asteroids of the Serpent Swarm, who would like to be good, constructive citizens. Some, I am told, worked to rescue humans in the devastation after the UNSN Ramscoop Raid. Already many of them work on human projects, and not a few in positions of trust."

Leonie interjected. "Rarrgh, Vaemar's . . ." Leonie could not think of the correct word—*major domo* seemed faintly ridiculous and few here would know what *verderer* meant—"chief servant, twice saved my life. The first time he stopped me from drowning, the second time he ran through fire and helped Dimity Carmody give me resuscitation when the traitor Henrietta wounded me." She had also saved the life of the kitten, its legs broken by the Morlocks and kept for live meat, who grew to be Karan, but modesty prevented her mentioning it.

A murmur ran through the gathering. The name of Dimity Carmody, the genius who deciphered the alien theory behind the first hyperdrive shunt, was a potent one here.

"Where is Dimity now?" someone asked.

"She is Vaemar's guest, and also his Ph.D. supervisor," said Leonie. "He has placed a guest-house in his palace at her disposal. She has the use of the laboratory and instruments. I believe ARM is aware of the situation." *And has probably planted something the size of a grain of rice under the skin between her shoulderblades,* thought Nils, *to track her movements and to detonate if she looks like leaving the planet without permission. Neater than a Zrrow. But it would be tactless to mention that now.*

The testimony of the Rykermanns, and the name of Dimity Carmody, had done much to swing the meeting.

"He may need a bit of coaching," the bearded man said eventually. "But there are quite a few kzin around here, and a helluva lot more spread around the planet. I say we should go for him. And just think of the look on the chancellor's face when our boy gets up to speak."

Vaemar and the abbot got out of the air-car and looked at the stockade. "You are sure this is in my electorate?" Vaemar asked. "It's a long way to the abbey and Grossgeister Swamp."

"Your electorate is pretty open-ended. I don't think officialdom knows about this place yet, it's too far away. But the villagers have been trading gold and precious stones for some months now, and buying all manner of things from horses to newspapers."

"Will they still hate all kzin, do you think? They must have come here to escape the Occupation in the first place," Vaemar wanted to know.

"There's your answer." The abbot pointed to a tall, bulky figure coming down to the stockade from the hills. It walked lithely and confidently. It saw them and headed straight for them. Vaemar moved in front of the abbot and patted his holster.

"Ho, kzin warrior, what do you here? The kzin is a mighty hunter!" Vaemar asked in the formal tense. The kzin's eye caught the red fur on Vaemar's chest, and his ear-tattoos. He began to go down in the prostration until Vaemar stayed him with a gesture. "Dominant One . . ." he began in the old style.

"That is not necessary," Vaemar reassured him. "We live in modern times now."

"Greetings, then, Great One and Human. I am Rrhougharrrt, the sheriff of this town. I keep the Judge's Law." Ruat showed them his badge with pride.

"I am standing for election for this district," Vaemar explained. "I would like to talk to the town, if that can be done without alarming the people here."

Ruat gave a very human shrug, although on rather a large scale. "I know nothing of elections and districts, Great One. I will take you to the judge, who will decide. Follow me."

They followed him to the gate, which was opened to allow them in by a gatekeeper who addressed Ruat in familiar tones. "Hi, Ruat, got some more visitors to join us?"

"I know not, Hans, but the Hero is of royalty. I take them to the judge."

Boniface and Vaemar were admitted with a polite nod, and the gate closed behind them. They looked around. It was somewhere halfway between a shantytown and a well-designed minor city. The houses were a bit rough but were in the process of being spruced up.

Children and kzin kits played together in the streets, the kits with buttons on their claws and Vaemar had seldom seen anything like it: man and kzin living together and a kzin sheriff who seemed to be on good terms with everbody. The kids showed not the slightest fear of him; they seemed to see him as a protector. They waved at him and *smiled*. And the kzin waved back and flipped an ear at them. Unbelievable.

"Judge, I have found some strangers. They came by aircar, it is outside the wall. The Hero wants to talk to the town, for reasons I know nothing of. You must explain it to me later." The judge looked up at them. He was sitting on a rocking chair on the porch of his house and smoking a pungent cigar.

"Lord Vaemar-Riit, as I live and breathe! And of course you are the abbot. I have never met you, but I have heard a lot about you. I knew your predecessor. I owed him a debt."

"But you have met Vaemar before?" the abbot inquired.

"Indeed I have, although under embarrassing circumstances, and with luck he does not recall me." The Judge was grave, so Vaemar decided not to recognize him formally, although it was not hard to recall the circumstances. Vaemar had been a mere kit at the time, but the events had been, ah, *memorable*.

"I have been selected as the conservative candidate for the Grossgeister electorate," Vaemar explained. "I would like to tell your people why it is important to vote for me. It seems a very vulgar thing to do, but I am assured that it is proper."

"Hey, you're going into politics? That's wonderful! Some of the men are out hunting or farming, but they'll all be back later. Can you wait two hours? We can have the whole town lined up for you by then. Not a whole lot of folk, of course, less than two hundred all up, but we are growing at the expense of some of the other villages further out. We can thank Ruat for that. He found gold and precious stones near here, which means we're rich now, and the word gets out."

"You have prospered," said Vaemar, as the villagers assembled.

"Indeed." It was obvious to the judge that Vaemar recognized him, despite the years that had passed. "And the sergeant . . . Rarrgh?"

"He heads my household . . . my palace staff.

"You have a palace? Times have indeed changed, O' Vaemar-Ritt!"

"Only a small one. But I find it is big enough. It is not on the scale of my Honored Sire's, but I find it is big enough for contentment."

"Then you are fortunate, as I have been."

Vaemar didn't need a soap box to stand on, had such a thing been available and strong enough to bear his weight. He checked with the abbot, who nodded.

"People, Heroes and humans, I am Vaemar-Riit. If you will vote for me next week, then I will represent you. My duty is to do what I can to help you help yourselves. I will do this if I am elected, whether you vote for me or not.

"I will have a say in the making of the laws. I will try to pass laws which I think are good for all this world. I shall exercise my best judgement."

There were six, no, seven kzin standing at the back, with men and women among them.

"If you want to ask me questions, I will try to answer them. Thank you."

It was probably the shortest campaign speech on record. It seemed to work. A kzin called out: "What is this voting? I have heard of it, but it meant nothing to me."

"You will be given a piece of paper with some names on it. There are little spaces after the names. To vote for me, you make a mark with a stylus after my name. If enough of you do this, I will become your representative."

"And if we have some trouble, we may come and ask your help?" a kzinrett asked.

"Yes." Vaemar was firm. "It will be my duty to give you help if I can."

The crowd digested this. "Will you favor the kzin? They are your kind," a human voice pointed out.

"No, I will do justice. I will be representing all of you, not just the kzin."

The crowd started discussing this with each other. Vaemar looked at the abbot, who nodded.

"Did I do that properly?" Vaemar asked the abbot on the way back.

"Looked pretty good to me," Boniface told him comfortably. "Think of it as practice for the rest of the speeches. Some may be a little longer when you're closer to Grossgeister. Tell them about the swamp."

"That will be good," Vaemar agreed. "I thought perhaps I could have spoken more, but could think of nothing to say."

"Doesn't stop most politicians," the abbot said drily. "I found it very refreshing."

"Ain't for me t' tell you how t' vote, Bill." The judge yawned.

"But you are gonna vote fer a *kzin*? I don't know I want to stay in this town, we got kzin all over the place, and I hate them. I hate them all."

"That's your right as a free man an' a fool, Bill Braun. How you can have strong feelins about a whole bunch of people you never even met is beyond me; I can only hate people I know pretty well, m'self."

"There you go, callin' them *people*. They ain't people, they's *kzin*."

"Way I see it, if you can have a talk to it, it's people. Don't much care about the shape or size or color," the judge told him. "Ruat is definitely people. He went into the river to fish out that kid was drowning last week, and he don't like water much at all. Would you still hate him if it had been one of your kids?"

Bill Braun glared at the judge. "We should have a human sheriff, not some goddam ratcat."

"No human sheriff could have heard the kid from that distance and moved so quickly. A human sheriff, and the kid would have drowned. 'Course, it's so much better to be fished out dead by a human than alive by a kzin, ain't it?"

Bill Braun couldn't think of an answer to that. He wanted to move out. He would have moved out. But his wife had told him that if he went, he went on his own. Damned women were more trouble than the kzin. And you couldn't beat them these days, even when they were sassy. Last time he'd threatened her, she'd screamed and that damned Ruat had been at his door in two seconds flat. Hadn't done anything. Just looked and asked if everything was alright. Had then explained that violence was against the Judge's Law. Except when it was required, as part of the law, of course. That, Ruat had explained, was *his* job.

The election day came. Vaemar and his mate Karan went around to every public place they could. They took Orlando and Tabitha, who were now nearly four years old, and were zooming around, mostly on all fours but occasionally toddling, and well behaved, all things considered; They also took their brand new kits, Orion and Arwen, who had opened their blue eyes but were still dazed by the world. Children came up to stroke them, because they looked so adorable.

After the count, the abbot could barely contain himself.

"Those two cute little fluff-bundles helped win you the election, Vaemar. You got fifty percent better numbers than your predecessor. The liberal was nowhere. And ten kzinti voted, which is a first. Next stop, the Bundestag."

Fifteen horses galloped east. The twelve riders carried rifles and side guns and were all in serious need of a shave. It was the better part of a day's journey to the village, and they had started late in the morning, so it would be nightfall when they got there. The three pack animals were roped to the horse of the last rider, who would have been recognized by the trader as a man who'd do anything to get money except work for it.

"The member for Grossgeister," intoned the speaker. Vaemar rose. This was his maiden speech, and he hoped it was going to work. The government looked up at him from the front benches, most of them with their mouths open.

"Madam Speaker, ladies and gentlemen. I stand before you as the first kzin member of this house, and as a sign that our two peoples can share this world under the rule of Law." There were a few "Hear, hear" sounds from behind him. The public gallery was packed, with several massive kzin standing among them. Journalists filled the press gallery.

"It would be possible for me to disburse platitudes about the fact that I, a kzin, should accept the role of this house, and that in doing so I might encourage other kzinti to engage with the political process, but to do so would be stating the obvious."

The chancellor turned to the man on his left. "We're going to have to get one of those damned ratcats in on our side of the house, or we're buggered," he whispered savagely. "If all kzinti decide to vote conservative because this one is, we'll lose everywhere. See to it, fast as you can. I don't care who he is, or what his politics are. We need a ratcat." The man nodded and scurried away. This was urgent. Vaemar had won a bye-election, but a general election was not too far off.

"Instead, I want to turn to the last finding of the finance committee. It is chaired by Senator von Höhenheim, who is, of course, of the upper house, and not answerable directly to this house. It is, however, this house which must ultimately determine proper priorities. And there is something which I find most unsatisfactory in this latest report. I hope to persuade both sides of this house that two grievous errors have occurred and that we must put them right."

Vaemar remembered to take a sip from a glass of water. Timing, proper pauses and the right buildup. Rhetoric was a weapon.

"First, there is the plan to drain Grossgeister Swamp. It is hard to understand how the government side of the house could possibly support this. The region is a complex wetland with a delicate ecology comprised of a huge number of species. That was where we found the Jotok, intelligent beings when developed, and there may yet be many others in their early stages. The dolphins breed there. To drain the swamp would be murder." That caused a buzz among some who remembered the Occupation. "I could enlarge on the damage which can be done when ecologies are disturbed, damage extending far beyond the immediate locality. If anyone doubts this, then listen to any competent ecologist. I have here some relevant papers which I shall table, and which demonstrate forcefully the serious risk of unexpected and malign consequences following meddling with a system as complex as an ecology."

Vaemar paused again after brandishing more documents than a human being could carry, and slapping them down on the table. (The *thud* made the government front bench jump.) The kzin sounded civilized; his soft, mellow voice carried not a hint of violence, but the sheer size of the creature was intimidating. The public gallery was absorbed, the press gallery appreciative and safely distant from the big animal. The front bench was not. Somewhere in their hindbrains, ancient terrors were triggered.

"And yet many millions of thalers were to be spent on this project, and no committee has been set up to consider the consequences. That surely cannot be allowed to go through. It would be irresponsible in the extreme; this house would be derelict in its duty if it did not set up a committee to review the plan to drain the swamp, and I am confident that any such committee would reject the plan as monstrous." Vaemar took another sip of water. So far, so good.

"Yet the examination of the *Valiant* has been stopped in its tracks. It might be thought that *I* would be the one opposed to an investigation which would likely bring opprobrium on the kzin. After all, by far the most likely explanation is that a kzin warship hit it and thought it destroyed. But truth must be faced down, no matter how fearful." Vaemar's voice rose in power and pitch: "We must learn to live together, and to trust each other. It is perhaps the most important thing for the future of our world that we do this. And trust must be based on plain speaking and on knowing the truth. Therefore I call upon this house to set up the investigation of the downing of the *Valiant* as most exigent business affecting our common future. My own most trusted servant, Rarrgh, has volunteered to go to provide security at no cost to the public treasury.

"I therefore move that the matter of draining the swamp be referred to a committee of all parties and that the house authorize an investigation of the *Valiant*." Vaemar bowed politely and returned to his seat, which had been greatly enlarged, strengthened and modified, but was still damnably uncomfortable. He must see about getting a *footch* installed. Several, in fact. That would be symbolically important, too. The house clapped for him, with wild enthusiasm from the conservative opposition, and more restrained graciousness from the government benches. The vestigial representation of the old Herrenmanner and the Progressive Democrats were pleased they had not been omitted. The public gallery mostly clapped, except for the kzinti, who made noises of approval. As maiden speeches went, it had the merit of brevity and the serious flaw of actually saying something. The chancellor would have scowled, but the press gallery had him in their camera sights. So he gave a benevolent smile instead.

The men arived at the village in darkness. Lights showed through the palings of the palisade that encircled the village; generators had been purchased and put to interesting uses. Eleven of the men dismounted, and some broke their breach-loading rifled muskets, loading them from bandoliers, while eyes watched them from the dark. The eleven crept up to the gate. The last man at the back sat and watched them, the three pack horses behind him sniffing the air nervously. His gun was already loaded.

There was a young man at the gate. Hearing the bandits, he opened the gate cautiously and peered out, shining a torch at them. Had they been marauding lesslocks, he'd have slammed the gate shut and given the alarm by blowing on the whistle he kept on a chain around his neck. Seeing humans, he called out to them:

"Hi, guys, who are you, then?" The lead bandit shot him, but did not kill him. The sound split the night more than the whistle would have done. The young man fell back, raised his own gun and shot the bandit stone dead, but it was too late. Inside the gate, the bandits shouted in triumph and fired into the air.

Outside the stockade, the horses were beginning to panic. One of the pack animals screamed, reared, broke the lead which tied him to the last man's horse and turned to run. There was a chorus of howls and the horse was submerged under a horde of lesslocks. The man caught the red eyes of the brutes and fired at them.

Lesslocks were so called because the species was clearly related to the Morlocks, but were smaller and squatter. They were less intelligent than the baboons they somewhat resembled, but were stronger and much more aggressive; they hunted in big packs of several hundred. They surged towards the man, who reloaded quickly and fired again before he went under a snarling mob.

Inside the stockade, deaf to the sounds outside because of their own firing, the bandits felt that things were going their way. The villagers were looking at them with horror, the women screaming. That was when Ruat and his deputies arrived. One of the bandits looked at a charging kzin, and tried to get off a shot. That settled things as far as Ruat was concerned. None of the other bandits even managed to aim; having five kzin warriors coming at you numbed the mind. The gates were dragged shut, leaving most of the lesslocks surging futilely about outside. The eleven bodies were torn apart. It made a bit of a mess, but, apart from the lead bandit's head, caught in the branches of a high tree where it had been flung, it could be tidied up easily enough come morning.

"Are we allowed to eat them?" one of the deputies asked.

Ruat pondered. He wasn't sure; he'd have to ask the judge for a definitive ruling, but he suspected not.

"No, we do not eat intelligent beings. Not unless they taste really good, and these won't," he explained. This seemed reasonable to the rest of the kzinti.

Outside the stockade, one of the lesslocks had picked up a musket. He found out how to break it, and copied what he had seen the man doing, taking a bullet from the bandolier and poking it into the breach. Then he closed the gun and pulled the trigger. It exploded and blew apart the head of another lesslock. Some dim sense of power came to the one holding the gun. It led the way back into the darkness, taking the gun and the bandolier with it.

The cross-benchers had taken the side of moral virtue and supported Vaemar's proposals when they had been made into a formal bill. This had allowed it to pass by a very respectable majority, to the discomfort of the government, which had opposed it on the principle that the opposition must always be wrong about everything. Vaemar had declined to be on the committee investigating the swamp-draining proposal, explaining that his presence might detract from the necessity of demonstrating complete objectivity. This was thought to be rather an eccentric perspective, but had, as it turned out, the effect of the committee feeling obliged to investigate the matter carefully and relatively honestly. The argument in favor of investigating the *Valiant* had some support from the anti-kzin faction, who hoped that it would show once again that the kzinti were murderous scum. The conservatives, joining with a minority who saw the force of Vaemar's argument that truth had to be confronted no matter how uncongenial, and another, larger minority, which had some serious suspicions about von Höhenheim and were worried about being seen to support him, again had the numbers, and the item passed. And so it was agreed that an expedition was to be sent out to do something about the sunken spacecraft. Rarrgh and the Rykermanns, Greg and Sarah, and Stan Adler, as well as a sizeable crew, and two other teams of Stan's news competitors were to go with it. This was going to be a very public event.

The motion-detector at the Rykermanns' door rang. Leonie awoke instantly, still with the reflexes of a guerrilla leader. The console by her bed identified the visitor as a large male specimen of *Pseudofelis sapiens ferox*. The lock identified the paw-print as Vaemar's.

The Rykermanns' ground-floor sitting room was equipped with a *footch,* the couchlike furnishing on which a Kzin warrior might recline. After shaking hands with Nils Rykermann, Vaemar presented Leonie with a small gold music box, mounted on what he said was Morlock bone, intricately sculpted. Rykermann felt his eyes narrowing very slightly as he looked at this. A valuable, if small, gift from a kzin of high rank was often the prelude to a request. He also knew, however, that this request would not come at once. A trouble with such requests was that, should danger be involved, the kzin would fail to mention it, politely assuming that all had as much contempt for danger as itself.

The robot butler brought appropriate food, and they chatted about the matters of Vaemar's estate, such as the doings of Rarrgh's increasing brood of kittens, and the work being done by Dimity Carmody, which Vaemar was sponsoring, on the further applications of Carmody's Transform. Finally, as if by chance, the talk drifted to the doings of Orlando and Tabitha.

"I would be grateful," said Vaemar, "if you would allow them to accompany you on the *Valiant* expedition. Rarrgh will go with you, of course, to keep them out of mischief, and Nurse. They should not be a burden."

It was not the favor Nils Rykermann had been expecting.

"My friend, may I ask why?"

"Because I am too tied up with politics to go myself, and I want them to start mingling with humans at the earliest possible age. An expedition into the wild will be an excellent introduction for them."

"They are very young," said Leonie.

"Not much younger than I was when Rarrgh, who was then Rarrgh-Sergeant, defended me at the last siege," said Vaemar. "There is an important matter at issue. You know only a small handful of female kzin have retained high intelligence. Karan is one. It will be a good chance to test Tabitha's intelligence under stimulating conditions."

"I do not think that is all you have in mind, friend," said Nils Rykermann.

"No, not quite all. My Honored Sire came to the belief, as a result of his experiences not only on this world, but on others earlier, that one of our species' greatest defects was the low place we gave to abstract knowledge. He had been on Chunquen, when many Heroes died because we kzin had no interest in Chunquen's seas, or the locals' submarine boats. When the Heroes saw their deaths coming upon them on the tips of nuclear missiles, it was too late to start learning. So he set out to study humans," (A trifle of awkwardness here: a lot of the preliminary part of that study had taken the form of dissection, but there was no point in reviving that fact now.) "But I know as a result of my own studies how many other areas there are that we have neglected. Seas take up about sixty percent of Wunderland's surface. I would like my son to have some knowledge of marine biology. The swamp taught me something of its fascination.

"Certainly, I do not want him to fall into the trap I have seen in the history of both our species—to grow up overly aware that he is a noble's son, living a life of ease and privilege, a Caligula, a Commodus, a Virritov-Riit. The abbot has mentioned this to me as a risk more than once. I want to start him on adventure while he is young. Something more that mere hunting for sport. Remember the Sage's Chant:

> *Knowledge, Oh Heroes, stands alone,*
> *Knowledge that comes with kittens' playing,*
> *Knowledge that comes with rampant slaying.*
> *A mighty weapon on its own . . .*

"Certainly I plan to get even more sons. But Karan has so far disapproved of other possible candidates for my harem. She says we must be modern." Leonie turned away to hide a smile. She could guess what form Karan's disapproval would take. "And, of course, one must be careful with the Riit bloodline.

"I was not much bigger than Orlando is now when I killed my first Morlock. We had come in wild country after Rarrgh put down Jorg von Thoma. I had slipped away from Rarrgh and entered the caves alone. I was no bigger than one of those Earth leopards at the time. Rarrgh disciplined me severely afterwards, but I believe he was secretly pleased with me. When he had finished he groomed me and fed me with some zinyah meat as a treat. I don't know how he had got hold of it."

"I must say I am looking forward to seeing the old *Teufel* again," said Nils thoughtfully, "and I guess he would not object to a field trip. But, my friend, I must be very clear about this. If Orlando and Tabitha are to accompany the expedition, they must be his responsibility, solely and entirely. You know how poor us monkeys' senses are. I cannot run an expedition and be watching those mischievous little balls of devilment at the same time. You know, my friend—and we have been through enough together for me to be able to take politeness beyond its limits by stating this—there may be danger."

"You speak frankly, but I forgive you. Much rides upon Orlando. But Rarrgh will be with them."

The mess inside the stockade had been cleared up, graves dug outside the palisade and the bodies buried. The mess outside the stockade was harder to deal with: fifteen dead and partly eaten horses and one dead man scattered about the place. Bits of the man had been eaten as well, but the body had been torn apart. Nobody could have recognized what was left without DNA analysis, and the thinking was simpler and more direct around the village. He'd got what he deserved. Likewise the other eleven bandits. The kzin deputies and Ruat had been given a sort of triumph for saving the villagers, a parade around the village on the outside and then once around again on the inside. Slowly, roles were evolving and beaten into habits. The judge was meticulous about the discussions that went around, joining in every one and letting his opinion be known.

Even the most obstinate of kzin-haters were coming around to the view that although kzinti in the abstract were murderous monsters, *our* kzinti were natural protectors. To the kzinti, something similar was happening. Although human beings in the abstract were natural slaves and food, *our* humans were basically, well, like kzin kits, essentially weak and helpless and to be protected. And the kits and children went to school together. It wasn't much of a school; there were only two classes, those who could read and do sums, and those who couldn't. They taught each other most of what they learned. They squabbled and fought indiscriminately and had to be punished when it got out of hand. Having buttons put on your claws was a dreadful disgrace to the older kits. The idea that the bigger kits should look after the little ones of both species, once planted, found good soil. The judge looked on his village with approval. If the folk in the big city could see how it was working out, here in the boondocks, maybe they'd have some hope for the future, he thought.

🐾 🐾 🐾

Further out, things were not nearly as nice. The kzin seldom attacked villages or even homesteads. They knew they had lost a war. They believed that if they did not observe the truce, they would die, and would deserve to die. The human beings were less tolerant and would have been happy to hunt the kzin down, but with the weapons to hand, this was impractical. Some had discovered this the hard way: Darwin strikes again. In the main, the species stayed separate and distrustful.

"Judge, there's a man here from out east. Some small village. He says they got attacked by lesslocks, and there's no survivors."

"Ask some of the men to ride out, armed. Oh, and take a couple of the kzin deputies with you. With you on horse and them on foot, you should be able to stay together. That's important." The judge was getting worried by the lesslocks. The numbers were getting unbelievable. Thousands of them in the neighborhood, and they were damned aggressive. They mainly hunted by night, and were cleaning up all the wildlife that moved except for fish. And they vanished for days or even weeks on end, suggesting a fair amount of travelling. Marauding lesslocks would overrun any homestead. Only a fair-sized village with a stockade and armed men stood a chance.

When the posse got back, it was to tell a terrible story. There had indeed been no survivors. The village had been small, had no stockade and had been swarmed. There were marks of the lesslocks fangs on the gruesome half-consumed bodies of nearly fifty people. But there were no guns. The guns and the ammunition had been taken. And one of the bodies had been shot.

The judge was worried. The village had defenses and could survive any ordinary attack, but the outlying villages, of which they had only partial and fragmentary knowledge, were another matter. And what if the lesslocks started attacking in daylight? The village could not sustain itself against a siege; their food was outside the stockade and already hunting was getting much harder.

"We're going to have to get help from the government," he told the men and kzin. "I hate to do it, I really do. Anytime a government gets its nose into anything they make a mess of it. But this time I don't see an alternative. So Hans, Ben, take some fast horses and get to Vaemar's palace. Get one of the deputies to run with you. Let Vaemar know the situation. He said he was here to help us help ourselves. Well, this is when we take him at his word. We need serious weaponry at the very least. Ride by daylight, come back by daylight. No night riding anywhere near here. Got it?"

"Got it, Judge, we'll be back as soon as we can."

Karan stood with her two younger kits held close, both squirming to free themselves. She was not as big as Vaemar or the deputy, but she was big for a kzinrett and had the sort of presence that made up for any lack of inches or kilograms.

"Vaemar is not here at present, he is in the Bundestag and will be in committee meetings after that. I am his voice. Tell me your troubles and it will be as if you told him."

Hans explained about the massacre and the threat the lesslocks posed. The fact that they had obtained guns and seemingly knew how to use them caused Karan to think hard.

"I must come and see for myself. I need to talk with your judge and to see the massacre. It is not that I doubt you, at least, not more than I doubt anyone, but I need hard facts, not second- or third-hand reports. If you return tomorrow, I shall be there before you. I shall fly to the village. I will bring some military people to give their assessment. Be sure that I take this very seriously and that Vaemar's promise to you will be kept."

The aircar held Karan, her new kits, two military men and one military woman. It landed outside the village after overflying it, and the judge, two men, Ruat and two kzin deputies came out to meet her. The combination of human and kzin in amity struck Karan as it had Vaemar. She had plenty of human friends, but this grouping had arisen quite independently. She saw something that nobody except perhaps the judge was capable of seeing: that the lesslocks were not entirely a curse. The dynamics which had made a man-kzin cooperation inevitable were intensified by the threat of the lesslocks. Intelligence was coming together to defend itself against a blind rage that had the numbers. Villages that had a mixed population were stronger than those which did not, and would survive. A sort of social Darwinism.

"Welcome to our village, my lady Karan," the judge said, hobbling forward on his stick. "I take it that Lord Vaemar is busy and you are his deputy?"

"Vaemar is busy in the Bundestag, but he knows of this matter, and although we had a slight difference of opinion on whether I should come in his place, and whether I should bring Orion and Arwen here, we are in complete agreement that this is urgent and needs to be handled immediately. I have come to observe for myself the massacre and confirm that the lesslocks have guns." Karan bowed politely, and let the squirming kits down, where they went racing around. It must be safe, it was mid-morning and the lesslocks were creatures of the dark. And nearly every species was kind to infants. The kits' big eyes triggered something protective across different species. No doubt there was a genetic recognition that the kits were too small to make a good meal, and it was better to let them grow bigger before eating them.

"Please come into the village, my lady. I suggest sending the aircar into hover mode just in case, but if you will follow me, you—" That was when the lesslocks attacked.

There were only a handful of them, but one jumped up out of the ground almost at the judge's feet, with a gun raised. The aircar had nearly landed on it. It was close, and much, much too close to Arwen, who gazed at it with astonishment. The judge threw himself in front of the kit and lunged. It had been a long time since he had acquired skill in fencing, and his stick was no schläger, but the tip went into the lesslock's eye, and the creature fell back and dropped the musket. Another lesslock stood and pointed its musket. The gun waved about uncertainly, the animal having only a vague idea of aiming. The barrel fell until it pointed at Arwen. The roar from Karan, the deeper roar from Ruat, the sound of a shot and the judge throwing himself in front of the kit happened too quickly to be distinguished, but Karan snatched Arwen back only a second before Ruat hit the lesslock and ripped its head off. The other lesslocks fled, and Ruat and the two deputies took them down within seconds. Karan looked down at Arwen. The bullet had emerged from the judge with the momentum of a thoroughly slugged baseball, and the kit had caught it in one paw, and was inspecting it to decide if it was edible. "No, dear, it's yukky," Karan pronounced, and took it from her and threw it in the long grass.

"You been hurt, Judge," one of the men said, unnecessarily. The bullet had caught him in the gut, and blood was pouring out from entry and exit wounds. Karan stooped and reached into the aircar for a first-aid kit. She bound the damage as well as she knew how, quickly and expertly. Then she placed the unconscious judge gently in the aircar. "Fly him straight to the hospital in Munchen. Fast as you can go," she told the pilot.

"I must go with him," Ruat rumbled.

"Good. And you," Karan addressed the female aide, "make absolutely sure he gets the top priority treatment as a matter of urgency. Send another aircar back to us as soon as you are airborne. Now, go!"

Ruat climbed in, and the aircar shot off. He didn't know what was going to happen, but without the judge, they would all be lost.

Karan stalked into the village. She was in a towering rage with herself. She had underestimated the enemy. So had the judge, and he might pay the ultimate price for that. But he had taken a bullet to save her kit, and that made a blood debt that would last forever. She was shown to the judge's house, which was also where he dispensed justice. The population, alerted by the gunshot and only partially informed, gathered and looked at her with some apprehension.

"I have sent your judge to the hospital. He has been seriously wounded by one of those *sthondat*-excreted lesslocks. Until he comes back, or you appoint a new judge, I am the Law East of the Ranges. I will do my best to give justice, even though I have not his wisdom." Her green eyes flashed, and nobody doubted her for a moment.

Vaemar needs to know, Karan thought. There was no necessity for visiting the scene of the massacre now; the basic fact of armed lesslocks was established beyond all possibility of doubt. Karan shivered with rage. The lesslocks now had an implacable enemy who would destroy every last one of them, whatever their inadvertent capacity to bring man and kzin together.

The judge opened his eyes to see Ruat's face framed by blue sky and the transparent upper shell of the aircar.

"Looks like I've taken early retirement," he wheezed. "I'm a goner, I guess. But it's been good having you as a friend, Ruat. You've done a good job."

"You must live, Judge, you must. We need you more than ever now." Later, Ruat was to treasure that *friend* word. Just now he had no time for thinking about it.

"We in an aircar?" The judge's eyes roamed.

"Getting you to be mended, as fast as we can go," Ruat told him. "Hang in there, judge," he implored. The judge tried to nod, but closed his eyes.

Ruat felt very out of place in the hospital. It was full of humans, and they were running around very fast, pushing a trolley with the frail, shrunken judge on it. They wouldn't let him follow them, nor the female military aide, who had handled all the negotiations and filled in forms. He looked around. A small man with a camcorder came up to him.

" 'Scuse me, but who was that guy you just brought in?" the little man asked.

Ruat looked at him. He seemed harmless. "That was the judge. He is a great and important man. He is the Law East of the Ranges, and I am his sheriff." He showed the man his badge.

"Really? A human judge and a kzin sheriff? That sounds kinda interesting. Tell me more," the little man said.

Ruat told him pretty nearly everything. It took some time and involved some food in a kzin restaurant, where the meat was really, really rare. In fact, still running. Although they were prepared to cook it, a little bit, for the occasional human customers.

Karan, through Vaemar, had ordered six drones equipped with anti-personnel weaponry. They were rare, and the military had been very nervous about releasing them, and had sent as many officers along with the controlling equipment. They stood in the village, not far from where the pig farm had been before it had been decided to temporarily shift it. It was already dark.

"We need to hunt the horde. Possibly several hordes. Can you get these things airborne without burning down the palisade?"

"Certainly, ah, ma'am. They should have no difficulty picking up a large number of bodies, even in the dark. Infrared capacity was noted in your specification."

"Then get them up there and quarter the district. Circle around the village and then look east. The beasts travel in large packs."

The officers looked at each other, and one of them shrugged. They had been trained to kill kzin, not take orders from one, but these were new and different times. Mental flexibility was definitely part of the modern job description.

"Very well, ah, my lady. We have six large monitors, one for each drone, and you will see what the drone sees. But please keep the newsmen well back."

The drones were released and went up on thin rocket flames. Karan watched the pictures they sent back. The village looked ridiculously small, but for a while she could see herself and the group inside the walls as green flickers against the darker ground. Those walls might have to be rebuilt from stone if this didn't work. The officers worked with keyboards and controllers, and the drones carefully avoided each other and surveyed the region. There were occasional flashes of bright green as small bodies roamed the woods and hills. But nothing like a horde.

"Further east," Karan ordered. The officers obeyed, and the six drones drifted off silently. "Deputy, do you recognize the area?" Karan asked one of the native kzin.

"Yes, my lady. That one is about a quarter of the way to the site of the massacre. And that one is flying over territory where we have seen solitary kzin who do not wish to join us."

It was perhaps too early for the lesslocks; the sun, Alpha A, had set only an hour earlier.

"Where would you expect the lesslocks to be at this time?" Karan asked.

"It is impossible to say with confidence. They seem to be moving far afield, which means starting early if they are to be back before sunrise, so it would not surprise me if they were further east and perhaps more southerly, since they have already devastated the region where the massacre took place. They are probably smart enough not to revisit the site. Although they will eat carrion, and may remember where their visit produced so many bodies. Of course, we buried them, but maybe they will dig them up again."

"What's that?" one of the newsmen asked, He had been taking pictures straight off the monitors. Others had been getting background shots of Karan and the officers, not to mention the villagers and particularly the kzinti.

"Ahh," one of the officers made an approving noise. "Hundreds of them. Each as big as an ape, moving on all fours in the main. I'll take us in closer."

"I've got another group," another officer remarked. "I should say at least a thousand of them. Going down to check up."

The two monitors dived towards the hordes. The bodies glowed bright green against the black background. They seemed oblivious to the vehicles above them.

"They must be lesslocks, but I need to be sure. Any way we can be certain?" Karan asked.

"*Fiat Lux*. Let there be light," an officer ordered, and a searchlight in the drone illuminated some of the horde.

"Lesslocks," Karan said with satisfaction. The beasts squinted up into the light, pausing. Some of them carried guns and had bandoliers slung around their squat bodies.

The drones rose quickly. Whether the beasts had the sense to use muskets against the drones was not at all clear, but a lucky hit could lose some very expensive equipment. A *very* lucky hit could do worse. Several of these present remembered the grossly asymmetrical war between the kzin Occupation forces and the Resistance that had flickered and smouldered in these red-jungle-clad hills. Human casualties in the end had been something like eighty percent of their original strength, but overconfident, unwary or unlucky kzin had suffered too.

"Destroy them. Every one of them," Karan ordered. The last part of the order was probably unnecessary, but Karan was taking no chances. With humans you could never be quite sure. Should lesslocks with guns escape into the great cave systems . . . and there was a question of vengeance. Another thought struck her even as she gave the order: many of the caves were still littered with the debris of decades of war. Not homemade muskets, but strakakkers and plasma-cannon, lasers and beam rifles. There were even stories of nukes . . . Let the lesslocks, now they knew of the principles of modern weapons, get hold of those, and . . .

This was what the officers had come for. The drones banked and tilted. A missile left the drone with deceptive slowness; it turned into the center of the horde and suddenly accelerated earthwards. Just before impact, it exploded into a vicious hail of slivers of steel and glass, and then detonated again into a ferocious flame of petroleum jelly. There was no microphone on the drone, but Karan had no difficulty imagining the screams of napalmed and razored bodies. She found it immensely satisfying. Something she had read once came to mind. *For the female of the species is more deadly than the male.* Kipling had got that right, she thought.

Both of the hordes were wiped out and reduced to roiling black smoke. No others could be found. A few individuals vanished like giant black insects into cracks in the ground, but they were very few. *You did not choose your enemies wisely*, Karan thought. The drones returned to land outside the stockade after inspecting the ground to make sure it was clear of lesslocks. The villagers cheered the officers and Karan with jubilation. The judge had been avenged.

Stan the Man had a lot of competition. One of his opposite numbers on a different television station had sneaked away from the southern continent with a less-than-convincing explanation involving a deceased relative. As if any newsman would put a relative, deceased or not, before the job. Unless the relative had been garrotted or hanged, drawn and quartered in a really grisly fashion, of course, when it would become a story, and one with a human interest angle.

The story of the village where kzin and humans lived happily together broke like a tidal wave. There were, it was true, a few other joint settlements, but in these they kept apart, in a state of watchful, suspicious truce. The fact that a human had taken a bullet for a kzin kit (pictures of Arwen blowing bubbles, and a slightly jealous Orion) showed what brave and noble people human beings were, which the human beings really liked, and pictures of Karan delivering justice cheered the kzin. Of course, there wasn't much justice to deliver, since asking the lady Karan to adjudicate on just which party had owned the pig and which the piglet seemed a bit, well, trivial really. So some issues had to be, if not manufactured, at least helped along a bit by kindly newsmen and newswomen. The justice Karan had delivered to the lesslocks went down well with both kzin and humans. Pictures of children and kits playing went around the planet. Pictures of dead lesslocks and of the massacre which had caused the retribution followed. People were proud of the brave pioneers who had gone out to face such things, and glad that they had kzin to help them. After the story hit, human beings went out of their way to be decent to kzin, a sort of acknowledgement that the surrender meant genuine peace. Kzin accepted that the truce was something more than a cessation of active fighting and looked as if it was going to last indefinitely. Some of the underlying tension that had outlasted the war began to dissipate. It was a slow process, but a man-kzin alliance was starting to look like something that could happen on Wunderland.

In due time, the Patriarchy also looked and wondered. So did other things.

The judge had also looked. Seeing his village on television had surprised him, and the enthusiasm with which telejournalists had pointed out children and kzin kits playing together and going to school together had helped his recovery. But it made him surprised when his visitor was announced.

"My lady, I thought you were holding down my job back at the village," he greeted Karan.

"It is not too demanding at the moment. Problems that they troubled you with, they fear to bring to me, lest my patience be shorter than yours. As it likely is," Karan confessed. "Mostly it is getting people to own up to being in the wrong when they are. They know inside themselves, they just don't want to admit it. Both our species suffer from pride, but yours is better at self-deception."

"Yes, we're really good at that," admitted the judge. "And can I stroke the kits? I think I'm entitled to."

"Indeed you are," Karan agreed, letting the two squirming bundles loose. "It remains a blood debt for all my family."

"Don't really know why I did it. I guess they just look so cute, and that damned lesslock so damnably ugly, my instincts kicked in before I had time to think. I'm not often noble when I have time to think, I promise you." He stroked Arwen who purred and rolled over on the bed to have her tummy tickled. Orion scratched his way up to join her.

"At least you have survived. We got you here in time, and they say you will make a complete recovery. You got the best treatment on Ka . . .Wunderland. My mate will meet all costs; it is the very least we could do to show our gratitude. I had to put up with a severe reprimand for exposing them to danger, and I *did* put up with it. Vaemar said I must feel very guilty indeed to be so meek, it was disturbing him. And when he gets a moment's free time, he wants to come and thank you himself."

"I look forward to renewing our acquaintance." The judge separated the two kits, which were practicing fighting with each other. "I get tired rather quickly still, and these kits are cute as buttons, but they are wearing an old man out. I hope to meet them again when I have a little more bounce to the ounce myself. Although I'll never have as much as they do."

Karan took them back and held them firmly. "I must go back to holding down your job. And I am very glad I do not have to hold it down indefinitely. You can be sure that my hopes for your early recovery are very sincere. The matron has promised me, however, that she will hide your clothes until she is satisfied that you can be safely discharged, so don't even think of leaving early. Know that I and my mate are forever in your debt. As are these little furballs." Karan bowed to the judge as he lay back. Karan looked back at him as he lay there. His eyes were closed with exhaustion, but there was a trace of a smile on his lips.

"It's coming in from the senator's own phone," the technician told Stan Adler. Stan was leaving for the Southland soon, and having a final check on one of his sources. "It's crazy. He can't be blackmailing himself." They looked at the string of e-mails. "Calls himself *Deep Throat* on the e-mails, and they come from a made-up email address, but I've traced them and they originate on the senator's own phone, like I said."

"Deep Throat. Rings a faint bell. Must check on what it means," Stan said, half to himself. "I guess it could be that the source is very close to the bastard and has access to von Höhenheim's phone. A girlfriend maybe. But it's a chancy business if von Höhenheim gets into the phone and finds out he's got an account he didn't know about. Particularly when he reads a few e-mails."

"You don't think he's trying some smart bit of misdirection? Accusing himself of something so bad that when the truth comes out it doesn't look anything much by comparison? Some charge he can easily prove false?"

"I wouldn't put it past the bastard," Stan admitted grudgingly. "And so far there's been no proof. Just some insinuations that could get the writer hanged anyway. Claims to have been in the KzinDiener. That mob of scum were passed by kzin telepaths, so there's no question they were traitors as far as humanity is concerned. They just loved the kzin, they'd do anything to show what adoring scum they were. I mean, you could make out a case for some of the collabos, they did at the trials. You know, they were doing their best to help the human race survive in the face of conquest. That sort of stuff. There may have been some truth in it in a few cases." This was a big admission coming from Stan; he took the view that sliming up to the cats was beneath any self-respecting human. But self-respect had been one of the early casualties of the war, which was why there was so much hatred of the kzin still around. It came not from the people who had fought to the end but from the people who hadn't. Stan could admire a formidable enemy, but he'd never doubted that they *were* the enemy. Now the enemy tended to be the scum who had temporized, particularly those who had found themselves on the losing side after the surrender. Oh, they had signed up mentally with the kzin, and now they felt betrayed. Those were the ones who really hated the kzin now. Those who had tried to side with the powerful and been let down.

They'd figured out that the kzin despised them and most of humanity despised them too. Well, that was what happened when you sold your soul. It was never a good deal. On the other hand, he had to admit, being eaten wasn't a good idea either.

He remembered too, the aged, haggard survivors of some of the Resistance groups from the early days. The kzin tortures, which everyone knew of only too well, since viewing them had been compulsory. The Public Hunts. Those who had not had access, or enough access, to the suddenly rare, precious geriatric drugs. The slow deaths of the diabetics (scores of thousands of them unsuspected in the days of autodocs) for whom treatment was denied until a makeshift, primitive plant to make the crude, long-forgotten treatments was set up. The cancer patients. Those of every age who died slave-laboring on the kzinti fleet's new spaceport. It was not simple.

"I figure he's someone close to the senator, and he's angling for immunity if he drops the senator into it right up to the neck. And all we know about him is that he hasn't got a phone, or not one he's prepared to use, but he has ready access to the senator's. Shouldn't be too hard, I'll get one of the researchers onto checking out the senator's staff. And his girlfriends, if any."

"We can't give him immunity, that's a legal thing," the technician objected.

Stan grinned wolfishly. "He may think I've got some sort of hold over a few judges or politicians. I'm not saying he's altogether wrong about that. He must also think I'd use it to save him in exchange for solid information. That's where he's badly wrong. This guy has been a treacherous shit to everyone in sight, and he is going down. But I'm happy to let him think he's in there with a chance; slime like this always feel they can con you into doing them some good. They'll believe they can manipulate their way out of any mess. Let's set him up to give us the real dope and then take them both down. So saith Stan the Man."

"Why do you have it in for this von Höhenheim, Stan? He may have been a bastard once, but he's not corrupt like so many of them."

"Not so far as we know. And nailing ex-bastards is good television. Besides, I hate those kzin-worshipping creeps. Now, I gotta run. "

The car was large and well-outfitted, strongly armored and armed like the fighter-bomber it had once been, with dorsal and ventral gun-turrets as well as forward-firing guns. Only its bomb-load was missing, replaced by a variety of salvage gear, and the seats which had once held attack marines had been partly removed to provide some kzin-sized accommodation. Orlando and Tabitha, however, were kept in a suitably strengthened playpen under the eyes of Rarrgh and a well-armored human nurse. They would not be welcome tearing about the car in flight and did not take kindly to being strapped in. They were, however, contented enough, standing on their hind legs to peer out through a port at the terrain passing below.

Nils Rykermann had not been particularly happy about bringing them, but Vaemar had been insistent. He had given detailed instructions to watch for signs of intelligence on the female kit's part. If she had inherited Karan's intelligence, the implications could be significant. Anyway, Rarrgh came with the kits, and he would be an asset in the event of any trouble.

Just now Rarrgh was flying the car. He was remembering another flight, the day kzin resistance on the planet had ceased, and he had escaped with Vaemar and Jorg von Thoma from the remnants of the kzin garrison at Circle Bay Monastery.

"So what happened to Captain von Thoma?" Nils Rykermann asked him. "I was still recovering from having the Zrrow removed from my shoulder. Removing it killed the surgeon and nearly killed me. We still didn't have proper autodocs deployed then. I missed all those months."

"I swore to protect him on the last day," said Rarrgh. "One of the last servants of the Patriarchy who remained loyal . . . I could not hand him over to the vengeance of your people. You shouldn't have been able to remove the Zrrow at all. We only accepted your parole because you were wearing it," he added.

"And because you put in a good word for me, I think," said Nils.

"We had fought side by side against the Morlocks. You and Leonie had saved my life when I was helpless. As least Leonie did—she dug me out of the rockfall instead of blasting me. And I think I know how else you used your fighter's privileges . . ."

"I swore to kill von Thoma many times during the war," said Nils. "But later I grew sick of killing and vengeance. Leonie showed me other things. The abbot released me from my vows. He said they were not good vows anyway. Mind you, if I actually did see him again . . . I had relatives, and students, who went to the Public Hunts, thanks to his police . . ."

"I am still sworn to protect him, but I suppose after this time it can hardly hurt to tell you what happened. And I trust you," said Rarrgh. "When we were a good way away from any human forces, I set him down, as I had promised him. He had basic survival equipment from the car. A food-and-water maker, a shelter-tent. I did not search him for weapons, but I imagine he had some concealed. He would have needed them in that country. When I checked it out later I found it was thick with tigrepards. They had multiplied without check during the Occupation, and the lesslocks were leaving their burrows. The fighting had destroyed many of their old food sources."

"I feel sorry for them," said Nils. "Like the Morlocks. They are unpleasant creatures, but they did us no harm till we attacked them."

Rarrgh still had trouble understanding certain human emotions.

"It was war," he said.

"Not their war."

Rarrgh gestured through the window to a ruined homestead on the ground below. "That might well have been their work," he said. "Of course, there might be other explanations . . ."

There was only the deep thrumming of the engines for a while.

"And there were other things," said Rarrgh. "Beam's Beasts, Advokats, Zeitungers . . . I thought he might not have survived. The Zeitungers were the worst."

"I know. I had one brush with them. One brush was enough."

"When I had established a secure and defensible bivouac for Vaemar and myself I went back to check on him, but he was gone. Whether he lived or died I know not. Later, when I was doing some work on the human farms, I tried to probe with a few questions. Some said they had seen a lone male human heading north, but there were many such wanderers then. There still are. Do you have a god that watches over travellers?"

"We have a saint. Saint Christopher."

"Ah. For us, the brave traveller, who dares the unknown, comes under the attention of Amara, third male kit of the Fanged God. But he lives on the Traveller's Moon, which orbits Kzin with the Hunters' Moon. I am not sure how much attention he pays to the goings-on of this world."

Senator von Höhenheim grunted. He had said relatively little so far, and had kept one wary eye on Rarrgh and the other on Stan and his two assistants. Below them the sea was shallowing and changing color.

"We must be getting close," Sarah said.

A gong sounded. A light blinked on the control panel.

"There it is. A nuclear engine, leaking but not badly. Let's get suited up." Now the radar was focused on the shape of the ship. The warcraft's sweeping lines, designed for high speed in atmosphere, were marred by obvious damage about two-thirds of the way down the hull. The after part had broken off and lay some distance away.

"That looks like a missile hit, all right."

They landed the car on a shelving beach about half a kilometer from the rolling hulk.

The Rykermanns and the Rankins headed out to the wreck in a

tender-boat. It had a translucent bottom, and diving was carried out through a central airlock. The high seas of Wunderland made this essential.

Had they been on a pleasure cruise there would have been plenty to watch. The seas of Wunderland teemed with life. Boisterous as the surface waves were, the sea a short distance down was tranquil.

The great curve of the *Valiant's* tail-part rose before them, somehow menacing in its sheer size. Nils steered the tender to the stern of the wreck.

"Look!" he said, rather unnecessarily, pointing. A circular hole had been punched in the banks of exhaust ports. Stan's people and an automatic camera on the tender were busily filming. Stan's competitors were trying to get better shots.

"Heat-seeking missile, I'd guess," Nils continued. "It must have got some way in before it detonated. Well, I guess there's not much to tell who fired it. The missile itself would have been completely destroyed."

"I would think," said Stan, "that such a missile would not have been very effective in space, where there would have been no point in running a chemical motor anyway. It has locked onto its target too neatly. As far as I know, these blockade-runners had ramscoops, which they detached and left in orbit to pick up on return. For flight in atmosphere they had chemical rockets—and hot exhaust ports. Especially in a system as dusty as this one, there would have been too much danger of a ramscoop picking up particles, not to mention enemy tactics like dropping compressed radon into it. I'd say it was flying on chemicals. "

"Meaning it was shot down in atmosphere."

"And look there!" said Sarah. Towards the nose of the great wreck, lights were burning behind several ports.

"The foward part is still air-tight." With strong modern alloys, designed for years in space, that was not particularly surprising.

"Could there be . . . anyone alive in there, do you think?" asked Sarah.

"It's not impossible. Those ships had mighty rugged life-support systems. It's been a long time, but the old design was expecting to be in space for decades."

"Try calling them up."

The results were ambiguous. No answer came, but a finely tuned motion-detector reported movement. Something was in there, about the size of a man.

"If he's been down there all these years he's not likely to be keeping a watch on the instruments," Leonie said. "He's not likely to be very sane, for that matter."

"We can't just leave things like this," said Nils. "We'll have to go in now, and find out. But we'd better go armed."

"We'll need cutting torches to clear the growth off the airlock controls anyway," said Leonie. "And to cut away any evidence we find."

"I think we should take a couple of beam rifles as well."

Their suits were designed for space but worked equally effectively under water. Von Höhenheim, who was too bulky for athletics, remained in the tender. A quick pass of the torch was enough to clear the growth off one of the derelict's forward airlocks. They stepped into the airlock and the water cycled away. The first thing that caught their eyes on the bridge was a translucent tank attached to an instrument console. It was nearly empty and the skeleton of a dolphin fitted with artificial hands lay on the floor. They removed their helmets.

"Kzin! I smell kzin!" Nils brought his beam-rifle to the ready. Almost without thinking, he and Leonie had gone into a back-to-back crouch, the muzzles of their weapons sweeping each exit from the lock. Leonie, still clumsy on her new legs, moved too fast and fell sideways. Sarah picked her up.

"That thing we saw on the motion detector," she said, "I'm sure that wasn't a kzin. It was too small."

"I don't care. Can't you smell them? Maybe it was a small kzin."

Violent headaches hit them. The Rykermanns recognized them at once.

"Telepath probing! That explains it! There is a telepath here!" Leonie screwed up her face and pressed her hands to her head.

"For God's sake! Rarrgh! Tell it we mean no harm! Tell it the war is over on this planet!" and then: "Tell it we have come to rescue it!"

The humans had expected no results. Nils and Leonie had to consciously override their training in such a situation and not think about eating vegetables (or—one of their teachers had been a Hindu—the capering monkeys of Hanuman), a drill designed to overwhelm a kzin telepath with nausea.

To their surprise, the humans felt their headaches subsiding. From one of the corridors a kzin emerged: small, bedraggled, a typical specimen of the kzin telepaths taken under the Patriarchial regime at birth and forcibly addicted to the *sthondat*-lymph drug, though perhaps looking somewhat better than the typical telepath that kzin commanders tended to use to destruction. Like all telepaths, language was no trouble for it. Its Wunderlander was fluent and colloquial and it spoke as close an approximation of human speech as its vocal arrangements would allow it.

"Don't hurt me!" it cried, falling face-downward in the posture of total submission.

"You have nothing to fear from us. Who are you and what are you doing here?" asked Nils, keeping the creature covered. This telepath was indeed small for a kzin, and plainly no fighter, but even so unwarlike an example of the kzin species would be able to dismantle a tiger—or a human—faster than the eye could follow. And their ability to inflict instant, paralyzing pain on the brain's receptor centers gave them an additional weapon.

"I was telepath aboard the cruiser *Man's Bone-Shredder*," the telepath told them, rising slowly. "Dominant One, there was a battle and I was taken prisoner. I was put aboard this ship."

That made sense, Nils thought. Telepaths were too useful to waste. They could be a mighty asset and it had been found that many had no cause to be loyal to the Patriarchy.

"Approaching Ka'ashi, we were pursued by ships of the Patriarchy, but evaded them. Then this ship was hit by a missile fired from the ground, and crashed. I had been placed in a restraining web so I was the only survivor of the impact."

"How did you know the missile came from the ground?"

"I read the captain's mind."

"Where are the bodies of the captain and crew?"

"I ate them. The bones are in there." He gestured to a closed door. I arranged them according to rank and dressed them in their uniforms. Do you wish to see them?"

The humans shuddered.

"It was all I could do to show my respect and gratitude," the telepath went on. "Apart from that there is a supply of rations. But I am glad that I have been found. I knew I was under water, but not how deep."

"Have any records survived?"

"I did not touch the computer's records. I am not familiar with human mechanisms and there were no survivors to teach me. I feared to touch the wrong controls. I read from your minds that the war is over on this planet, and the Patriarchy has been defeated. I am glad. My kind warred in secret against the Patriarchy as we might. I hope you will take me to be with others of my kind."

"It's a wonder you survived all that time, and a greater wonder you are still sane," Leonie told him.

"My caste has had long experience of living on the edge of sanity," the telepath told her drily. "And I have less than six months' food left. I should have had to take a chance on surviving the airlock naked before long. I have found comfort in isolation, but I should have been obliged to forsake this place soon."

The ship must have been retrofitted with the hyperdrive, Nils realized, and prudence would have made them provide food for a full crew for several years in case it failed. And two years of food for a full crew would have enabled a single individual to survive this time. And yes, solitude would have been better than company for a telepath. The pain of other minds would have been far worse.

"We will need to get a kzin-sized suit down to you," Leonie said.

The telepath nodded. Kzin did not easily show emotion in front of humans.

"Tell us," said Stan. "You read the captain's thoughts at the end?" Leonie was prying out the bridge recorder.

"Only in flashes. I dared not distract him or the other humans. For the ship to lose all control and crash, I thought I would be lost too. I huddled in the restraining web. We ran long and far before the missile caught us, with many evasions. The captain was clever, but not clever enough."

"But you picked up something."

"Of course."

"Say on. Tell us all you know."

"The missile's signature identified it as a *Hero's Slashing Claw*."

A short-range ground-to-air missile, barely capable of reaching the fringes of space. Though they could not be sure, Nils and Leonie thought they had been issued by the Patriarchy to KzinDiener forces. To prevent their misuse by humans, the later models had had identifiable radiation signatures, though whether the keys identifying these still existed was another matter.

Greg and Sarah returned to the surface and brought down a kzin spacesuit from the car. It was far too big to fit the telepath well, but it was adequate for a short, one-way trip.

"I don't trust von Höhenheim," said Nils. "If he is not entirely kosher, the recorder might be proof of that. I think I'll keep it out of his way until we're all snugged down and ready to leave. And don't let him know this kzin is a telepath."

"He *looks* like a telepath."

"If von Höhenheim asks, tell him the kzin has been eating badly lately. Also, he looks too well-grooomed for a telepath. I suppose because he hasn't had to use the telepath sense for a while."

Feeling there was nothing to be gained by alienating the telepath, they asked him if there were any possessions he wished to take with him, but there were none. Nils and Leonie had by this time made a watertight bundle of all the bridge recorders, and they returned to the surface. Rarrgh, who was trying to follow Vaemar in being a modern Wunderkzin, tried not to treat the telepath too contemptuously.

"You had better collect the kits," Nils told Rarrgh. Orlando and Tabitha, under Nurse's anxious eyes, had been playing in the sandhills above the beach.

"We must come back when we have time and examine this place," said Leonie. Storms had piled the margin of the sea with all manner of flotsam and jetsam, including the carapace of some large crustacean.

Nils also walked down to the tidal zone. It was hard to remember that he had been a professor of biology once. No one paid attention to Senator von Höhenheim. He quietly reentered the car. A shot from its dorsal gun-turret fused the sand to glass, barely in front of the human party's feet.

Nils wasted no time in demanding to know what was the meaning of this. He brought Leonie down with a flying tackle and rolled with her down the side of the dune. The others did the same.

"Bring out the kittens," von Höhenheim ordered through the loud-hailer as the car rose and hovered above them.

"What do you want with them?" asked Nils into his com-link.

"Hostages. They are two of the most valuable beings on this planet.

Can you imagine the consequences if their Sire were presented with their fried carcasses?"

"I can imagine what the kzin would do to *you*. And the human government wouldn't stop them."

"I saw you bury something when you came ashore. It may have been the bridge-recorder. I will trade it for the kits' lives."

"And what about our lives?"

"Killing you would not be useful to me."

"I'm glad you have enough sense to see that."

"I have a private island with a laboratory and autodocs. It is equipped with memory-editing facilities. Agree to have your memories of what has happened here wiped, and you will be returned to Munchen unharmed."

Nils did not believe him for a second. But his head was buzzing. It was not the full tiger-headache of a telepath's probe against resistance, but he recognized it. He thought at the telepath, "*Do you understand what has happened? Make a circle in the sand if you do.*"

The telepath made a circle.

"*Help us, and Chuut-Riit's son will be under a life-debt to you. Use the Telepath's Weapon.*"

The telepath injected himself with a spray he had concealed in a pocket of the vest-like garment he wore.

"What are you doing?" boomed von Höhenheim.

The telepath went limp. His eyes rolled up. He struck at the human's pain centers with all his force.

The car jerked sideways in the air, suddenly out of control. Rarrgh made a mighty leap up onto the wing, his prosthetic arm smashing through one of the skin-fittings—a refuelling port, The car slewed further and came down hard. Rarrgh had pulled himself onto the wing or he would have been crushed beneath it. They dragged von Höhenheim out unconscious after closing down the engines. Stan's people had video-recorded the entire episode. This included Tabitha racing to Rarrgh and pulling bits of wreckage off him and licking his face while mewing frantically; Orlando had been a poor second. When the footage was shown in Munchen, Karan and Vaemar watched it with enormous satisfaction: it certainly looked as if the female kit had bred true. With any reasonable luck, so would Arwen, although it would be years before they could be sure. And all the kits were safe.

🐾 🐾 🐾

"What do we do with the bastard?" Stan raged. "That business of trying to take a hostage and promising us a memory-wipe is as good as a confession! It's gone out on television, and most of our audience want to know why he's still alive."

"Due process," Nils answered phlegmatically. "He's under house arrest, but the legal guys are still trying to formulate a charge. Threatening a couple of kzin kits doesn't look enough, we have to get to motive. And he's had the sense to say absolutely nothing. Or his lawyers have told him to stay silent."

Stan pondered. "I think I know how to nail him," he said at last. "There's the emails from his sidekick, Deep Throat. It has to be Grün. He's been hinting at enough to send them both down. It's time he came good. Or bad, in this case."

Von Höhenheim faced Grün. He had been allowed to return to his old office while wearing an anklet that told police where he was, and he had found Grün there waiting for him, and sitting in *his* chair.

"Good to see you, Senator," Grün had said cockily. He stood and made way for von Höhenheim, with a little bob that was loaded with irony.

"And may I say how disappointed I am that you are under house arrest for trying to steal the records of the warship you were responsible for shooting down."

"Bah. They have nothing on me that cannot be explained," von Höhenheim snorted. "So I was planning to kidnap two kzin kittens. That was on the television, I saw it. The question is why? Do you doubt that a good lawyer will have a dozen explanations which redound to my credit? Oh, an illegality perhaps, but one a great many humans will have sympathy for when my lawyer explains my motives. And they don't have any kzin on jury duty, so I expect to get a good deal of sympathy. And my lawyers have already ensured that I shall not have to go before a telepath; the argument advanced was that my well-known hostility to kzin would lead to not being able to trust the telepath's findings. And the court bought it."

"As long, of course, as there is no other evidence in your complicity in shooting a missile at the *Valiant*?" Grün rubbed his hands together.

"Who could possibly provide it?" von Höhenheim asked. He looked narrowly at Grün.

"I could, Senator. And I would be willing to go before a telepath and have it confirm my honesty on the point. Unless, of course, I were to get some consideration, financial consideration. Rather a lot of it. You are a wealthy man, Senator. You did well out of the Occupation as a leader of the KzinDiener. Better than I by far. I would think that if you were to give me half of that wealth, it would certainly buy my silence."

"So you think you can blackmail a von Höhenheim, you slimy runt? That is a mistake." The senator drew his pistol and aimed it at the suddenly terrified Grün. "Say your prayers to whatever gods you bow before."

Grün started to babble. "You must not threaten me, Senator, this is being re—"

The senator shot him between the eyes. The body was hurled backwards, arms and legs flung wide. Von Höhenheim considered. Getting rid of the body should not be impossible. The sound had not been loud, and the building was empty at this time. What was it the disgusting creature had said. "This is being . . ." Being what? Being recorded? No, it was not possible. He looked around frantically. He saw it. A camera stuck on the wall above the door. He aimed carefully, fired, and saw it explode into flame and a shower of sparks. He smiled grimly and looked around for a chair to stand on, so he could rip the thing down. He reached out for one sturdy enough to take his weight and started rolling Grün's body out of the way with his foot.

That was when the phone made a *ding* sound. He hardly ever used the thing, where was it? The sound came from the corpse, and von Höhenheim found it in the top pocket, and looked at it. He had mail. With a heavy feeling in his stomach, he checked. There were six messages, all from different television news channels. He opened the first and read it with mounting horror.

"Thank you for your video. It will be checked out by an editor for possible use within the hour."

Removing the anklet had been difficult, but he had been able to aim the gun carefully. However, the blast had burned his ankle. At least now he could walk without being traced by satellite, and he had some hours until it was light. Money. He must have money, as much as he could carry. The safe held more than that. He filled his pockets with gold coins and looked around. He had little time. Getting the anklet off would notify the police that it was no longer being worn, and at some point a computer-generated message would be sent to a human being, but with luck, not until the morning.

Von Höhenheim limped to the door, glanced once at the corpse with contempt, and went out. So, he was ruined. A video of him shooting a blackmailer was the end. But he would not give in without a fight. The world was big, and there were always opportunities for a man of resource. He would go east. There were towns out there now, he knew.

"My word, come in out of the rain; it's a terrible night, not fit for man or beast." The kindly old abbot held the door wide, and von Höhenheim dragged himself in. He was beyond exhausted. He'd been running on empty for a day now and his foot was burning in constant pain.

"Come in here. At least I have a good fire burning—we'll soon have you warm and dry."

It was like being a child, and being comforted by this old man. Von Höhenheim shivered uncontrollably and accepted the support that the old man gave. This abbot looked to be a hundred, but he was tough and wiry enough to support von Höhenheim all the same.

The fire was in a grate that was big enough to burn a log as big as a man, and the abbot led him to a chair that was directly in front of it, and added logs to the blaze. Again, the old man was stronger and more energetic than one would have expected, von Höhenheim thought.

The abbot bustled about and brought blankets back with him and wrapped them around von Höhenheim as if he were indeed a child.

"You are limping, show me the cause. We all had to have some degree of medical skills when I was younger, it was a survival skill," the abbot said gently. Then he looked over the damaged leg, tutted to himself and went outside the room. Von Höhenheim listened to the storm outside, the wind howling as though in torment, and the gusts of rain on the windowpane battering against the glass.

When the abbot came back, it was with some sort of salve. He knelt by von Höhenheim, took the exhausted man's boots off, then his socks, and applied a handful of the salve to the wound. Von Höhenheim gasped as the stuff stung.

"Antibiotic, not a powerful one, and with some herbs to help. I see from your boots and feet that you have come a long way," the old man said. He went back to another chair, which he placed close to von Höhenheim's, and then seated himself. He looked intently at von Höhenheim. There was only kindness in his eyes, but kindness was no use to von Höhenheim. They sat and looked at each other.

"Yes. I walked from Munchen. It has not been easy."

"My word, that does go some way to explain the state of your boots. Well, you are most welcome to rest and eat. Today is my birthday, you know, and you are welcome on that account too." The old man smiled happily.

"Thank you, I would be most grateful. I can pay, I have some gold." Von Höhenheim was stiff. The last thing he needed was pity. Pity might break him.

"Oh, no, we cannot take money," the abbot sounded almost shocked at the idea. "It can be my birthday present, you see."

"It is usual for the visitor to give the present, not the person whose birthday it is," von Höhenheim pointed out.

"Oh, but of course; but you see, you only get food and shelter, and to keep your money, I suppose. But *I* get the blessing of doing a fellow human being a kindness. Worth so much more, don't you think?"

Von Höhenheim didn't. In his view the old man was a fool, but it would have been undiplomatic to say so. He watched as the old man shuffled off to return with bread, cheese and meat, and a jug of ale. He gave von Höhenheim two plates and a carving knife, placing them on a little table he drew up next to von Höhenheim's chair.

"We have made a very nice liqueur here for many years," the old man said with a beaming smile, sitting down again. "When you have finished, I shall get you some."

"Thank you," von Höhenheim mumbled through a mouthful of cheese-and-beef sandwich. He was ravenous. He needed the ale too, his throat was dry. He wolfed the meal down and drank the ale.

"If you are still hungry in an hour or two, perhaps some fruit, but it would be unwise to eat too much too quickly," the abbot said. "Let me get you that liqueur. I am sure you will find it soothing."

He did. Von Höhenheim leaned back in his chair and sipped the liqueur. It sent a warm glow right down his digestive tract. Combined with the warmth of the fire, he was able to feel the aches in his bones start to ease.

"Rather pleasant being inside, with the storm held at bay, don't you feel?" the abbot said chattily. "You must stay for at least tonight, of course. The beds are rather hard, we would hardly pass for a hotel. You can have one of the cells the brothers used to use."

"Are there many people here at the abbey?" von Höhenheim asked.

"Oh dear, no. We used to be a thriving little community at one time, although we suffered badly during the occupation. But it is so hard to find people with a vocation these days. We had a deluge of vocations during the war and occupation, but the death rate was high. At present our few remaining monks and brothers are away on an agricultural course. I am holding the fort. I have some novices and helpers who come to help with the Jotok pools, but they do not live at the abbey." He sighed regretfully. "No, I am virtually alone these days, save for a woman who comes in once a week to do odd jobs. I think she enjoys looking after me, so I let her do my washing for me. Not that there's a lot of that." He laughed.

The fire roared and crackled, and outside the storm raged and spat at the windowpanes. There was a long silence, and von Höhenheim felt sleep stealing over him. He felt almost safe. He wasn't, of course, he never would be again. But then, safety was an illusion—he'd always known that.

"Let me take you to your cell," the abbot said comfortably. "I have made up the cot for you, and you should be quite warm. I hope you sleep well."

In the morning, von Höhenheim raised himself out of the bed with some reluctance. The storm had passed in the night, but his aches and pains had not. He dressed hurriedly and left the small room, almost a cell, but with no lock on the door either inside or out.

He explored briefly. A kitchen garden was visible through a window, and he could see a blue sky with some straggly white clouds. Then he picked up the smell of frying bacon and found the abbot up and cooking breakfast.

"Oh good. You are awake. Isn't it a beautiful day? Go to my study and wait by the fire, I shall bring both our meals in together."

The study was the room he had been taken to last night, and there was a new fire roaring away. The walls of the room were lined with old-fashioned books; he had not noticed them last night. He went and looked at the titles; mostly theology, but with some popular and not-so-poular science books. Von Höhenheim sniffed contemptuously. The abbot was one of those intellectual people he despised. A soft man, this abbot, interested in ideas. What use were ideas? A man had to be hard, to be practical. It was a miracle the abbot had survived the Occupation.

The abbot came in carrying two large plates with bacon, eggs and mushrooms. Von Höhenheim helped him place them on small tables, and the abbot vanished to return in a moment with knives and forks, none of which matched.

"Here you are, now eat. I've given you three eggs. Very nutritious eggs."

The abbot gave thanks, very quietly, then they ate in silence. The abbot had given himself about half of what he had given von Höhenheim, so he finished first. He waited politely for von Höhenheim to finsh, then took out the plates and cutlery. Von Höhenheim waited for him to come back. He didn't like the thought of what he had to do next. He could hear the running water as the abbot washed everything.

The abbot bustled back and sat down. "Now we can talk. I have a feeling you've a lot to tell me."

"No. I have to leave now. And I fear I must tie you up and gag you. Nobody must know I have been here."

The abbot looked into von Höhenheim's eyes. "On the whole, I'd prefer it if you shot me," he said with infinite patience. "Oh yes, I detected the gun in your pocket while I was wrapping blankets around you last night. You see, if you were to tie me up, I should certainly starve before I was found, and I have an aversion to rats. Silly, I know, but there you are."

Von Höhenheim drew his gun.

"It has already killed one man. He deserved it and you do not, but I am desperate." He levelled the gun at the abbot.

The abbot ignored the gun and looked into von Höhenheim's eyes.

He showed no fear whatever, but he looked a little sad.

Von Höhenheim looked back, and his finger tightened on the trigger. He closed his eyes.

"I think you ought to look," the abbot said patiently. "You might botch the job if you have your eyes closed."

Von Höhenheim opened his eyes, and the abbot looked into them sadly.

Von Höhenheim took a deep breath and tried again. Why was it so hard?

His finger tightened, then he slumped and put the gun back in his pocket.

"I can't do it," he said savagely.

"That's good," the abbot said in relief.

"Good for you, you mean," von Höhenheim snarled at him.

"Oh, who can tell? I meant good for *you*. It would be dreadful to have to kill someone. You would find it very difficult to live with, don't you think? Your conscience would give you terrible pain. It already has, you know. I can feel it. But I wouldn't feel anything, I'd be dead. Or perhaps if the stories are true, I would be somewhere else."

Von Höhenheim glared at him.

"Some people don't seem to have a conscience," the abbot explained, "but I think we all do really. It's just that if you keep telling it to shut up, it sort of loses specificity. You know there is something wrong, something badly wrong, but you don't know exactly what, so it just becomes a general wretchedness. And some poor souls live their lives that way. I think that is what hell is. And they never find out." He shuddered, as a man glimpsing horror beyond words.

"Conscience! You babble of nothingness," von Höhenheim snarled.

"That's just silly," the abbot told him calmly. "It's one of the most important things in this wide and amazing universe. What was it stopped you killing me? Such a small thing, so easy to do, but you couldn't do it."

"I still could, and if you annoy me with this prattle, maybe I will," von Höhenheim shouted at him.

"Perhaps," the abbot answered prosaically, as if it hardly mattered. "I think though that you should ask yourself why this so-called prattle is making you angry. Do you think it could be because it's about a great truth you have been trying to deny for a long time?"

"Nonsense," von Höhenheim replied.

"Would you like another glass of our liqueur, do you think?" the abbot asked him. "It's good for the nerves, and I think you could do with some."

Von Höhenheim made a noise of intense frustration, and the abbot took this as agreement and bustled out. In a moment he returned with an ancient bottle and a single glass. He glugged a healthy quantity into the glass and gave it to von Höhenheim, who was feeling bemused.

"Try that. But don't drink it too fast, you need to savor it. We went to a lot of trouble to get it right."

Von Höhenheim sipped the drink and looked at anything but the abbot. The fire was burning nicely. Outside, birds were singing.

"Tell me about it," the abbot said softly. "It often helps, you know."

"Since I cannot leave you alive, I suppose I might as well," von Höhenheim said savagely.

And he told the abbot, "I was a leader of the KzinDiener during the Occupation.

"Servants of the kzin?" the abbot asked.

"Yes. We all but worshipped them. And they betrayed us in the end."

"Well, false gods do that, you know. It's one of their distinguishing characteristics," the abbot pointed out reasonably. "How did they betray you?"

"They lost the war. They were so strong and so beautiful. But they lost."

"I see," the abbot said thoughtfully. "Yes, I can see that might look like betrayal. But I daresay they did their best, you know. The mistake was to worship them; they are only animals, after all. Intelligent, of course, and with souls, no doubt. Much like us, really. I suppose the trouble is that some people need to see their gods in a very human form. A failure of imagination or perhaps perception, don't you think?"

"What do you mean?" von Höhenheim asked suspiciously.

"Well, the trouble is, God is everywhere you look. So some people don't see Him at all. I find that amazing, but it's true. I suppose it's a bit like an ant not seeing a human being, they're just too big. The world is so full of wonders, and some poor folk just don't notice. And we all have a hunger for the transcendent, and if we don't notice it because it's everywhere, then when you see a kzin prowling, and you've never seen a kzin before, I suppose for those poor people, it must look as if it's what they've been searching for all their lives. A tragic mistake, of course, but one can see how it could be made."

"I don't understand you," von Höhenheim said angrily.

"I think you do, you know. I think you saw the power and the glory and fell for what is really only a poor copy of the real thing. Of course, we are all made in the image of God, all of us, man and kzin alike. But it's only an image, not the real thing."

Von Höhenheim's mind was in turmoil. Yes, he did understand, at least in part.

"Where are all those wonders you speak of?" he asked.

"Oh, my. Haven't you ever seen a green shoot coming out of the bare brown soil? Isn't that a miracle? Aren't you a miracle? That anything should live among this vast whirligig of suns is a miracle, as is the whirligig of suns itself. Just think of the galaxy turning in endless patience, for time beyond comprehension. We can talk glibly of billions of years, but the mind cannot grasp the wonder and the majesty of it. *The heavens declare the glory of God, and the firmament showeth his handiwork.* And if that were all it would be enough; but it is only a tiny part. There is life, there is intelligence. And you and I are a tiny part of that, and we can see something of the wonder. Well, I can. Maybe you can't."

Von Höhenheim was silent. Something inside him was crying. The abbot was right, there was wonder in the universe, as well as atoms and galaxies. And he had never really seen it. Not until he had been shown.

"There was a man named Saul," the abbot said, looking at him in sympathy. "Very like you, I should guess. Full of certainty. Very competent, very clear in his thinking, but perhaps lacking in humor. And he took the road to Damascus in pursuit of what he thought was important work: making life difficult for people he hated, actually. And on the way, God spoke to him. That sort of conjures up a deep voice speaking out of heaven, but I find that hard to believe. God speaks to me quite often, but he doesn't do it with sound waves, you know. It's more commonly a sort of internal niggle, a sort of spiritual itch that you just have to scratch. And sometimes it's a great warmth that spreads right through me. So I'm inclined to think it was likely that Saul had something similar. He had a sudden insight into what he was doing, and it shocked him so much he went blind for a while. Or so the story goes. It's a very easy story to believe, for me."

"What happened to him?" von Höhenheim asked.

"He became someone else. He changed his name because of that. All of a sudden he figured out how to be happy. God asked him why he kept trying to turn against the road, to do the wrong thing, and he suddenly realized he didn't have to. What had looked the easy road became very hard, and what had looked impossibly hard was suddenly inevitable. So, he became another man. A man who could be happy."

"I wish I could become another man," von Höhenheim said, and the abbot heard the yearning in his voice.

"Well, I daresay getting to the point where you want to and see that it's possible is the hard bit," the abbot said cheerfully.

Two days later von Höhenheim waved goodbye to the abbot and set out to the east, walking steadily. In his last words, he had asked humbly if the abbot would report his presence.

"No. I am not answerable to man, but to my God and my conscience," the abbot had replied firmly.

Having waved back, the abbot went into his study and thought. "My goodness, I think I've performed a miracle," he said aloud. "Well, You did it, of course, but You let me be the one it was done through."

He fell to his knees and looked up to a heaven he saw quite clearly.

"Oh, thank you so much, God," he said happily. "That was such a wonderful birthday present."

A long time later . . .

A solitary figure came slowly through the dark. He was obviously footsore, the gatekeeper thought. Come a long way, and lucky to make it without bumping into a tigrepard.

"Can I rest here the night," the stranger asked. "I can pay. I have gold."

"We got more o' the stuff than we know what t' do with, but yes, you can stay the night. If you want to stay longer, you'll have to talk to the judge an' see if he agrees."

"You have a *judge?*"

"Sure we got a judge, an' a damn good one, too. We even got us a sheriff an' a couple o' deputies. An' you sure better not piss them off, I'm telling ya."

The stranger was passed inside and directed to Ma Jones, who had a spare room and was prepared to serve food to people who looked reasonably clean. With the traffic they were getting these days, she might find she was running a hotel before long, the gatekeeper thought.

In the morning, the stranger appeared before the judge. No, the *Judge*, the stranger told himself. The judge was sitting at ease in a chair, smoking something that could pass for a cigar most places. He looked up.

"G'day, stranger. Where you from?"

"Ah, I come from Munchen," the stranger told him.

The judge looked at him hard. "Seems to me I've seen you before, stranger. Long time ago. And more recently in one of they noospapies we been getting' since we got enough hard money t' pay for them. Frivolity I call it, but some o' the folk around here like it, an' it's a free world these days. Thank the Lord."

The stranger looked at him carefully.

The judge looked hard right back at him.

"Seems t'me you might just be on the lam from what some folks call justice," the judge told him.

"And you too, Herr Jorg von Thoma," the stranger said.

The judge laughed. "That one won't fly, Senator von Höhenheim. Sure, that was my name once. And sure, I came out here and lived alone in the valley for years. And one day another man came, and then another with his wife, and we lived reasonably close, for help if we needed it, mostly against the lesslocks."

"Some sort of species related to the Morlocks?" von Höhenheim hazarded.

"Yep. Shorter, more like chimps or baboons, and not too afraid of the light. And varying from being a damn nuisance to a lot worse, until recently when we done taught them a lesson not to mess with man. Or kzin. But now I'm sort of in charge here. Working in the government meant I was good at organizin' and arguin', and these people needed a lot of that. So now, hereabouts, I *am* the government.

And the Law. These are my people; I stand by them, and they'll stand by me. They understand loyalty. So do the kzin we have here. Anyone calls for me to come back to Munchen and face the music is wasting his time. I won't go, and even if I wanted to, nobody here would let me."

Von Höhenheim digested this. "You were a better man than me," he admitted. "You cooperated with the kzin, but you didn't shame yourself. I adored them. I worshipped power, and they seemed to have all of it. It didn't work of course, I understand them better now. They could work with you, thinking of you as a servant. I claimed to be a servant of the kzin, one of the KzinDiener, but they knew better. I admired them, hell, I worshipped them for their power, their strength; I saw them as living gods, I wanted to abase myself before them, to adore them. Me they despised. Perhaps the ancient gods of man always despised those who would abase themselves. Those who respect power and do not respect themselves."

There was a silence.

"And how do you feel about it now?" the judge asked, shaking the ash off his cigar.

Von Höhenheim thought. "I do not know. I am running from an attempted kidnapping and also a murder charge, but the man I killed was slime. Worse than me. But I was slime too. I have nothing to be proud of. I have sought power all my life, and now I see that it was nothing. Once I met a kzin telepath who had been living in a sunken wreck with skeletons. He was grateful for life, and when the moment came, he did his duty. He was nobody important, he will be forgotten, but he did his duty. And because of that, some of the evil I had planned was undone.

"I had a long time to think while I was walking here, it has taken me months, and on the way I stayed at the abbey and talked to Abbot Boniface. He showed me what I was, all in gentle words, most of them questions about why I'd done what I did. I told him everything, it just poured out of me. Ashes in the mouth. There was nothing of value in any of it, and it leaves nothing in the end but contempt for the self. The little triumphs seem so empty, the setbacks devoid of meaning. I thought it was all about me, but it wasn't. I am nothing. Plaited reeds, blown through by the wind."

"Yeah. That's all any of us are in the end. It's good ya found it out. Most don't."

There was another long silence.

"I will go further east. Maybe one day I shall find somewhere I can stay, somewhere where they won't know me. Then I shall have only to live with myself. That will be hard enough."

"Better stay here, stranger. Now you figured out what you are, ya can do some work and earn a place here. I'm gettin' old. These folk here are the usual sort. You know, mainly stupid and silly, but also mainly decent and kind. They need the help o' someone with more sense, someone who is prepared to take care o' them and stop them doin' dumb things . . . yes, and to love them. I could do with a rest. We may need a new judge East o' the Ranges before too long."

There was another long silence. "You would appoint a murderer, a cheat, a liar, someone who has abased himself before the kzin?"

"That's politics, ain't it? And maybe want of courage and self-respect, which can be learned. You're here because they caught ya out. Don't get caught out again. An' the best way is t' be middlin' honest. Ya know, the most successful cultures on old Earth were those that engaged with the rest of the world and learned all the other culture's best ideas. Now we got the kzin t' learn from. And they tell the truth. And hey, it works better than you'd think. Your big nemesis was a kzin. Vaemar-Riit. Seen it in the noospapies. Learn off him. That's the smart way."

"If I could start again . . ." there was dreadful pain in von Höhenheim's voice, and a kind of yearning.

"It's a big, big country, stranger. An entire planet. Room for people who see they screwed up and wish they'd done things differently."

"I spent my entire life screwing up," von Höhenheim said bitterly. "I worshipped power. It took a lot of walking and thinking and talking to the abbot to see it, but *What shall it profit a man if he gain the whole world and lose his own soul*?"

"Then now would be a good time to change strategies, don't ya think?" the judge asked cheerfully. "I had time t' think too. Long ago. And I got a gift of mercy I never deserved. From a kzin warrior, a sergeant, with a sense of honor as deep as a well. And kindness from Vaemar-Riit, no less. So I owe those guys, I owe them big time. And ya know what they say? They say, pass it down the line."

"You are a great man, judge. I could never fill your shoes. But I will do all that I can. If you will give me mercy, then I will try to earn it."

"Right, then ya can find Ruat, our sheriff, an' ya can tell him I have appointed ya his clerk, so ya can learn the ropes. Have to get ya one o' them starry things made up for ya to wear. Ya might have t' explain what a clerk is. He's a kzin, an' still learnin' stuff."

The former senator swallowed. Well, the kzin could only eat him, he thought. He squared his shoulders. This was a new life, a promise, something shiny and wonderful had this moment opened up before him. He had been forced to look into his own soul, and seen the wretched *smallness* of it. He was more than lucky to have a second chance, and he wasn't going to mess this one up. If a kzin sergeant could have a sense of honor as deep as a well, then a man could at least try to equal that.

🐾   🐾   🐾

HERITAGE

by Matthew Joseph Harrington

This story is respectfully dedicated
to the descendants of the Bounty survivors
on Norfolk Island.

❧ HERITAGE ❧

THE UNSN CARRIER *YORKTOWN* had been an experiment which might not be repeated.

A colony ramship, started by Skyhook Enterprises and completed just before the end of the First War, had been fitted with hyperdrive and gravity compensators at the beginning of the Second, making it the largest warship humans had ever constructed. Much of its interior was hangar space for singleships sheathed in superconductor, which allowed them to go through a ramfield without scrambling the pilot's nerve impulses. The carrier's mission had been to: a) accelerate to relativistic speed, b) reach the kzin home system in hyperdrive, c) reenter normal space, d) wreak multiple kinds of havoc with the *Yorktown*'s drive and field as they decelerated through the system, e) drop off its singleships to destroy targets of opportunity, f) take a close turn around the star with the field stirring up flares, g) pick up the singleships, h) accelerate out of the system, and i) go into hyperdrive as soon as they were out of the singularity.

They had gotten as far as "a." Then they were spotted by the battleship, which had possibly been scouting ahead for an invasion; the kzinti were a little less reckless than they'd been in the First War.

Captain Persoff had the *Yorktown* take evasive action as the kzin fired weapons and began matching course, but a ramship is not built to dodge. Over the intercom, Monstro, as the commander of the fighters was known, said, "We can take him out, Captain. Get in close untouched and slice him into chum."

"Then you'd better," said Persoff.

They had only been waiting for the order. Forty dolphins locked, loaded, and launched.

The kzinti had sixty-four fighter ships and the best tracking systems in Known Space. Out of forty targets, they got two. They were completely unprepared for an enemy that maneuvered instinctively in three dimensions. They quickly altered their tactics to attempt to ram the *Yorktown*. The fact that getting within a thousand miles of the carrier would be fatal only meant that they aimed very carefully. The *Yorktown*'s beam weapons were diversions of the main drive, and none of the kzinti got within fifty miles except as vapor.

The kzinti had learned the Lesson of the Laser in the First War, and the outer layer of their ship was water tanks. It vented steam wherever it was perforated, and this not only kept the damage from penetrating further, it acted to diffuse and disperse later attacks.

On the other hand, water vapor also interfered with the kzin sensors as it cooled and formed ice crystals, and after about an hour of battle, Captain Persoff began moving the *Yorktown* closer to the kzin ship. At a thousand miles the ramfield would wreck an unprotected nervous system, but the kzin ship was well-shielded from that, judging by the uniformity of the venting. However, at half that range, the ram drive itself could be aimed with precision, and the only effect of the superconductive sheathing would be to make sure the kzinti all roasted at the same time.

The kzinti realized what was happening just before the carrier got into aiming range of the ramship. The enemy's fusion drive suddenly lit up, but apparently enough damage had been done that this was a bad idea: most of the conical aft segment turned white and evaporated.

Half the universe turned bright blue, and the other half vanished.

You don't put a man who isn't a plasma engineer in command of a fighting ramship. You don't. Not if you want your ship back. Persoff opened the ramfield constriction to minimal power production, just enough for life support and the gravity planer, and began easing the ship over to the singleships one by one.

The dolphins were all dead, killed by synchrotron radiation from the relativistic protons being diverted by the ramfield. When the kzin ship had exploded, something must have happened to its gravity planer, and it and everything else in the ramfield, inside some unknown but significant level of ram flux, had been accelerated in the direction it had been aimed. What was left of the kzin ship was glowing by its own light, which suggested some of its ammo had gone up after the powerplant blew.

Captain Persoff was moving in on the last one when Astrogator Conreid announced, "I've worked out our speed and heading, if you want them."

"Can't hurt," Persoff said.

"Speed is approximate, calculated by comparing the wavelength of that glow dead ahead with the microwave background of the universe. We're operating at a tau factor of about fifty to one, which works out to a velocity of point nine nine nine eight C. At full impulse," like most math types, he loathed describing the effect of a gravity planer as "thrust," "we can decelerate to zero in about five hundred and seventy-nine days, give or take one. That's our time. By then we'll be about forty lightyears away from Earth. Our heading was a little trickier, since nothing looks right, but my best guess is we can steer enough to pass our target about 200 AU out. I can't figure out a way for us to get closer without risking the field collapsing. Moscow Motors overdesigned the scoop as a matter of habit, but the ramfield was never expected to have to deal with flux at this speed. One of the little private-sized ships they were building toward the last could have done it, but of course one of those would have been useless on a mission like this. However, we can hit them dead on if we jump laterally in hyperspace. Drop out just outside the singularity, dump most of the water since we won't be needing it now—" He didn't seem to notice the instant hostility of the rest of the bridge crew at the callous remark; the better sort of technical brain tends to miss these details—"hit it with the drive to disperse it widely, and let it spread through the kzin home system ahead of us."

Persoff nodded, had a grabber bring in the final singleship, and said, "If we don't mind dying before we see if we hit anything. When we came out of hyperspace we'd have hydrogen inside the ramfield, moving at a whisper short of lightspeed relative to us. Allowing for mass change, I'd say over a microgram within the ship itself. Secondary radiation from collisions should come to about half a million rads."

"Aw, crap," said Conreid. "Here I thought I had a way for the fins to strike one last blow. I know Monstro would have wanted to." Someone with normal empathy would have looked depressed. The astrogator looked really annoyed.

"So where do we come to rest?" Persoff said.

"Not real sure. There's a little cluster of stars in that direction that we'll have to pick our way through, and it's hard to tell what's beyond them. Old kzin charts we got in the First War don't show any missions that way, probably because the stars are too blue to suit them. Captain, may I suggest we get those singleships back?"

"I had intended to. What's your reason?"

"We can use the engines as laser cannon on the way back."

"Mr. Conreid, I like the way you think, but there's every chance we'll have to strip them for parts. The ramfield is just barely handling deflection, and we'll be nursing it pretty carefully for the next twenty months."

Conreid nodded. "In that case, sir, we should dump the water as soon as possible."

"Less mass to decelerate, good thinking."

"That too, sir, but what I had in mind was smashing the crap out of anything in our way."

Persoff blinked. "Such as what, that the drive laser won't vaporize?"

Conreid spread his hands, palms up. "Such as whatever the *Eva Peron* ran into. Their matrix ionizer was as good as ours is, and they weren't going as fast."

"Persuasive. All departments report."

One by one, he heard from everyone at their battle stations that the ship was intact and no further enemies were available. The last was hyperdrive systems, and Kershner told him, "I don't think we can use the hyperdrive or the hyperwave at all, sir."

"Explain."

"The mass of everything else in the universe has increased by a factor of fifty and a bit. At this speed, a rock that's normally small enough to ignore turns into a boojum, coming on too fast to spot when we charge up. The hyperwave is even more fussy than the drive when it comes to general background gravity, and it's my belief it'll be wrecked if we turn it on. Also, we'd have to record a message and play it back slowly for them to understand it, and I honestly have no idea what relativistic effects do to whatever the hyperwave medium is anyway. I also don't know if our tau factor would carry over in hyperspace, or what the transition effects are if it doesn't."

"Recommendations?"

"Let's not find out."

Persoff nodded. "Stand down to Condition Yellow and prepare to jettison water." He thought about it. "Astrogator, that water will spread out enough for some of it to go through the kzin system, won't it?"

"Yes, sir." Conreid suddenly smiled, which he rarely did. "Ought to screw things up a little."

"Or a lot. Our combat pilots are getting burial in space. Work out the trajectory that gives them the best chance of going through the system. The funeral will be at the start of the midwatch."

The chance of attracting someone's attention with the com laser wasn't even discussed. Nobody would be wasting time monitoring a frequency that was less than two percent of normal.

The funeral necessarily took place while they were at Alert stations, as the ship was still in constant danger and would be until they at least managed to get below about point eight G. That wouldn't be until they were well past kzin space. On the bright side, aside from a few rare and lightly-armed antique courier ships, the kzin didn't have anything that could catch them on the way through. As long as it didn't run into anything, the *Yorktown* was safe enough.

It rankled. Kzinti weren't the only ones who'd changed their viewpoint during the First War. They had become more prudent as the reckless ones charged into overwhelming enemy fire, but humans had become more aggressive as the conciliatory ones were eaten.

Persoff established training drills in combat and ships' systems. Not everybody was qualified to learn everything, but all of them were capable of learning something, and knowing more would make them better fighters. Someone—he never found out who, but he suspected it was Tokugawa, who in addition to his other duties was a historian—put up a sign in the rec room that said:

KILL KZINTI. KILL KZINTI.
KILL MORE KZINTI.

IF YOU LEARN A NEW JOB
YOU WILL BE BETTER
AT KILLING THE ORANGE FREEMOTHERS.

It had a profound effect on enrollment in the classes being offered.

A bigger problem was the ratio of sixty-eight men to nine women, which led to some serious fights until Persoff bluntly ordered the women to set up a rota of when they would and would not be available to any particular man. One man had to go into the ship's organ bank before this was accepted, but after that there were no more fights—or attempted rapes.

His own partner of choice was Newmar, the ship's master at arms, who had astonishing balance and a relaxed attitude about fidelity—which was good, because he had to pay some attention to each of the other women now and then or risk the appearance of favoritism.

The mission was never intended to last more than eight weeks. Holding the ship and crew together for more than a year and a half was a strain he'd never anticipated.

He got the remaining seventy-six of them through alive, and sane, as far as he could tell.

Persoff declared a celebration when they got down to point eight C, which was their intended cruising speed. In the midst of it, Potter, the communications officer on duty, interrupted him with the news that he was picking up a radio signal from a nearby system—transmitted on what, allowing for Doppler effects, must have started as a one-meter frequency. "It's got to be from humans, sir."

"What does it say?"

"Well, that's a problem. It's some kind of dot-dash system I'm not familiar with. Short groups, repeated."

"What would they say if it were Morse code?"

"'OSO OSO OSO,' over and over."

People of merely high intelligence need not apply for special missions, and Persoff had not been made the leader of this crew for nothing. "It sounds like someone trying to send an SOS who doesn't know Morse."

Potter was no slouch himself. "Good grief. Got the dots and dashes reversed."

"Exactly. I'll be there at once. Call Conreid and Kershner and tell them to join me on the bridge."

Conreid showed up barefoot, and Persoff forbore to ask what he'd interrupted. Kershner had been sleeping, and was wearing a bandolier of flasks of tea. When he arrived he was foggily opening a nicotine patch. "You can smoke if you want," Persoff told him.

"Can't stand the smell," Kershner said, glaring at the patch as he worked the adhesive layer off one corner. "I just want the IQ boost."

"Oh. We're getting a signal from human beings in a system—how far away?"

"About two lightyears," Potter said, "almost lateral to our course."

"Right. I want you two to plot a course that'll take us through hyperspace and come out at a point that'll bring us to a halt in that system when we're done decelerating."

"Oh. Okay. A little over fifteen days uphill from the source, then," Kershner said.

"You worked that out just like that?" Persoff said.

"Hell, no," Kershner said. "But I remember how long it was supposed to take us to ramp up to this speed." He freed the patch, put it on, opened a flask, drained it, and said, "Then what?"

There had been complaints about Kershner's manner from officers all through the trip. Hesitant ones. He'd been one of the corpsicles revived for training duty in the First War, and no one was entirely certain whether his behavior was due to an attitude problem or a touch of thawing damage—what the ARM called Ice on the Mind, and the corpsicles, even less politely, called Freezer Burn.

Some of them had been known to milk it for all it was worth. It would have been easier to deal with if so many of them hadn't been the best in the world at something or other. Kershner, for example, had an intuitive grasp of hyperspatial relationships that rivaled that of Carmody herself. The odd part was that he wasn't that much of a mathematician.

"Then we do it," Persoff said.

"Okay."

Kershner earned his pay as they came out of hyperspace. In a civilized system there would be beacons and beams providing constant, clear, insistent instructions about where the inhabited sites were and how to match course. This place just had the one repeating beacon, which wasn't even enough to ascertain the plane of the ecliptic.

Nor, indeed, the extent of the local Oort halo. Something—just what wasn't clear on the films afterward, but it must have been rock—sheared away a chunk of the outermost ram ring about three seconds after they returned to normal space. When they were checking, the tapes also showed that Kershner had them back in hyperspace something like a hundred and forty milliseconds after the alarm sounded, and they came out again a couple of seconds after that.

"We still have deflection," Persoff told his crew after checking, "but that ring has to be rebuilt before we can collect fuel. We've got enough to make rendezvous, and what the planer can collect will run the ship while we make repairs. Kershner, that was some sweet piloting."

"Thank you, Captain," Kershner said, barely audible over the sound of his suit recycler starting up.

"Need anything?"

"Maybe new kidneys? I think I've ruined mine."

Conreid found the beacon again, assessed its motion from the frequency changes, beat drums, burned incense, and gave an opinion of where the ecliptic was which proved to be accurate to within a tenth of a percent.

The planet was weird. It was Earth-like, but lower in density, and had a thicker atmosphere and no moon, and according to what was believed about planetary development that was just wrong. Earth had had much of its lightweight crust knocked off by a major collision, the debris had formed Luna, and the excess atmosphere had been stored as carbonates while things cooled. Just to make things more confusing, this place had too much nitrogen, about twice as much as Earth. Almost half as much as Venus.

There were huge icecaps, a lot of shallow ocean, and not much land. All of the land was islands, and all the islands had volcanoes, with the solitary exception of one big equatorial one. The source of the beacon was in synchronous orbit over that.

The source was colossal.

As they approached it kept getting bigger. It must have been half a mile long, not even counting the big spikes sticking out of each end. There was a hole in the side that the *Yorktown* would have just fitted into. Persoff, unable to find anything like it in the database, finally called Tokugawa as they were maneuvering for a better view of one of the spikes, to have him look at the images they were getting of it. He couldn't believe humans had ever built a ship that big.

At his first glance the history buff screamed, "Get us away from that!"

Persoff had the planer at thirty gees before Tokugawa could inhale for the explanation. It was too late. This spike was a railgun longer than the *Yorktown*, and it threw one rock.

Drill called for everyone to be in suits for maneuvers, and the planer had moved the ship somewhat, but six men died when the rock hit, and most of one end of the ship was sheared off. It was the end the ram was attached to.

Persoff wrecked the railgun with a plasma shot and set about the serious business of getting them onto that island. There was no way they could stay in space to repair the ship. Half of the bio converter had gone with the ram.

He took his time setting the ship down, which was the best part about gravity planers: you could land a ship that was open to space. The bad news about the landing site was also the good news: almost all the island was covered by trees, in perfect rows, which meant that there were definitely people who thought like humans here. Kzinti liked loose forests with large clearings, Jotoki liked groves with pools in the middle, and the sonar-using Kdatlyno kept trees widely separated when they allowed them around at all.

Up close, the trees were mostly pines, which implied humans again; someone else might have taken over a world with a human ship orbiting it, but no race that wasn't from Earth could stand the smell.

The *Yorktown*'s planer cut out just as they settled, and everyone and everything aboard gave a little bounce as the lower local gravity took over. Persoff froze, then said, "Emery, what was that?"

"I don't know, Captain, but half my board just went black," she replied. "The cutoff point . . . looks to be just about where that shot hit us."

"Sweet reason. We just made it. Tokugawa, what was that ship? —Tokugawa?"

"He hit his head when he fell, sir," said his assistant, Fiester.

"Tanj. How is he?"

"I got him to sick bay right away. He was doing well when I left."

"Good grief, how fast were you moving? We just got down."

"No, sir, not just now; he fainted when they shot at us."

"Fainted?"

"Passed out? Went all pale and blotchy—"

"I'm familiar with the procedure. Sick bay, this is the captain, connect me with Tokugawa."

"He's not well, sir," said Meier.

"Now, Doctor," he told her.

"Doctors," Kershner muttered.

"Sorry I funked, sir," Tokugawa said.

"I gather you had reason? What is that ship, anyway?"

"It's the Galaxias, sir. Built by Sinclair Enterprises in 2164. It was supposed to be the first manned ramship."

"I never heard of it."

"No, sir, it was headed in this general direction and disappeared in a big flash of light. It just dropped out of the news, and references to it disappeared."

"That's weird."

"Not really. The UN didn't want any bad publicity for the colony ships, and the ARM had draconian powers over the media even then. It was an experimental design, too. Had a whopping big Sinclair accelerator as part of its drive."

"I would think they'd have noticed pretty quickly that it doesn't really reduce inertia," Persoff remarked.

"Not from outside the field," Tokugawa agreed. "The thing is, they mounted the generator on a spike that extended way in front of the ship, and used the field as a nonmagnetic ramscoop. Everything went in just fine, but when it tried to get out the aft side of the field, it slowed way down and gathered at the middle. That was what got fed into the fusion drive. Worked great in the tests, and they kept solid objects out of the path with an early version of the medium ionizer all later ramships use, a big blue laser aimed forward from inside the field. Came out as X rays, vaporized everything. I guess the kzinti noticed the laser, attacked, and got fried like the ones we met. I was afraid that was the end pointed at us. Instead we got the exhaust accelerator."

"Why was it so big?"

"Generation ship, sir. They were planning to go outside the plane of the galaxy and terraform planets, setting down colonies every century or so. The starting crew was three hundred, and they meant to expand to six thousand on each leg, retaining the best gene patterns in the crew for the next trip. They had embryo banks, seeds, bacteria, the works, mostly in stasis. They must have used the accelerator on the planet," he added.

Persoff frowned. "Explain?"

"They couldn't have had much choice about where to stop. The planet here would have been the right distance from the primary, but with no collision and no moon it would have been more like Venus or the lowlands of Plateau. If they separated the landing vessels and stocked them as lifeboats, they could have expanded the accelerator around the planet, so it radiated heat five hundred times as fast as it absorbed it. Let me see—Doctor, this computer link doesn't work."

"You're injured," came her voice.

"My hand is fine. See?" There was an exclamation and the sound of a smack. "Ow. Thanks. Now, yes, nine or ten years would be enough time for the carbonates to form, then they'd have the field timed to shut off, and seed algae and so forth."

"You sound like you were there."

"Oh, it's an old idea. John Smith, an exile on Mars, came up with it before the First War as a way of terraforming Venus. He wanted to leave part of the atmosphere out to let the nitrogen boil off, then add water, and helium to keep the water from breaking down, like Jinx has."

In spite of the urgency of the situation, Persoff had to ask, "Where was he going to get that much water?"

"Callisto."

"The Jovian moon? The ships would roast in Jupiter's radiation belts."

"No ships. He wanted to hit Venus with Callisto. Ion thrusters. For some reason he couldn't get the UN interested in moving a planet almost as big as Mars past Earth's orbit."

Kershner made a noise Persoff would normally have considered medically alarming, and put his face on his control board. Persoff was trying not to grin himself. "I would think not."

"No. Anyway, Smith should be happy to hear it works, if we can get the news to him."

"He's still alive?"

"Was when we left. He's one of those people who does really well in low gee. Has some weird medical condition that prevents osteoporosis, actually has to have excess calcium cleaned out of his cells on a regular basis. I've heard it suggested that's inherited from our Pak ancestors."

Persoff was not about to get into that can of worms. "Thanks. So the survivors planted these trees. Good."

"Trees? Good lord, that's a lot of trees. —Sir, we didn't damage any, did we?" Tokugawa sounded badly worried.

"No. You think they're sacred or something?"

"The Galaxias complement were handpicked, so I doubt they'd have fallen that far back, but I'm sure they're deeply revered."

"Well, it's not as if we have to cut them all down or something," Persoff said. "Get some rest. I have to check on my ship." He signed off and said, "Damage and system reports."

"What do you mean, we have to cut them all down?"

McCabe, the strongest man aboard, and conceivably the strongest anywhere who wasn't from Jinx, hunched in on himself as if expecting to be hit. "The only way we can get off this planet is a launch catapult, sir. The planer is fried, and a lot of the hull is unsound. What we have to do is cobble together something that'll get a work crew up to that hulk in orbit and strip the accelerator field generator for parts. That should allow us to fix the planer up there. The thing is, we don't have the resources to construct an aerodynamic vehicle in less than years. We have to go straight to space all at once. No room to launch on fusion drive, because the ram's shot, so we'd have to use the singleships for thrust, and they're so hot the backwash would slaughter everything for miles. And they can fuse protons, so we sure can't launch from the water. So we have to slap something together and fling it up there and leave the main fusion plant on the ground."

"How many years would an aerospace ship take?" Persoff said.

"That depends on how many local inhabitants there are, and how fast they can learn. If they're as smart as the Shogun says—"

"Who?"

"Uh, Tokugawa, sir. It's kind of a running joke in Supply."

"Go on."

"If they're that smart, I'd say we can have an infrastructure in place in ten years. Otherwise we're looking at a couple of generations while we get the population up."

"And building a spaceship would be faster than that?"

"We've already got spaceships, sir," McCabe said. "They're just not built to fly inside an atmosphere. I was going to use three fighter drives to let the orbiter maneuver in space. —And then of course we'll also have to reassemble the *Yorktown*."

Persoff sighed. Then he frowned, looked straight up, and stared very hard at the ceiling, as if seeing through it. Slowly, he said, "How long would it take to install the hyperdrive in a ship that still has a working ram?" He looked at the storesmaster again.

McCabe gaped at him, then pulled out a flaptop, unrolled it, and began working the problem out. "We'd have to do hull and systems repairs to the hulk at the same time, but it's still less than the time we'll spend building the catapult," he finally said. "Maybe ten percent of what it'll take to refit our own ship. Which we could put aboard and repair there."

"Get together with Curtis in Engineering and work out what you need to do." When McCabe winced, Persoff said, "What's wrong?"

"He yells all the time."

"That's because he won't accept a transplant for his hearing problem. He was running the communications in Munchen during the Hollow Moon incident. The pulse, when it went up, blew out one eardrum. Stayed at his post with blood running down his neck and the gain turned up for the other ear, so it screwed that one up too. They patched the drum, but if he ever sounds like he's really angry, just ask to see his medals. That should keep him distracted for about half an hour."

"He's that proud of them?"

"There's that many. Since you've got clearance for this mission, I'll authorize you to hear the story of what really happened. Don't ask him unless you want to hear it all, and really don't ask unless you want to know something you won't ever be able to tell anyone. I had to learn it to assess his value for this mission, and I wish I hadn't. Go see him now."

McCabe saluted and left, looking thoughtful. He was the only crewman who still fully adhered to military courtesy after all this time. He didn't ask anyone else to, and his response to those who'd made fun of him had always been, "Permission to speak freely?" Nobody granted it twice, because they never made fun of him again after granting it once. His lecture on the purpose and value of military courtesy was sensible, cogent, and, when you considered that it was delivered by a man who might well be able to rip your arm off, gradually terrifying as it developed its theme: military courtesy allows trained expert killers to work together in difficult conditions without unnecessary loss of personnel.

There were others who had resumed using it, but only around McCabe.

About ten percent of each end of the island was loose rocks, which, since it was volcanic rock and there were no volcanoes on the island, meant it had been put there. Persoff had set the ship down near the west end, about halfway between where the trees ended and the rocks began. The trees at this end of the rows were saplings, while those near the east end must have been planted almost as soon as the colonists had landed.

Nobody had sighted any humans on the island, and nobody could figure out why. After Tokugawa's reaction, Persoff had no intention of starting to chop down trees until he'd talked to the locals, so he was planning parties to explore other islands and find some. They'd need cars and stunners, and the stunners were the bottleneck; not many had been included in the ship's manifest, and regs required officers on watch to wear them. Curtis had built three more from spares for the ones they had, but Persoff had wanted to send out at least six parties. There were lots of islands.

The bad part of being a commanding officer was making everyone think you weren't working hard. He was supposed to be relaxed and confident. One of the things that troubled him badly was the fact that all through the first night, the ship in orbit had been displaying lights. Bright ones. It wasn't the power available that worried him, since the ship dated after the invention of both black magic and electronic batteries, and half of it was in unfiltered sunlight all the time. It was the fact that its beacon had stopped transmitting when the lights began. The ship was displaying a flexible response to circumstances. Not inconceivably it had recorded their landing site. It might well be charging its com laser.

Other than abandoning the ship and scattering to the four winds, there wasn't a thing they could do about that.

After the first night, Persoff had left his exec, Thurston, in charge, and taken a car to East Point so he could fret over the preparations uninterrupted and without making everyone panicky.

So that was where he was when the canoe showed up.

It was an awfully big canoe. If it had been another shape or style he'd have thought of it as a ship, but the oars and the hull's lack of boards constrained his thinking.

As it came to shore, he realized that it hadn't constrained its maker's thinking. It had the look of a dugout, but it was almost twice as wide as the biggest tree on the island, and there surely couldn't be any trees twice that age on the planet. The ones behind him must have been planted the day they got here, which was surely no earlier than 2305, and more likely later. The accelerator trick, if they'd used it, wouldn't have given trees more time to grow, it would have killed them from lack of sunlight. Therefore they had stuck the trunks of two or more trees together to make this, well enough to keep the leaks down to something manageable.

It came directly toward him, and as it got close he still couldn't see any seams. They must be awfully good at making canoes by now, but this was unbelievable.

On the other hand, selection for starship personnel had been even tougher then than it was now, and the next man after Persoff on the promotion list at the Manhattan Space Academy in Kansas had just won the Wisowaty Award for resource management. (At last update he was part of the supply liaison to the Belt Fleet, and had once succeeded in impressing them. It was no small thing, to impress a Belter when it came to making effective use of resources.)

There was a man at the prow, calling back to another man at the stern, and they seemed to be the only ones facing forward. Pilot and steersman, he guessed. The sides were too high to see much but heads and shoulders of anyone but those two men. All the rowers had longer hair than the men. The standing men wore shirts, but the shoulders of the rowers were bare.

The men were also beardless, and that abruptly stuck him as an accomplishment. They certainly had no docs to depilate them here. A history teacher at MSA had had Persoff's class remove their facial hair with the sharpened steel wafers that had once been used for this, and his respect for the courage of the men he now saw was considerable.

The canoe struck the beach and continued up it further than he would have imagined possible. The pilot jumped ashore as soon as it stopped, turned, and called out, "Ropes!"

All the rowers jumped out. They were twenty nude women, and they hauled the canoe further up the beach until the pilot said, "Rest!" They dropped the ropes and ran to play in the surf. The steersman came forward and jumped out, and the two men, both in shirt and shorts (how had they made them?) came toward Persoff. They were both gnawing carrots. "Have a carrot," said the steersman, holding out a spare.

Not wishing to offend, Persoff, who hadn't eaten a carrot since he was big enough to spit, said, "Thanks," and took a bite. It tasted a lot better than he remembered. Of course, he was used to them cooked.

"We've got maybe ten seconds," said the pilot. "Is your mind being read? He'd have stopped when you bit it."

Persoff stopped chewing to stare, then said, "No. You were expecting kzinti?"

The two looked at each other, then at Persoff. "Yes," said the pilot. "You're wearing clothes, but if they were rational enough to use cover they might think of that too. It's my job to think of things like that. I'm Tom, the Johnson for this vessel. This is Ron, our Denver."

"Micah Persoff, Captain, commanding officer of the carrier *Yorktown*."

The two local men looked astonished, then came to attention and saluted.

Persoff returned their salutes. "It's lucky for me you showed up so soon. I was here planning missions to find the colonists."

"Colonists?" said Tom.

"We came here because the ship signaled us that someone had landed," said Ron.

"What do you mean, 'colonists'? We're stranded." Tom appeared to be getting upset.

Persoff shook his head. "Force of habit. I tend to think of settlements off Earth as colonies. We need to talk with you about getting off the planet again."

Tom nodded shortly. "Of course. Ron, give the All Clear."

Ron turned to the canoe and bellowed, at a volume Persoff found painful, "It's okay!"

Eighteen men, all chewing, stood up and began methodically unloading their crossbows. The women, serious now, returned to the canoe, where men who were done early began tossing them clothing.

Persoff stared, put it together, and said, "You were going to ambush the kzinti?"

"If they were here," said Tom. "They wouldn't read a female's mind right away."

"How would you ambush them in ten seconds?"

"Oh, Ron would have knocked you out."

Persoff looked at Ron, who had a low-gee build and seemed skinny at that. "How?"

His head hurt less than he would have expected, and he was lying before a brand-new hut, near a campfire, surrounded by women. "How many fingers do you see?" said the nearest, holding up a hand.

"Five," he said, "three of them folded."

"Talks like a Johnson," said another woman. She was prettier than the one who'd spoken first, and that was odd, because they all had about the same set of features. "Good stock, I bet."

"Well, he's starship crew," said yet another.

"I still think the basic stock might be deteriorating. They send off all the best."

"And I still say—Hey, he's right here, we can ask. Captain Micah Persoff, does the UN Fertility Board store sperm samples of men who go out to fight the kzinti, and make the samples available from the ones who did really well?"

Persoff was still a little stunned, and it took him a moment to follow the question. Then he said, "Yeah, any citable accomplishment is an automatic Birthright. Women who use donations get low numbers in the queue, too."

"See!"

"How'd you figure that out?" he said.

"It's the only thing that makes sense. Otherwise you'd all have been eaten before you got here."

"They still could have repopulated from colony worlds," said a woman who'd spoken before.

"Lightspeed and too busy."

"Loyalty and conditioning!"

"Alienation."

Others had begun chiming in, and it was getting loud. Persoff said, "What happened to me?"

"Oh, you got knocked out," said the woman who'd spoken first, all the rest shutting up.

"I'd figured out that much, but how?"

A man's voice—Tom—broke in. "Lateral impact near the left end of the mandible turns the head far enough to jar the brain stem." He got into view, raised his hand, and snapped his fingers. "Shuts you off like a bucket of wet sand on a small fire. But without the steam."

"Speaking of which," said the first woman.

"I thought he'd be waking up soon—not yet, in fact; he's tough—and he should have some things explained to him. And first he should have an apology. Captain, a Denver is identified by decisive action. Unfortunately it isn't always preceded by thought. Often that's a good thing, since it lets a Denver act without fear. Not always. I'm not familiar with your habits of speech, so once it was clear you were alone I should have had him stand further from you. I'm sorry."

"Apology accepted. How did he get so fast? I didn't even see him move."

"That's because he did it when you blinked. An early hint of the Denver gene complex is when a child seems unobservant but, now and then, somehow does some difficult thing exactly right. Which is not the same as doing the right thing. Incidentally, would it be possible to analyze people's DNA when your ship is back in operation? Working all this stuff out by inductive reasoning is quite a burden."

"You Johnsons do fine," said a woman.

"I never said otherwise. It's just hard."

Several women cleared their throats, and Tom looked like he'd suddenly remembered something he should never have forgotten. "Sorry. Captain, is your neck in pain? We can't do real regeneration, but I used the things we do have that improve healing ability."

"Actually the only thing that hurts is my teeth," Persoff said, touching his cheek. There were things sticking out of his skin. "What are these?" he said.

"Sutures. You'd lost a tooth. I had to go in from the side to make sure circulation was restored. They should come out now, in fact." He reached into a bag sitting nearby, and took out tweezers that looked like bamboo, and a small pair of scissors with clay handles and obsidian blades.

As threads were snipped and pulled out of his face, Persoff was able to distract himself by being deeply impressed with the quality of the tools. Ever since the kzinti attacked, History of Technology was a prerequisite for combat officers, so he knew fairly well how difficult those instruments had been to make.

He suspected even his teachers didn't know it nearly as well as the people here, whose ancestors had grown up with the "everybody play nice" version of social development. They must have had to learn everything down to rock chipping from scratch.

Tom put some goo on the holes and said, "Wash your mouth out with this."

Persoff obeyed, but regretted it at once. Once he'd spit it out, he said, "What was that?"

"Everyone asks that, but nobody ever likes the details. It's something that bacteria won't live in. You won't have to brush your teeth for a few days."

"I've never had to."

Tom studied him silently, then said, "May I take it that the process that prevents that still works? On your ship?"

"Absolutely. There's something I have to discuss with your people."

Tom nodded. "The Hales aren't all here yet."

Persoff said, "The Hale clan are in charge?"

"That would be 'is.' The word 'clan' is singular. And they're not a clan, they're a type. We'd be in a sorry mess if we chose leaders by heredity."

"You have elections?"

Tom waited until most of the crowd was pretty much done laughing. "If we chose leaders for their ability to talk people into things they'd all be Blackers!" he said, grinning.

"Sounds fair," said the woman who'd said he was good stock. She was joking.

"Of course it sounds fair. That's the point, isn't it?" Tom said, followed by more laughter. When that had diminished, he explained, "Hales are identified by character, same as everybody else."

"Who chooses them?"

Tom looked confused. "Chooses?"

"I think he means identifies," said the woman who'd just spoken. "They identify themselves. Anybody can see it. This is interesting. Captain, you clearly have a Hale job, but you talk a lot like a Johnson. How were you chosen?"

Persoff, who was starting to worry that he'd been hit a lot harder than he'd realized, said, "I took placement exams to qualify for the Academy, and after I graduated, the people in charge put me where they needed me."

"They all sound like Wellses," she said, to general agreement. "A Wells helps out wherever she can be useful," she explained.

"She?"

"They're usually women, like Blackers or Schafers."

As Persoff opened his mouth, Tom said, "Blackers keep track of things and give advice. A Schafer trains."

"They're teachers?"

"They train children, yes, but they train anything. Animals, plants—the plant that produced the sutures I used on you, for instance. Didn't hurt coming out, did it? When we landed it started out as flax, and the fibers would have soaked up some of your blood, which would have clotted. We have bad stories about those days. There were people hurt in the last landing." He looked grim.

Persoff could just imagine. "How many landing craft did you have working?"

"One," said Tom.

Nobody added anything to that. Persoff sought anything to say that didn't involve asking if anybody had ended up being left on the *Galaxias*. They would learn that anyway, if McCabe's plan worked. He remembered about the trees. "I wanted to talk about—"

"They're here!" someone shouted from down on the beach, and most of the people around him left. Six remained.

The woman who'd spoken first said, "It'll take a while to sort out protocol. Meanwhile, do you prefer Blacker or Wells?"

"For what?"

"Sex. It's getting really difficult to find partners with low consanguinity, and yours is zero. So, Blacker or Wells?"

"Uh, Newmar, as a matter of fact. She's our ship's master at arms."

This was greeted with glum expressions. The woman who'd spoken just before the last said, "You have female crewmen."

"Nine, in a current complement of seventy. We lost six men when your ship fired on us."

"Oh hell," she said. "I don't think anyone expected to be found by anyone but the kzinti. I'm awfully sorry about that." There was a chorus of agreement.

Lacking a useful comment—"me too" seemed tactless—he said, "What do I call you?"

She looked stunned for a moment. "You don't know our names, of course! I'm Sophia, this is Betsy, that's Liz, she's Susan, and they're Eva and Donna." She'd alternated between types, which he took to be Blackers and Wellses. Blackers seemed more intense, Wellses more amiable.

"Hey," said Betsy, who'd spoken to him first, "their ship only had a complement of seventy-six."

"Seventy-seven. And forty dolphin fighter pilots. Those died when the kzin ship blew." They'd been the reason the *Yorktown* hadn't included any Wunderkzin, since dolphins became insanely hostile in the presence of kzinti. There had been training incidents.

Betsy said, "But the only way that could be enough people is if you have hyperdrive." They all went quiet.

"We do."

It was half an hour or so before he had another quiet moment. By that time they'd learned more than he'd realized he knew about hyperdrive and hyperwave. The first interruption came when a large man—no, a man the size of Tom or Ron, who had built himself up with exercise—came over, shook hands without using a neurotically insecure bonecrusher, and said, "I'm Henry, currently the senior Hale. Understand your ship's damaged. We'll be glad to help. How many of us can you take back on this trip?"

"It depends on whether we can fix the *Galaxias* once we're in orbit. My storesmaster thinks we probably can, and we have better technology than when it was built, so conceivably thousands. How many of you are there to take back?"

Henry looked at Sophia, who said, "Last count was four thousand nine hundred and three, breeding and sterile. Call it five thousand until we can check."

"I have a crewman who says the *Galaxias* was designed to hold up to six thousand," Persoff said.

"That was before the battle," said Henry.

Sophia recited: "'Ship's original complement was three hundred and two, with thirty-eight survivors after the collision. Thirty-one were in coldsleep and had to be awakened via emergency protocol, resulting in impaired cognition. The remaining seven included the two stowaways, who were instrumental in getting the *Galaxias* back in working order and the awakened into functional condition, respectively. When the ship reached a system with an adaptable planet, the only survivor of the original mission was the pilot. He died bringing the last of the supplies and the ship's complement, then numbered one hundred and three, to the surface. He was the only casualty of the ferry trips." She looked at Persoff and smiled. "That was Stuart William Denver. It was by his order that records were kept of accomplishments, and full acknowledgement given to stowaways Marion Johnson and Russelle Wells, without whose work none of us would have lived to get here. Stuart with a 'u,' Marion with an 'o,' Russelle with a final 'e.' The distinctions are made because one name derives from a profession, and both other names were then considered sexually ambiguous."

Persoff nodded, wishing he could think of something sufficiently respectful to say about that pilot. Then he frowned. "Johnson, Denver, Hale, Wells, Blacker, and Schafer make six," he said. "Who was the seventh survivor?"

"Foote," said a voice from outside the firelight. An old-looking woman stepped forward, propping herself up on two canes. "James Foote."

"Foote with a final 'e,'" said Sophia.

"He financed the *Galaxias*," said the old woman. "He was a planner."

"One man paid for that thing himself?" Persoff said, thinking of the Cyclopean ship he'd seen so briefly.

The old woman smiled. "He was a good planner. My name is Eden. Currently I'm the senior Foote. There are seldom more than eight or nine of us. Everyone else is good at some form of implementation, but original planning is too abstruse."

"Then I guess you're the one I need to talk with about cutting the trees," he said.

Everyone else had been quiet, but up to then they'd been breathing. It got quieter.

"Out of the question," Eden said. "Those are our history. The first of them were planted by the Pilot's own hand."

"The thing is, to get off the planet we'll need to build a launch catapult."

"Do it on another island."

"We can't move the power plant off this one."

"We'll help you make others. There may not be much smeltable iron, but there's sure plenty of thorite."

"All the other islands are volcanic."

"There are ways to drain off the magma, we've just never gone to the trouble."

"They'll take time."

"We've waited a couple hundred years so far."

"Goddammit, we're forty years overdue on our mission already!" Persoff bellowed, then shut up, ashamed.

She frowned. "What's your mission?"

"We were supposed to attack the kzin home system, but we were attacked before we got there and flung this way when their gravity planer blew."

"Just like us," said Eva.

Eden said, "You mean, you need to cut the trees to beat the kzinti?"

He actually felt the air go out of him. "Uh, well, yes."

"Then cut the trees," she said, and her voice broke. She turned to Henry and said, "Go tell the rest of the Hales, and make sure everyone's at the first trees, first thing, morning after tomorrow. Captain Persoff, there's something we'll want to do before you start cutting. It's going to take us at least a few days. Will that delay you, or are there other steps you can take while we're doing that?"

Things were changing too fast for him. "I doubt we'd be able to start cutting for weeks," he said.

"Good. Then we can do this properly. If you don't mind, Captain, it would be better for your nerves if you were back with your ship while the news is spread. I have arrangements to make as well."

"It was out of the question, but now we can cut them? Just like that?"

She gave him a look that made him wonder if he'd make it to his car, but all she said was, "Yes, Captain, just like that. Be at the first trees on time if you want to know the story."

When he took the car up, he saw hundreds of campfires below. The entire population must have come—and if they never cut the trees, then they'd brought the firewood with them. Yet they were letting him cut them, if it meant striking against the kzinti.

He set the car to take him back to the ship, wished he drank, and got on the radio. The tech on duty was Blackwell, who was evidently startled out of watchstanding trance by the call: "Is there an emergency, sir?"

"No, I'm just coming back early. Pass the word that I've met the locals, and they are disposed to help." Had he said "friendly," it would have told his crew that he was under duress. "I did get a minor injury, but they treated it. I want Meier to look at their work. Some of the things they've come up with are likely to be useful."

"Yes, sir. May I speak freely, sir?"

Wondering, he said, "Granted."

"The ship doesn't feel right without you here, sir. Mister Thurston's a good man to work for, but I'm glad you're coming back early."

"Thanks, Blackwell. Fact is, I didn't feel right being away from the ship. Persoff out."

Meier kept exclaiming under her breath, and finding more things to exclaim over with every instrument she used. "Did you know your jaw had been broken?" she finally said.

"It was?"

"By some kind of blunt impact. Right at what I would judge to be the weakest spot, if that's not a silly thing to say about a jawbone. It's had two pins put in, which the autodoc says are made of cellulose, gelatin, and powdered sterile bone. New bone is already growing as your cells digest the protein. The tooth they restored is pegged, but that seems to have been done out of sheer thoroughness, as it's already taken root. And as for the scars, if I hadn't seen you without them I'd swear they were weeks old. You're absolutely right, I do want to see what else these people have got. It's like they had to reinvent medicine."

"I think they did. I didn't see any equipment from their shuttle, so I think it must have sunk in the last landing. I'd sure want to keep that stuff handy."

"It wouldn't have worn out, either," Tokugawa said from his bed. "Those old colony ships had equipment that was even better than required by law. And in those days you could go to the organ banks for making defective lightbulbs."

"Don't exaggerate," Meier said.

"He's not," Kershner said, walking in. "I hated the idea of organ banks when they thawed me out, so they had me read about one case. Indicator light on a paranoid's autodoc burned out. He killed off an entire family, root and branch. I still hate organ banks, but I have to admit the only other thing that could possibly be appropriate for that degree of negligence, when you know how serious the risks are, is eternal damnation. Which is difficult to enforce. You need a demon on monitor duty, at least."

"They get the paranoid?" Persoff said.

Kershner froze in place, mouth open, an odd habit he had when he couldn't retrieve a piece of information. It could be disturbing, but he had fewer quirks than a lot of other ex-corpsicles. "I'm sure they must have, but I can't call up the details. There was something weird about his case. But I was talking about the manufacturer. Three people went to the organ banks for negligent homicide. It was open and shut. One didn't do maintenance on a monitor that supervised the filament composition, one was the middle manager who used to fire employees in quality inspection for failing too many products, and one was the interviewer who hired the manager and gave her instructions about keeping costs down. If any one of them had been doing a diligent job, the killer would have gone on being treated properly. What really capped it for the jury was that the ARMs investigated all the other lamps they'd sold over the same period, and found two more of inferior quality. We're talking a specialty light here, made specifically for 'docs." He frowned. "I wish I could remember— I do recall, the guy who did maintenance on the 'doc in question had to have some serious therapy. Totally blameless, but it was eating him up."

Kershner didn't look much happier than the man he was discussing. "Did you have a report for me, Mr. Kershner?"

Kershner came out of his funk and said, with a different kind of gloom, "We've got no spares for the hyperwave. It looks like when the railgun shot us, a piece of the bulkhead spalled through that locker. Since I have to use parts from the 'wave for redundant systems in the drive, we won't be in contact with Earth until we get there."

Persoff considered, then said, "And after forty years the war may have been won already, and if we carry out our mission we may be starting another." What a freemother. He carefully did not say that aloud.

"I'm afraid so, sir."

"The people here hold the trees we have to cut in very high regard, and they've given permission based on the idea that it'll help win the war."

"I'll explain the situation to them, sir," Kershner said.

"Thank you, but it's not your duty."

"Beg pardon, Captain, but it is my specialty. If I'm standing by, explaining the fine details as you refer them to me, it'll look to them like you're avoiding responsibility. I think it'd better if I explained before you said your piece."

"Are you trying to let me off the hook, Kershner?"

The hypertech looked startled, then grinned. "Just this once, sir. It is your first time."

Meier and Tokugawa both made strangled noises, while Persoff just rolled his eyes. "Are you off watch, Kershner?"

"Oh, yes, sir."

"Then go engage in optional activity," Persoff said. "Consult McCabe if you're not certain of the term. Dismissed."

He brought his crew to the beach as the locals were assembling for whatever they had planned. Full dress uniform, no exceptions. Tokugawa was still in a float chair, but Meier was able to get his blues around his neck brace. The only grumbling anyone did was the sort that was used to complain about the weather, since everyone understood what these people had agreed to give up.

They thought they did, anyway.

Persoff took his senior officers to where most of the orders were coming from, and addressed the elders there. "Before we go on, there's something I need you to know. Even if everything works right, we may not be able to strike against the kzinti. It took us decades longer than planned to get here, and the war may be over by now. We can't find out until we get to a human world, because we won't have the hyperwave. Mr. Kershner can explain the technical details if you wish."

One very old man said, "Johnson. I can see a civilian vessel just carrying spares, but I would expect a fighting starship to be able to fabricate replacement parts for everything it used. Why can't you fix the hyperwave?"

Kershner stepped forward. "Sir, it isn't practical to put something of that complexity aboard a vessel. The parts we need are of mixed composition, and have to be made to standards of molecular precision."

The Johnson—apparently The Johnson—nodded and said, "That's to produce an effect that's necessary for the thing to work."

"Yes, sir," Kershner said, looking surprised.

"What's the effect?"

Kershner gave a faint sigh and began explaining hyperwave physics in baby talk, as if he were describing it to a journalist.

The old man stopped him after no more than fifteen seconds and said, "It sounds like you're setting up a standing wave to maintain a constant peak pulse, because keeping the whole system at that power level will burn it out."

Kershner stopped dead, blinked about nine times, and said, "Yes."

"How big is it?"

Kershner held up his thumb and forefinger a little ways apart.

"The Blacker?" said The Johnson.

An old woman said, "Yes?"

"What's the stuff for alloys in constant friction, very rare?"

"Rhenium?"

"That's it, thanks—Why can't you run the wave at full strength through a cubic foot or so of rhenium? There's plenty of asteroids."

What Persoff knew about this subject he had mostly learned from journalists' work, but it must have been a good idea, because Kershner got all excited. "That could work! People still think of rhenium as too rare to be used for most things, but you're right, there's lots of asteroids! How did you think of it?"

"Captain Persoff described hyperdrive, and we spent yesterday discussing possible causes for the Blind Spot effect and working out implications. It seemed to us that in hyperspace, normal matter must be the local equivalent of a massless particle, which accounts for the standard speed."

"That's right! Captain, permission to—"

"Denied. It'll wait until after we've attended the ceremony."

"Yes, sir."

"We don't mind," said The Johnson.

"Yes, we do," said someone who must have been The Hale. "Captain Persoff, there's been some discussion, and the general opinion is that the ship's organics will have to be replaced. Since the trees have to be cut anyway, it'll be best all around if they're used for that. And we'd appreciate it if you could use everything from the first row there. Roots and all."

"Thank you, that'll help a lot." They were taking it a lot better than he'd dared hope.

The Blacker stepped forward. In the moment before she spoke, Persoff had a chance to notice and realize a lot of things that he hadn't fitted together before. To begin with, she was wearing something that actually looked sort of Polynesian: a necklace of long, sharp teeth. Old teeth. Kzinti teeth. He'd been assuming the *Galaxias* had merely fired, survived, and gotten thrown this way, but that had to be wrong: they knew what the kzinti called themselves, which meant they'd had prisoners, and they'd forced them to learn English, because they didn't use kzin loan words. Near the Blacker there were other women, in hearing range but not close enough to interrupt, who were dressed in clinging outfits of orange fur, extremely worn in spots.

He was suddenly very glad he hadn't been able to bring any Wunderkzin. Something had happened back then, and these people made damned sure they remembered it.

"Captain," said The Blacker, "are you certain you wish to be part of this? It can be a strain even for us, and we grow up with it."

"You're helping us, and we couldn't do without you. It seems to me we have to show our respect."

"Then you do understand," she said, and turned and led the other Blackers west, toward the trees.

Eden came to his side and said, "She jumps to conclusions sometimes. Do you have recording devices?"

"Yes, why?"

"Use them. You'll see." The Foote walked after the Blackers.

"Recorders on, everyone," Persoff said.

At the trees, the procession halted, and all the adults moved to let the children through. The only grownups near the front were carrying babies. The Blacker waited until the *Yorktown*'s officers were near, then said, "Pay attention. We can never do this again. People have come to take us home. You must say goodbye to your family." She put her hand on the nearest tree.

"This is James Foote, who gave up everything he had to build the *Galaxias*. It was he who extended the field around the ship after the enemy boat rammed us, so that the drive would destroy its mothership and leave them dependent on us no matter if we won or lost. When he was dying he asked to be frozen, so that he could be buried on the planet he always hoped to reach. This was a tiny island then, but the Pilot crushed rock, buried James Foote, planted this tree over him, making the first true soil in the world, and brought rocks from other islands to protect it from the tide, and so we have done ever since when we bring our dead here." As she moved to the next tree, all the children came up and touched the first, one by one. Last of all, mothers took their infants to the tree and guided a hand to touch it, so that each baby could be told later that this had been done.

Persoff was in something like clinical shock. This was their cemetery, and their museum.

And to beat the kzinti they were willing to cut it all down and grind it to pulp.

"This is Captain Jonas Hale, who was blinded fighting the officer of the kzin attack boat. He advised the Pilot through as much of the trip as he could, and was the best friend the Pilot could have wished for." One by one, they all touched the tree.

"This is Olga Blacker, who kept us all from going mad, by listening to everything we needed to say, and reminding us of the good things." The procession continued.

"This is Russelle Wells, who sneaked aboard to be with her boyfriend, who had lied and wasn't actually part of the crew. She raised thirty-one infants with adult bodies into people who could raise children of their own, and never once had to hurt any of them." The Blacker bowed to the tree before moving on.

"This is Lavinia Schafer, who taught kzin prisoners English, and then taught them to answer questions. And outlived them all." The Blacker clenched a fist and raised it overhead in salute.

"This is Academician Marion Johnson, who made so many ruined things work that we could spend two days and a night naming them all, and who got aboard the *Galaxias* in a crate because he was judged too ill for space travel. He showed us how to cool the planet we needed, and died while we were waiting."

The seventh tree was touched with special care. "This is Stuart William Denver, who brought us here in a damaged ship through uncharted wilderness, who gave us all hope when we despaired, and who landed all of us and all we needed to live on this world, and died of his burns after getting the last passengers out of the lander as it sank." She kissed the tree. One by one, the rest did too. After the children had moved on, the adults moved in to do the same.

As she moved on to introduce the next rank of trees, Persoff, who was blind with tears, heard Kershner say softly, "And the kzinti call themselves Heroes?"

🐾   🐾   🐾

THE
MARMALADE
PROBLEM

by Hal Colebatch

❧ THE MARMALADE PROBLEM ❧

"I THINK I'VE SOLVED the Marmalade problem," General Leonie Rykermann told her husband, Nils Rykermann. "The monastery."

The Marmalade problem had been preoccupying her thoughts for some time. Had Marmalade been reared on Kzin or on any kzin-ruled world, it is very unlikely that he would have survived childhood. However, he was reared on Wunderland, after Liberation, and had lived to be a problem.

What the circumstances of his birth were, no one knew. After the cease-fire there had been many orphans, kzin and human, wandering the scarred surface of the planet. Some formed savage feral gangs. Marmalade had been found, very near death, not far from Circle Bay Monastery. He had been clutching a locket, engraved with a sigil such as were issued by Conservers of the Ancestral Past.

Instead of killing him the farmers had obeyed the abbott's instructions and handed him over to the monastery's care. It appeared he had previously been selected for telepath training—so much he could tell them, and the telepath syndrome generally produced smaller and weaker creatures than the huge fighting kzin—but he remembered very little beyond that. He fetched up at length in the orphanage where Leonie Rykermann was trying, in the face of considerable opposition, to turn parentless kittens into *Wunderkzin*—kzin who might cooperate with the humans on Wunderland.

Leonie was a patient, dedicated woman, and had established understandings—friendships even—with some kzin, not least Rarrgh, the Senechal of Vaemar-Riit, prince of the kzin on liberated Wunderland, while Orlando, Vaemar's eldest son, regarded her with fierce possessiveness.

Very few humans knew more of kzin psychology (if that was the term for it), and she and Rarrgh had saved one another's lives— indeed, that was how they had met. But though she was relatively used to dealing with kzin, including young kzin, she found Marmalade a handful.

The problem was not the usual one among young male kzin of wild, reckless bravery and aggression. Marmalade was a coward. Not merely cautious as Vaemar-Riit sometimes was (and as he had tried to teach Orlando to be), but obsessively, unreasoningly fearful. It was probably something to do with his aborted telepath conditioning, allowing him to feel empathy for other creatures' minds, but not how to control or use this faculty. His mind had been opened for telepath training but not trained further, and fear had run wild in it. It might also be because he had the typical telepath's physical weakness, which marked him out in the rough-and-tumble of the other kittens' play and hunts. Some cowardly kzin compensated for their condition with cunning, but Marmalade had no particularly large ration of that.

When he had been taken sailing on Wunderland's seas, in the boisterous low-gravity waves, he had clung to the boat's mast with all four limbs, shivering with fear. When the orphanage kits were taken for a brief excursion into sub-orbital space, he had been found trying to hide from the rollcall, and during the flight he had disappeared, to be found crouched under a bunk, flooding the cabin with fear- pheromones.

He was not only afraid of real dangers, like lightning storms and flash floods, or animals like the poison-fanged Beam's Beasts or tigrepards, or the crocodilians and other carnivores of nearby Grossgeister Swamp such fears would have been more than bad enough in the eyes of a real kzin, even a humble noncombatant, but Marmalade was frightened also of innocuous things like noise, crowds and strangers.

Leonie had soon realized that Marmalade was a problem. He had to be kept separate from the other kittens, who would have made short work of him if they had been given the chance. To turn him out to make his own way on Wunderland would have been an equally certain death sentence. His very "name," ridiculous and meaningless, would be taken as a deadly insult to a kzin of real Name should he encounter one. Not only were there kzin at large, there were also fanatically anti-kzin humans, survivors of the Occupation, who, peace treaty or not, would attack any kzin they found alone and vulnerable-looking. In the orphanage he was kept in a sort of protective custody, in one of the isolation units, but plainly this state could not go on for ever.

There was no point in Leonie even asking the kzinti she knew well, like Rarrgh or Vaemar, for advice. They, she knew, would simply consider him a disgrace to the Heroes' species. Vaemar might live as a modern, Wunderkzin prince, but he was not as advanced as all that. Rarrgh and she had an odd bond and a strong one between them, dating back to the day he had received his Name, but he was an old senior sergeant of the Patriarch's armed forces, and the motto of senior sergeants of all races tended to be: "There are no excuses for anything!"

They *might* give him a chance to prove his worth in a death-duel, but she would not bet on it, and anyway, weak and slow as he was, he would be bound to lose. Leonie herself could beat him in the practice arena, wearing heavily padded protective clothing, for he did not know how to even try to fight. And it was a rough rule of thumb that in hand-to-hand combat, a real kzin was the equal of about forty humans. That was not a guess. That kill-ratio had actually been achieved many a time, though of course guns tended to equalize things. (Specially trained Jinxians, the heaviest bipeds in known space after the full-grown male kzinti, might do better with long-practiced scientific kicks and blows, but only, it was understood, at the cost of their own lives. They would get in one strike and no more.)

Anyway, Marmalade was neither fighting kzin nor telepath. He had no other special gifts that would justify his continued existence, even in Wunderkzin society, even as a mere noncombatant. His stooped gait, hunched shoulders and scuffling feet proclaimed "weakling" and "victim." Fortunately for him, "coward" was less easy to recognize, simply because among kzinti of all classes it was so rare. And yet, there was something about him that touched Leonie. Perhaps it was the fact that she had seen him trying to be brave.

"You're not thinking of making a monk out of a kzin, are you?" Nils asked her. "Even a kzin like Marmalade. The abbot is a kind old man, but I can't see that he'd stand for it."

"No," said Leonie, "not a monk."

It was reading the old classic *Brideshead Revisited* that gave her a clue to the solution. "Listen to this," she told Nils: "Monasteries, it says here, often had a few odd hangers-on who don't fit into either the monastic order or the world."

"Yes, I know there are a couple like that at Circle Bay. Old men the Occupation drove crazy, most of them. Drunk half the time."

"Why not Marmalade? He could be useful without having to take any vows or anything. I know he's weak for a kzin, but he's still stronger than any human except maybe a male Jinxian. And he speaks Wunderlander."

"What could he do?

"Plenty. In the book, the man who can't do anything else becomes a sort of under-porter. He could do odd jobs."

Kzin intelligence is baffling to humans. They could solve problems brilliantly, and most of them, if put to it, could be quite inventive mechanically, but they had strange blind spots. It was because of those blind spots that the wars lasted long enough for humans to get the hyperdrive. Having a kzin about the place, especially a kzin as docile as Marmalade, might be quite useful, not to mention the fact that his mere presence would be an effective deterrent to human thieves or outlaws, of which post-war Wunderland had more than its share.

The abbot, when the suggestion was put to him, was happy enough to take him in, providing the government supplied him with kzin infantry rations and other upkeep and he left the monastery's animals alone, except for herding them if necessary.

One of the monastery's main efforts was to build human-kzin cooperation, and this looked like a good opportunity to advance it. The abbot, turning the matter over in his mind, foresaw generations of monks going out all over the planet, and beyond, remembering the kzin as a quaint, harmless character who had been part of their novice days. It was perhaps overly optimistic of him, but the abbot was by nature an optimist. Anyway, he was pleased to do a favor to the Rykermanns, two of the greatest heroes of the Resistance, and with a degree of official power. A hut was found for Marmalade and he settled down to an undemanding life: fetching and carrying, placing and changing flowers in the monastery chapel and the Abbot's study, moving furniture and farming implements, and, when he had overcome his timidity over them, tending the infant Jotok in their breeding ponds. There were even a few lines about it in the news.

Nils Rykermann, as a member of the Legislature, held a weekly "surgery" to hear constituents' problems. A few days after they had left Marmalade at the monastery, he had two unusual visitors.

There was nothing unusual about their being unusual. There were plenty of odd types on Wunderland, but these were something new to him: a human and a kzin, both old, small and withered-looking, the human with a long white beard, and a wise, kindly face, the kzin with white fur on his muzzle and about his ragged ears. Nils found himself warming to the old man. There was something intrinsically good projected even in the deep, thoughtful timbre of his voice. Otherwise, the white hair at least gave them a curiously similar look. Wunderland had had a long period under the Occupation when geriatric drugs had been available only to high-ranking collaborationists and Resistance leaders like Nils and Leonie, and it was plain that the old man had not been one who had qualified to receive them. They carried a bundle.

The human introduced himself as Pieter von Pelt; the kzin was nameless, and apparently spoke neither English nor the Angdeutsch-like Wunderlander.

They had, von Pelt explained, been prospecting in the Jotun Mountains and had come across a wrecked kzin ship, shot down in the war. The wreckage was much scattered and there was little worth keeping, but they had found the ship's logbook and, intact, the elaborately sealed metal container of the Patriarch's urine which every kzin capital ship carried. Like any packages the Rykermannns received, it was X-rayed and found to contain liquid, with a thick, solid top and bottom. It was sealed with an elaborate seal. Leonie pointed to a design on its side. She took it and examined it closely.

"Like Marmalade's locket."

"Ask him if he knows what it is?"

The old prospector and the old kzin spoke together in the slaves' patois. The Rykermanns, who often had to deal with kzin who still considered monkeys' attempts to use the Heroes' Tongue a deathly insult, the surrender notwithstanding, could follow it, though there was no reason to betray the fact. It was, they gathered, the sigil of the captain of the ship, scion of an ancient aristocratic kzin family, which had been attracted to Wunderland from a distant planet by rumors of the easy pickings to be had there.

How did the old kzin know this?

He had been one of the ship's officers and had escaped in a boat, carrying the jar with him, von Pelt explained. He had attached himself to one of the local magnates. He had buried the jar on landing and had retrieved it only lately.

The war had ended shortly afterwards. He had followed the progress of the peace negotiations from a distance, and though it had taken him some time to adjust to the idea of kzin and humans living together in peace, he had adjusted. They had met when prospecting and had joined up. Such alliances were becoming less uncommon and the human authorities welcomed them.

He was also able to throw a little light in the mystery of Marmalade's origins. Among the Admiral's kittens there had been a small, weak one which had seemed to exhibit the telepath syndrome. As soon as he could be weaned, admiral had had him isolated to protect him from the other kits. Telepaths in the family were not anything to be proud of, but too rare to be wasted. The ship's own telepath had been ordered to begin work on him. He was to have been sent for more advanced training when the ship was jumped by a squadron of *Dart*-class fighters. When the ship's gravity planers were failing, and it was falling towards the surface, most of the crew dead and the engines about to destabilize, he had been jettisoned in one of the ship's boats. He could have come down anywhere. When Nils Rykermann told them about the kitten, the old human prospector was moved.

"Poor little chap," he said. "After my . . . partner . . . told me what had happened to him in the battle, I wondered what his fate had been. I was never able to hate the kzin, you know. An old desert-rat like me, living in the back-blocks. I was fortunate, I know. They left me alone and I left them alone . . . I hardly even saw one until after the war, though I was able to help a few humans, and I'm glad of that . . . I'm glad he's been looked after."

"He's quite appealing, in a way," said Leonie. "I know fear makes some creatures into bullies, but he is quite gentle."

The pair wished to present the precious jar to Vaemar-Riit. Of course, they had been put to considerable expense travelling from the Joyuns, and if anything could be done to recompense them for their outlays, this would be appreciated. Nils Rykermann promised to speak to Vaemar about the matter, and they left, taking the jar with them. The Rykermanns, who were glad of a chance to spend a day out of the city, flew to Varmar-Riit's palace the following day and told him the story.

"The seals are unbroken, you say," he put to them. "Urrr . . . it would go well on the mantlepiece." No one said as much, but there was an unspoken thought in all their minds that it would do something to reinforce the legitimacy of his position and help reduce the stigma of "collaborator," which, among some kzin, he had never entirely lost. "And this . . . this *Marmalade*?"

"A kitten," said Leonie, "a weak kitten. A failed telepath, I think. Or rather, he was separated from other Heroes before the training began." It was just permissible, given her relationship with Vaemar, to describe the kitten as "weak." Some, after all, were born so, and could not help it. But for a human to describe one kzin to another, even Vaemar (and she knew Vaemar would die for her if Honor required it) as a coward . . . !

"It would be useful if he finished his telepath training," said Vaemar.

"I think he is too old for that."

"I should like to have a look at him, anyway. "

Leonie was not happy at the prospect of Vaemar-Riit meeting Marmalade, but there was no argument she could put against it. She was unhappily aware that if Marmalade disgraced himself before the greatest kzin on the planet, the consequences could be unfortunate.

The day of the presentation was cool and cloudy. The kzin did not need to wear the hats and sunglasses which sometimes gave them an odd appearance. Vaemar, with his mate Karan, Rarrgh, and other members of his household, were dressed in finery, Rarrgh with his two ear-rings on prominent display. Also present were the Rykermanns, the abbott, and several other human dignatories. Marmalade was to be presented to Vaemar-Riit.

However, Terrified of the gathering crowd, Marmalade was nowhere to be found. Leonie, the abbott and Rarrgh went in search of him while Vaemar and Nils Rykermann took refreshments.

Using Rarrghh's *ziirgrah* sense and his artificial eye with its infrared vision, they eventually found Marmalade cowering in the darkest corner of the monastery's old and disused chicken coop. Rarrgh, shocked, was in favor of tearing him to pieces then and there, as a disgrace to the Heroes' Race, but Leonie, to whom Rarrgh also was secretly devoted, talked him out of it, saying Marmalade was under her protection. The fact that Marmalade was still young enough to have retained the juvenile spots on his fur may also have inhibited Rarrgh—though mature male kzin sometimes killed kittens, they also developed a protective reflex towards them, and Rarrgh now had new kittens of his own. Still, Rarrgh was boiling with rage and vicarious shame, perhaps, indeed, to the extent that his *ziirgrah* sense was affected by the effort of keeping his emotions in check.

With somewhat more difficulty, Leonie talked Marmalade out of his hiding place. "Will he hurt me?" he asked, gazing up at Rarrgh with huge, terrified eyes. In all her dealing with kzin, Leonie wore unobtrusive but very strong armor under her clothes. It was just as well, for Marmalade seized her arm for comfort, too frightened to retract his claws, now looking down with fear at a small mouse-like creature that had been eating some spilled grain. Rarrgh seized the arm and threw it off her. Marmalade's claws had not penetrated Leonie's shielding or drawn blood, but still Marmalade was closer to death than he had ever been in that moment.

They joined the little crowd. Fortunately, there were a number of other kzin in the gathering, and this made Marmalade a little less conspicuous, at the back of the group and partly hidden from the VIPs on the ceremonial dais by a tree-stump. He was, if anything, even more frightened of telepaths than of ordinary kzinti, and Leonie was relieved to find there were none present. Some drums, an important part of many kzin ceremonies, were produced, and Vaemar's younger kittens danced on them.

Von Pelt and the nameless kzin brought the jar forward and placed it on a table covered with cloth of gold. Marmalade, Rykermann noticed, looking a little nervously behind him, was staring at them with an unusual intensity. The pair bowed to Vaemar-Riit. Then, with a few well-chosen words from the old man, they stepped modestly back into the crowd. Their aircar was nearby.

The next part of the ceremony called for Nils Rykermann to present the jar to Vaemar on behalf of humanity, an enduring symbol of the respect in which humanity held him. Vaemar would then make a speech of acknowledgement, to be followed by a feast for which two sorts of food had been prepared.

Marmalade's telepathic sense was dormant and unschooled but not completely absent. Screaming a single word, he burst out of the crowd like a rocket, scattering humans and kzin left and right. He snatched up the jar and ran with it to the edge of the crowd. He threw it to the ground and flung himself upon it to cover it before it exploded, scattering hydrofluoric acid in all directions.

Between the acid and the explosion there was not enough left of Marmalade to place in a shrine. One of Vaemar-Riit's kittens bears his name.

LEFTOVERS

by Matthew Joseph Harrington

🐾 LEFTOVERS 🐾

UNLESS HE WAS STAYING over with a woman he'd met, Buford Early slept in his autodoc. At his age most people died in their sleep, and while he wasn't as afraid of dying as most people, it struck him as an undignified way to go after surviving five wars. On the other hand, his psychist program told him it was really a way of distancing himself, since the lack of a bed in his apartment meant that any woman who came home with him couldn't stay over herself. The clincher, however, was that it was the most comfortable place he'd ever had to sleep.

He was not accustomed to being startled when he woke up.

He was certainly not accustomed to being so badly startled, ever. There was a head floating outside the observation window.

It was a head of truly astonishing ugliness, resembling nothing so much as a really cruel caricature of a dragon. A bulging snout of a nose hung over a rigid and lipless bony beak, whose molar-textured gash extended back to the hinge of the jaws. Huge ears flanked a face with the texture of boiled leather, which had been crammed into the bottom third of a swollen bald head, which looked as if someone had overinflated the brain and then stuck another on in back.

Which was more or less what had happened. The thing belonged to a Protector, which meant that the human race was about to begin a long period of being micromanaged like so many small and rather stupid children.

Buford reached into the receptacles adjacent to his hands, but instead of finding a stunner and a one-shot puncher, he felt only small pieces of paper. He brought them up to look at them. Each had one word printed on it: COLD.

Next to the head, his robe, draped over nothing, waved itself at the window. He'd have to bide his time, keep his mind off the subject, wait for a chance, and take it. Meanwhile, he opened the lid of the 'doc, sat up, and said, "George Olduvai?"

The Protector rolled its eyes and said, "Puns are the pornography of mathematicians. Jack Brennan is dead."

"How did that happen?" he exclaimed, taking the robe as he got out.

"A weapon whose programming he hadn't supervised himself activated a laser and cut him in half at the waist. Aberrantly careless, I suspect suicide. As a breeder he seems to have been sociable, so he never got used to being the smartest person he knew."

As Early tied his robe sash, he felt for the coil of Sinclair filament in the capsule at the end. The capsule was there, but it held another piece of paper that read COLD. "So who are you?" he said, crumpling the paper and tossing it toward the cleaner.

"You can call me Ursula."

"You're female?" he said, then winced at the gaffe.

She let it go. "If memory serves. Let me get you a sandwich," she said, and the control panel started doing things.

"Can I see something besides a head, please?"

"Sure." A pressure suit appeared below the head, mostly covered with pockets. It looked like a suit of medieval armor that had just been swallowed by an enormous mutant potholder. Though she didn't have the accent, it was like a Belter's suit, with a conspicuous and distinctive emblem on the chest. The picture was of a wheel station, seen from along its axis, and covered with weapon emplacements, with two of the eight spokes shot away on either side. "How's grilled cheese and bacon suit you?"

"Actually I was planning on cooking the roast I have in the freezer."

"Sorry. Gone."

He goggled at her. "That was five pounds of cultured beef!"

"Marshall Early, Pleasance was conquered almost a year ago.

We're at war. I was hungry. And anyway, you got cheated. That was grain-fed—I distinctly tasted gluten peptides." She handed him a plate bearing a sizzling handmeal. Doubly annoyed though he was, his mind was working; sandwich was an archaic term used by his generation and by Pleasanters, which suggested she was the latter, and must have had some fairly interesting experiences in the past year. He bit into the sandwich.

About a minute later, she handed him a hot towel and a bulb of cold milk. After he'd used both, he said, "That was good."

"Want another?"

"Yes." As that was being handed to him, he said, "I haven't used the 'doc foodmaker in too long. I didn't remember it was this good."

"It wasn't. I rebuilt it when I was reprogramming the 'doc to remove the Puppeteer bug from your head."

She was fast: she caught the sandwich three feet off the ground. "The what?" he said.

"Bug. The reason you've been so much more relaxed and easygoing since you were wounded in the Third War."

"Fifth."

She waved a hand. "The one before this one. It's why you've been trying negotiation."

"Well," he said, "they say a pacifist is just a general who's been shot."

"In the brain."

"Sorry?"

"'A pacifist is a general who's been shot in the brain.'"

"That's not how I remember it."

"Of course not, you've been shot in the brain. I replenished the boosterspice supply while I was working on the 'doc, you'll get up to speed soon."

"That couldn't have been too hard."

"Whatever makes you—ah. No, boosterspice is not based on tree-of-life, it just activates some of the same inert gene complexes. If a Protector wanted to make people younger, the stuff would repair gene damage instead of just patching over it. Good for about fifty years. Here, eat. I've also added a beetle to the 'doc programming. It'll spread into other 'docs, so they'll recognize and remove the implants in other people after yours gets its regular update from the manufacturer. Humans have been doing entirely too well at fighting kzinti. There were supposed to be a couple of more wars to get you into shape."

"For what?"

"For whatever the Puppeteers need you both to fight so they don't have to. It's a dangerous universe out there, and they want lots of cannon fodder between them and the rest of it."

"Ursula," he said, "that's paranoid, and this is me saying it."

"Marshall," she said, "I'm a Protector. I don't act on supposition. I confirmed it."

"How?"

"Interrogated a Puppeteer."

"I thought they killed themselves if anyone tried that."

"They do. Not only that, there's automatic reflexes that kill them in various ways if you prevent them from doing it voluntarily. Took me fifteen tries until I had them all covered."

This time her hand was right under the sandwich. She led him to his desk, where he sat, and shook, and said, "There are fourteen dead Puppeteers now?" ("Conniptions" didn't begin to describe how they would react. "Extinction" might.)

"Don't be silly. I just recorded one and kept editing the pattern. I noticed the transfer booth system was bugged, so I took advantage of that." She handed him another bulb, and he ate and drank in silence as he thought about this.

When he was done, he said, "You duplicated a Puppeteer?"

"Hell, no. I just flat-out kidnapped him, then replaced the original recording when I was done and sent him on his way. With a few minor edits, so he didn't notice the discrepancy in the time."

It occurred to Early that she'd killed the original.

She must have been able to read his face and body language better than he could imagine. "You do realize that, unless you assume the existence of souls, a transfer booth kills the user and delivers a replacement," she said. "It's how you can tell no Protector has ever been to Jinx. There are people who believe transfer booths don't send the soul along, and on Jinx that means the only way for them to get from one End to the other in a reasonable time is by suborbital craft. A Protector would have put a hullmetal tube through the planet for them to use."

"You'd go to that much trouble and expense to humor a superstitious belief?"

"You let people vote."

He didn't have an answer for that.

"Anyhow, that was why Lucas Garner suppressed the human-built version back in the twenty-first century. That and the fact that you could, technically, make copies of anyone who used one. He reckoned you'd have to make murder legal."

"Can you? Copy people?"

"Sure. Of course, blacking out the entire planetary power grid for eight months to charge up for it would be a bit of a giveaway. Garner wasn't so hot on the math part, more concerned about souls."

"Do we have souls?" he said.

"How should I know? And why would I care? Souls are of significance after death. That puts them just exactly out of my jurisdiction. My job is to keep you all alive and reproducing and happy enough to stick with it."

"The Mor—" he said, and shut up.

"The Morlocks on Wunderland took an interest because they had never been exposed to the concept, and were too busy to think the implications through."

"You know about them."

"Of course. I even know whose fault they were. Relax, you're not in trouble for approving Project Cherubim. I'm a Protector, I expect breeders to screw up."

"You have a problem with creating Protectors to fight the kzinti?"

"I have a problem with creating an army of immortal nursemaids to supervise the human race."

"They were exposed to a lot of radiation on the trip. They were supposed to live just long enough to win the war."

"Interesting theory." (Somehow she made that rhyme with "you schmuck.") "One of the reasons I think Brennan's death was suicide was, if he'd made an effort to survive, he could have recovered. I know I could. Anything that doesn't kill a Protector outright can heal."

"You said he was cut in half."

"Top half still worked." She patted his arm. "Don't worry about it. All the human Protectors from Home are headed for the Core to kill off the Pak, and I have serious issues with manipulative parents. I might add that you, personally, are very lucky that the plan failed."

His mind raced but got no traction. "Why?"

"Marshall, who did you consider the sexiest woman in the world when you were growing up?"

"Well, you know, it's been hundreds of years—"

"Buford."

He looked at her and remembered who, or rather what, he was trying to be evasive with. "Leslie Cordwainer."

She got a pad out of a pocket, scribbled on it, and said, "Not bad. I take it the pendulum had swung back to Rubens."

"Hah. No, the Dead Wirehead look was in full force. She kind of stood out."

"Literally. Mine weren't that big. Now, can you imagine what her sex life was like?"

"I have been known to manage not to for days at a time now," he said mordantly.

"Sorry. But I need you to imagine that, thanks to you, she has become an asexual, superintelligent killer, having nothing which would qualify as a conscience by your standards, and with reflexes so fast she can dodge pistol slugs, cells with internal reinforcements that would allow her to survive a few hits with nothing more than bruises, and bones and muscles so strong she can take the gun away and rip it apart," she took a breath, "who remembers every detail of her sexual history and knows where you live."

He made a noise in his throat, and she turned to get him another bulb. While she was getting it he opened his desk, only to find several more pieces of paper that said COLD. "Hey, where's my cigar lighter?" he demanded.

"Obviously I took it."

"Well, dammit, give it back! It's a priceless heirloom, maintained and handed down from agent to agent for over six hundred years."

"I should just think it has been. I found eighty-two different ways it can be used to ruin somebody else's day. Eighty-three if they don't smoke. You'll get it back later, I don't want you wasting time. You had enough to eat?"

"I want a cigar," he grumbled.

Her rigid face was as capable of expression as a Noh mask—

exactly so: when she turned it to change the shading, she displayed a new mood. She detested tobacco smoke.

"You mind if I smoke?" he said, prepared to see if Protector hide would blister.

"Hell, I don't mind if you catch fire and burn to the ground like Miss Havisham. You've spent almost three hundred years making my job harder to do." She opened his cigar box—he saw another slip of paper—got one out, snipped the end, handed it over, and lit it for him.

"Is that a wooden match?" he said after the first drag.

"They're supposed to preserve the flavor."

"I just—mm, it does, thanks—I just think that's a little extravagant."

"Marshall, this planet has ten million square miles of forest. That's about a trillion trees. Cut down one percent a year and that's five tons of lumber per flatlander, with another five tons of foliage and slash for reductive petroleum synthesis. That resource is the principal factor that keeps the dolphins from taking over the plastics industry with their corner on the algae market. You've started to believe ARM press releases."

Early took a gloomy puff to avoid answering. She was right. Then he said, "Who's Miss Havisham?"

"Early selective-breeding reformer, precursor of the Fertility Board. Marshall, I need to find the other Freezer Banks."

"Other?"

"The only one I can find in ARM records is under this building."

"They were combined right after the start of the First War," Early said. "What was left. They were just about emptied out."

The mask turned again, to become forbidding and cold. "Transplants?"

"Sergeants."

The Protector blinked six times. Then she got her pad back out and scribbled on it again. She had damn long fingers, from the extra joint that gave a Protector retractable claws. The effect was exceedingly creepy. Without looking up from the screen, she said, "A lot of things that frighten people are hardwired into the brain from Pak days."

"How did you do that without seeing my face?" he said.

"Your body language changed." Ursula lifted her gaze again, and he paid attention to her eyes for the first time. They were pretty. It was a jarring contrast with the rest of her looks. Also, the pupils were different colors—one red, one blue. "That was your idea too."

"Yes."

"That was brilliant, and this is me saying it. Well done."

"What kind of frightening things?" he said, embarrassed.

"It's a long list. For example, revulsion at the idea of old people having sex comes from the fact that the Pak were accustomed to anyone past menopause becoming physically asexual. Bald people are intimidating. And before boosterspice, children used to be afraid of kissing Grandma."

"I remember."

"So you would," she said, nodding.

"I don't get why, though."

The mask shifted, and she was about to tell him something unpleasant. "Protectors recognize their descendants by smell, and can detect the mutation of a single codon. Any creature not under protection is a threat to descendants. And Protectors make maximum use of resources. When someone big and wrinkly leans over close enough to smell you, there's a chance you're about to be eaten."

He didn't want to believe that, but he had quite a good memory—and that was exactly the way he'd felt about his grandmother the first time he'd been shown to her.

It would have shown on his face to someone not nearly as smart as she was. "You're safe," she said.

Badly wanting to change the subject, he said, "What do you want with the Freezer Banks?"

"We need generals."

"There's not an intact head in the lot," he said.

"Not a problem. I plan to use sections of at least three brains each and splice them together, rectify the DNA, and use the combined experience to make encyclopedic geniuses. I'll grow them new bodies."

The thought was ghastly. "Three sets of memories? They'll be insane!"

She shrugged. "Insanity in a breeder is about as serious as warts on a leper. I have a Sinclair accelerator, so I can provide enough therapy to get the personality fragments to establish a working relationship. They'll have the advantage of being genetic supermen—superwomen, rather, since the rectifying process would treat a Y chromosome as a defect."

"Are you talking about nanomachines?"

"Right."

He snorted. "Good luck with that. We've had people working on that since before I was born. They always break down."

"I know. Brennan saw it happening, made nanotech that attacks all other nanotech, and turned it loose. I have to do all my work in a chamber that's been cleared of the hunters."

"What in hell did he do that for?"

"Marshall, consider what may be defined as nanomachinery. When photosynthetic life began releasing free oxygen as a byproduct, it exterminated almost everything on the planet and replaced it with its own kind. The plants you live with and eat aren't nearly as efficient at using light as what I've made. And that's just an intentional feature. Can you imagine what someone might make if he screwed up? Brennan may have been a quintessential Belter, but even his imagination was good enough for that."

Early reeled. "That's a hell of a note for Weeks," he said.

He evidently didn't have to explain who Weeks was. "When I looked in on him he was moving in that direction. Would have made a 'bot that hunted the hunters. Fortunately I stopped him before he could do any damage."

He closed his eyes. "He's dead?"

"Humph," she said. She didn't grunt, she pronounced it. "Thanks to Phssthpok and the Morlocks, people think of Protectors as casual murderers. It's most unfair. I'm not casual at all. Besides, as soon as I saw him I realized he was a Cellar Christian."

Early hated that term. "Religion has never been prohibited."

"No, just heavily edited. And a good thing, too. Weeks was raised on source material, and he's peculiar even for a breeder. I altered my cloaking system, appeared in his room, and offered to teach him all the secrets of nanomachinery in return for his soul. I expect he's still at church."

Early stared, gaped, and said, "You're a fiend."

"You know, that's just what he said. Slightly different emphasis, though."

Early got up, breathing heavily, and went into the bathroom. Here and there, where his weapons of opportunity had been, he found a few more notes that read COLD. It was getting annoying.

It became more annoying when he realized he didn't need a shower. He got out casual clothing, dressed, and said, "I like taking showers."

"You can switch off the 'doc's body cleaner if you're just going to sleep. It wasn't very good, so I redesigned it while I was undoing the Puppeteer hacks."

Something that had been bothering him—besides Ursula—came to a point: "I was wounded before humans had encountered Puppeteers," he said.

"As one of the great philosophers of the Fission Age often said, 'That turns out not to be the case.' The Puppeteers were interfering with human society, and erasing the memories of any witnesses, well before the First War." After a flash of annoyance so brief he wasn't sure it was something she intended as a message, she added, "You'll recall they got their name because there was a Time For Beany revival. 'Puppeteer' is a cute, harmless name. One of them chose it. They arranged the revival and the timing of the first contact."

"You got that from the one you questioned?"

"Didn't need to. I had an extensive entertainment database that predated the editing of ARM records. Cecil the Seasick Sea Serpent had two eyes." She began scribbling again, and muttered, "Give me a bit, that's the fake one."

Appalled, he said, "Why didn't anyone notice that in the secure data?"

"They got to that too—I keep meaning to get around to doing that holographic indexing system."

"But nobody can get into that."

"Nonsense, I did. And they've had computers for millions of years."

"How did you manage that?"

"I could tell you, but the shock would be so great you'd revert to infancy and I'd have to erase your memory back to before we met."

"Come off it, I'm not that fragile."

"You always say that."

"What?"

She looked up, all innocence. "Oh, nothing."

A few moments after the transition from horror to severe exasperation, Early recalled that Jack Brennan was suspected of having undertaken a number of elaborate and disturbing jokes. One had been the extermination of the Martians. He was getting off lightly.

He looked at the screen she held up to show him and saw three grayscale images side by side, the first two grainy. One was the Cecil he remembered from the cube. The second was similar, but with two eyes and some more details to the features of the head. The third was a Puppeteer's head, which looked almost exactly like the first image. "The middle's the original?"

"Correct."

Early frowned. "How long?"

"Long enough to sic the kzinti on us in the first place. Locating a slowboat in interstellar space requires a technology well in advance of kzin capabilities. Brennan had made us too nice to be good cannon fodder, and the kzinti were too feral to take the job, so they decided to use both races to do selective breeding of each other. Calm down, I planted some surprises in the Puppeteer when I put him back. Have to erase my own memories of them before I talk to any Outsiders, of course, but I can promise you if they're still in contact with us in five hundred years they'll be much too busy to manipulate human lives."

Early made certain his face and body didn't shift and reveal his feelings.

So she noticed the stillness instead. "Relax, I won't either," she said. "I'll make some generals, they'll win the war, and kzin culture will be altered to the point where they won't feel compelled to start another. The only thing I've done to alter Earth's culture is rig autodocs to remove Puppeteer bugs and arrange for water from Lake Mead to reach Death Valley."

"You did that? It looks like seepage."

"Thank you."

Early snorted. "And it's not enough to make it habitable."

"No, but it's enough to make it more bearable for borax mining. True, the spaceports at Perth and Nairobi will get a little less business, but the important thing is that the price of boron will go down."

"I wasn't aware that was a vital resource."

"It's used in linac-fusion plants. They're small, but they don't need a fusion shield, so they don't need an ARM presence to guard them from Gangreens. The ARM personnel budget will have to be cut, and with fewer ARMs around, nations will be able to show more independence. This will lead to petty quarrels in the UN. You need more practice not getting along."

Early didn't like that, but the part of his brain he thought of as a Roman judge had to admit she had a point. "How did you do it without disturbing anything else? Nanobots?"

"Oh, no, I wouldn't turn something like that loose unsupervised. It . . . hm. It's too hard to describe without a few months of teaching, you don't have any words for some of the forces involved. You don't even have terms to use in a plausible lie, like the one about how a disintegrator works."

That confused him. "I thought it reduced the charge on electrons."

She shook her head. "And a slug pistol causes little pieces of metal to appear inside things. Another great Fission Age philosopher likened a man surrounded by forces beyond his comprehension to a mouse on a battlefield. A little difficult to explain what's going on. The standard explanation of a disintegrator is like telling that mouse that humans are throwing things at one another. It leaves stuff out—like why the disintegrator doesn't turn to dust."

"So give me the mouse version," Early said, annoyed again.

She shook her head again. "That's the disintegrator example. Explaining the porosity trick would be more like trying to make the mouse understand that all this stuff on the battlefield is going on because a teenage French girl was prettier than her mother, who resented her and made her finish up some rye bread that had gone bad and should have been thrown away. The concepts just aren't there."

He recognized the example; he was a military historian. "Is that a serious explanation of Joan of Arc?"

She shrugged again. (In a properly run world, with her Protector's shoulders, that would have made some kind of dramatic noise.) "It explains the visions, and some of her work displays the behaviors of an abuse survivor. It'll do."

"How come you don't sound like Brennan?" he said.

"I'm not in a hurry," she said. Before he could tell her that was hardly an answer, she said, "Sorry. This may come as a shock to a respectable ARM, but sometimes people with an agenda have been known to say and do things that are misleading."

"If sarcasm was a physical substance, I'd be getting a rash."

"Ooh, good one—Brennan could have sounded any way he wanted, but he was planning to steal a starship. He presented limitations he didn't possess, to create a sense of security."

"Like not letting Garner smoke, because he 'couldn't help himself'?"

She stood as straight as she could, which wasn't very, and said, "Very good! And the story he told about how he killed Phssthpok. Claimed he stunned him with a blow to the head and crushed his throat. Sheer fantasy; Protectors don't stun. The injuries on the corpse in the Smithsonian suggest he broke the Pak's elbows with a Martian's spear, cut the nerves—glass is sharp enough, if you have a Protector's strength behind it—then strangled him before Phssthpok could heal enough to use his hands again."

"I thought Ph—the Pak was stronger than he was. And a better fighter."

"Marshall, the Pak store calcium phosphate in their mitochondria. As a reserve to rebuild broken bone it's wonderful, but it displaces ATP. It's as if every cell in the body has water in the petrol tank. The trait has been bred out of their human descendants, largely though suicide. Jack Brennan was at least thirty percent stronger than Phssthpok, and he would have been able to use any fighting move he'd ever seen on the cube. His biggest problem was leaving a presentable corpse."

"But that didn't have anything to do with his getting the Pak ship. Why would he lie?"

"Same reason everyone does. Saves time."

He took a final puff as he tried and failed to think of a counterexample. It did all boil down to saving time. He stubbed out the cigar and said, "Time for what?"

"Time he'd have to spend later, if breeders knew he was alive, and had traps set for him when he came to make alterations. Ready to go rob some graves with me, Igor?"

"If you can turn invisible, what do you need me for?"

"I don't want the stuff to just disappear, it'll upset too many people. I prefer to make it look like the appearance of these generals is the result of breeder activities."

"And you trust me to keep quiet?"

"A paranoid certainly grasps the concept of self-interest. You're a breeder, but you're an awfully smart one."

He wasn't sure whether he felt flattered or patronized. He decided he could do both. "Okay, got your shovel?"

She patted a pocket by her left knee. "All set." While he was trying to decide whether she might really have a shovel in there—it could be a foil-covered balloon, and stasis fields were easier to make than the ARM ever wanted anyone to know—she handed him an earplug and said, "This will let you hear me. If I have a question, I'll stick to yes or no, just nod or shake your head." A bubble helmet deployed over her own head, and she disappeared again.

He put it in and said, "What if I have a question?"

"Oh, like you'd trust my answer," came her voice, soft but clear. "That'll evaporate in a couple of hours. If you decide there's something you'd believe, get out your phone and write it unless you think it's an emergency. Then I'll stun people and erase memories afterward."

He nodded, then went out the door.

On the long walk down the hall to the elevator—he'd had an apartment near an elevator back when he was (good God!) in his twenties; never again—he said in a low voice, "Just what's the plan?"

"Shipping the materials to a secret lab offworld, where a crazed doctor has a plan."

"So we're sticking to the truth."

"Hm! Right."

"I surmise you have most of the arrangements in the system already," he said.

"Of course."

"Enthusiasm is no substitute for experience," he said, and every part of the corridor was swept with sonic cannon except where he was. He dove for the hatch that opened up in the wall, went five stories down a slide that he'd swear hadn't been that steep in the drill, came out into another hallway, and rolled against a transfer booth, whose door popped open. He wasn't even tempted, he knew she could trace him if he used it. His phone was obviously bugged, so he came to his feet and ran to the emergency phone. Hand on the scanner, he said, "Marshall Buford Early crisis priority to Osiris Chen."

The screen lit up.

It said COLD.

A bag of rocks wrapped around the back of his neck, and a rubber ball fitted neatly into his gaping mouth. Ursula's head appeared next to his.

"Huh, yeah, what, Buford?" said the Chief of Internal Security.

Buford Early heard his own voice come out of Ursula's mouth. "Ozzie," she slurred, "I jus' wanna tell you, you're a rilly beau'ful person."

"Where's the picture?"

"Oh, off, 'm naked."

There was a pause. "And you had to call me up at 3:18 to tell me."

"Din wanna forget again. You deserve to know, an' you can tell everyone I said so."

"Oh, I will," said Chen, who assuredly would.

"You gessum sleep now," Ursula said, and the phone shut off.

The ball came out of his mouth, and he looked at her and said, "You unbelievably horrible bitch."

"What? He sounded glad to hear it."

It was boasted, in White Medical's advertising, that nobody who used one of their 'docs every day had ever died of any of a number of ailments. The list included apoplexy. This turned out to be true.

When he had calmed down somewhat, largely due to lack of breath, Ursula said, "Do you know why ARM HQ security has never been breached? It was designed by Jack Brennan. The cheats are conspicuous, to me. And you really hoped you could catch a Protector."

"Hope is a virtue," he muttered.

"Hope is a narcotic, and it kills more people than wireheading. As witness the planet Pleasance. Marshall, you are free to waste your own time, but wasting mine is an act of sabotage in wartime. Do it again and I'll dose you with something that'll make you compulsively truthful for about five hundred hours, then turn you loose at the Belt Embassy. The next three weeks will be historic."

He'd been doubting the existence of such a substance until she used that last word. Given some of the things he knew about what the ARM had done over the centuries to minimize Belter trade advantages, the term was precisely accurate.

"And by the bye," she said as her helmet formed again, "no amount of practice will create talent."

"What?"

"My reply to your trigger code. I found it an unusually foolish statement."

"My father used to say it, back when I was starting to date." It suddenly occurred to him that his father used to get divorced every ten years or so.

"You might want to listen to someone smarter than you for a change. As in, 'Protectors don't stun.' The sleep center is under voluntary control and can't be triggered by an external signal, and the tissue is too tough for a shockwave to shut off circulation, those being the two ways a stunner can work." Her head vanished again.

The trip down to the Freezer Bank was without further incident.

Doctor Massoglia was IN, according to the little card on the door. It always said that. He'd checked once, and the other side of the card did indeed say OUT, but he'd never seen that side in use. He seemed to live here.

What the tanj, lots of people had apartments in the building; why not one in your office?

He'd always have ice at parties.

He shook that thought off and entered his ID in the reception screen. A few moments later, an astonished-looking woman he didn't know came out of another room and said, "Good morning, Marshall, I'm Jane Rancourt."

"Pleased to meet you, Doctor."

"Jane."

"Buford. Is Martin up? It's about the new project."

In his ear, Ursula's voice said, "Penzance."

He got the reference instantly, clenched his teeth, and said, "Penzance. You get a memo?" The damn tune would be running through his head for years, he just knew it.

"Just today. Well, yesterday. I wasn't expecting anyone at this hour, though."

"It's the only time I'm not doing something else. And the appeasers are less likely to get wind of it if it's done quietly."

"I'll call him." Jane went back into her office.

"Penzance?" he muttered.

"It's at least as good a codename as 'Overlord' or 'Desert Storm,'" Ursula said. "And much better security than 'Cherubim.'"

"I wanted to call that 'Pumpkin,'" he said.

"The kzin are highly literate and fond of alien fables. They'd have understood it was a reference to transformation."

Early was shocked. He hadn't thought of that himself. He'd been thinking of sweet potatoes, which he loathed in pie. He liked pumpkin pie, that's all. "What codename would you have given it?"

"Supposing I was silly enough to do it, you mean? Mighty Mouse. Complete irrelevance. Of course, there'd be some minor risk of them stocking up on limburger, but the Protectors would be in pressure suits most of the time anyway. Dummy up." Massoglia was coming out.

"Hey, Buford."

"Marty. Sorry about the hour."

"Nah, makes sense. And you are always Early." The only enjoyment he got from that tired old joke was hearing Ursula's beak grind at the pun. "You want the full tour at last?"

"Not hardly, but I'm taking it. How much did the memo tell you?"

"Splice and clone, and they need at least a quarter of a cortex per donor. Personally I think if the Belt wants genius lunatics they should start with the guy who thought this up."

"Who says they didn't? They need more than one."

"Might as well take you straight to the Beneficiaries, then. Not many of those. This way." He led Early down a corridor and through a doorway.

Corpsicles had once been kept in separate Dewar tanks. Later they were more numerous, and space was at a premium, so most had been packed in rows, side by side.

Not these. There would have been too much risk of getting the parts mixed up. As they passed one carcass, Early said, "Good Christ, what happened to him?"

"Run over by a sugar train. Wore a lottery bracelet, so he was frozen," Marty said without looking. "Everyone asks that," he added, clearly accustomed to people wondering how he knew which one.

"Lottery?"

"It was a fad for a while to have local lotteries award freezer slots as prizes. If we could ever get him stuck back together right he'd have a lot of money waiting for him."

"How did a guy that lucky get hit by a train?"

"Crossed the tracks when the barricades were already down. It was a jurisdiction where pedestrians had right-of-way."

"So he expected the train to stop for him? I'd have made the freemother pay for the engineer's therapy! A jaywalker never has the right-of-way."

Marty just grunted agreement.

In Early's ear, Ursula's voice said, "We do not want that brain."

Early nearly choked from trying not to laugh aloud.

Fortunately, he was able to let it out when Marty said, "He's probably not quite what you're looking for."

This chamber had originally been excavated as a bomb shelter, which, since the building overhead had once been where the UN held its meetings, said something about the original General Assembly's opinion about their own effectiveness. Dividers and equipment had gone in during the First War, while the delegates met under a mountain in Switzerland. They got to the end of the ranks of bodies, most of which reminded him of people he'd last seen right after a battle, and got to a section near the end that struck him as different. Early immediately studied his surroundings to see why.

The lighting was better. The windows over the bodies had no frost on the inside, meaning they were of a different material. The ID tags at each body were of hullmetal, with the lettering inset, and given the properties of hullmetal, that meant they'd been formed that way. "These are the Beneficiaries," Marty said. "People who couldn't afford to be frozen, or hadn't thought of it, so strangers who admired them paid for it or took up collections. They were all heroes to someone. This is Wu Kim," he said, pointing to the left half of a woman whose right side had not been entirely found. "Tiananmen. A few of the people who got the body out and on ice in time later ended up in the First War. Not too surprisingly, they all distinguished themselves."

"Tiananmen?" Ursula said in his ear.

"Chinese word meaning Waco," Early remarked. Marty glanced at him and nodded.

There were only sixty-one Beneficiaries, and Marty had something to say about them all. The last and earliest was Hugo van Trast. "He was still at Caltech when he came up with the rejection buffer," Marty said.

"What did that to him?"

"Carlists. They blamed van Trast for the organ bank that saved the life of Francisco Bahamonde. They kind of overlooked the fact that that same organ bank also saved the life of Marissa Colby, who invented the fusion shield and replenished the depleted fishing grounds and gave us free water. She was on vacation in Majorca when she was exposed to some kind of pesticide. You know, the ones they used in the period when DDT was illegal? Really horrible stuff—There are royalists today who hold annual parties where they burn Bahamonde in effigy."

"I don't know why. He's still dead," Early said, shaking his head.

"Take them all," Ursula told him.

"Tag them for shipment."

"Some don't have that much brain left," Marty objected.

"We can at least get their DNA," Early said without being told. "These are miracle workers. The kzin get smarter with every war. We could use some miracles."

Marty nodded, but looked sad. He looked around at the dead, made a gesture with his right hand which could have turned into a wave if he hadn't stopped it, and said, "You need any others?"

"I hope not," Early said.

Marty nodded again. "Was it Napoleon who said he'd rather have a general who was lucky than one who was smart?"

"It's been attributed to him," Early agreed, "but look how he turned out." He studied Marty. "You'll miss them, won't you?"

Marty nodded. "I liked to sit here and read. It was a good feeling, to be with the best people their times could produce."

"Get a DNA cheek swab from him," Ursula said. "Imply that he's got this job because he's the most diligent organizer willing to do it. That'll make him feel better."

"Martin," Early said, "they need orderly minds to sort their memories out. How would you like to have any good genes you carry added to the mix of every general they're made into?"

"I think I'd like it a lot."

Back in the elevator, Early murmured, "That was a damn nice thing to do."

"I like when I can combine that with doing a good job," Ursula said. "I also like when someone displays intelligence. You picked up on the idea right away."

"Thanks," Early said, keeping his own counsel.

It didn't help. "I see. You got the purpose and the method, but you thought I was just being considerate. Two out of three."

"Two out of three—"

"—Is a D, Buford."

He was fuming by the time he got back to his apartment. Ursula became visible again, and he went over to his desk and gave the nearest leg a vicious kick. It broke off, bounced against the wall, and rebounded where he could grab it. He turned and aimed the stub at her. "You missed one," he said.

"And you missed my companion," she said.

"Are you serious? 'There's someone behind you'? That's the oldest trick in the book."

A huge, gloved feline hand reached over his head and plucked the puncher out of his grasp.

"Actually, the oldest trick in the book is kidnapping a couple of teenagers, brainwiping them, waking them up in a prepared habitat, and saying, 'I made you out of dust and I made her out of one of your ribs,'" said Ursula.

Early turned carefully and looked at the indubitable kzin in his apartment. His suit looked like it was made out of balloons. "Oh, hell," Early said.

"I thought it was 'hello,'" said the kzin. "Human languages are weird."

"I need to recreate the roast I ate earlier. Stun him and put him back to bed, then we have to get moving to arrange the supposed wreck of the ship with the bodies."

As the kzin brought up his other hand—the one with the stunner—the only thing Buford Early could think of was, *I am the very model of a modern major general*—

He saw the room tilt, then stop as he was caught. The rest was silence.

Unless he was staying over with a woman he'd met, Buford Early slept in his autodoc. At his age most people died in their sleep, and while he wasn't as afraid of dying as most people, it struck him as an undignified way to go after surviving five wars. On the other hand, his psychist program told him it was really a way of distancing himself, since the lack of a bed in his apartment meant that any woman who came home with him couldn't stay over herself. The clincher, however, was that it was the most comfortable place he'd ever had to sleep.

He was not accustomed to being startled when he woke up.

Certainly not by a group of stern-faced guards. He checked his weapons by reflex, but left them; he'd spent his entire career doing what he believed was right, and however someone had disagreed on what that might have been, shooting his way through his fellow ARMs wasn't it. He opened the 'doc and said, "Do I get to eat?"

"You're not under arrest," said Smith. The Marsborn agent was the only man he recognized. "But we really do want to ask you an awful lot of questions. The ship you sent off last night has disappeared."

"Ship?"

Smith squinted, then said, "Aw, tanj, he's had an erasure. Assume lethal traps and search the place."

"I can point things out if you like," Early said, utterly at a loss. Why would he have an erasure?

"You might have had some things erased," Smith said.

Early got up, went into the bathroom, showered, dressed—he'd apparently remembered to run the laundry last night, all his clothes were in the cabinet—and went to the kitchen to start the roast.

After a while he heard an exclamation and came to the doorway to see who'd made what mistake. They were all standing at the desk looking at the screen. Smith looked at him and said, "Where the fuck did you get this crystal?"

Early spread his hands, shook his head, and went over to see what it was.

It was in kzin script, with a running translation down the side of the screen.

If it was genuine, it was the entire kzin order of battle, including the target schedule for the current war. They were making copies already.

He must have had an erasure to protect the identity of one king-hell insider in the Patriarch's Palace.

"If this checks out," Smith said, "that funny business last night isn't going to cause you much trouble. You'll probably be promoted to a directorship to keep you out of trouble, but I imagine you'd find it difficult to get out from behind your desk under the weight of all the medals anyway. Marshall, you're either the smartest man alive, or the luckiest."

The copying was done, and the screen reverted to a desktop that wasn't his: a reclining woman he'd never seen before, almost entirely Caucasian, nude, built like he liked 'em, and smiling at the camera with what looked much very like love in her eyes. Below it was perhaps the most unnecessary caption imaginable:

HOT.

🐾   🐾   🐾

THE WHITE COLUMN

❧ ❧ ❧

by Hal Colebatch

☙ THE WHITE COLUMN ☙

THE LIFT TOOK ME DEEP UNDERGROUND, past five decks of steel and concrete, the guard glaring at me and my own escort, and apparently deciding he hadn't quite got an excuse to shoot us. The site was well hardened.

General Burkholtz greeted me at Level 5 and took me through the second retinal identification. Then our far-seer was to be presented to me.

"We've tested him at short range, sir. To show us, under top secrecy of course, headlines of newspapers from different parts of the world, from a few weeks ahead. In each case the newspapers, when they were printed, were exactly as he had pictured them. It works for sounds as well—he recorded a new symphony before it was written. It was just a matter of fitting phones on the opti-encephalograph."

"Why not just have him read all the future documents, then?"

"He can't see to that degree of visual detail. And also because in every previous case where such an ability has been present in some degree, it very rapidly burns itself out. It did with Basil Shackleton. Already we are starting to get flickerings in the pictures he 'transmits.' Once the ability has gone, it doesn't come back. We don't want to waste it, sir. He's the best we've ever had, but judging from the rate of 'flickering' we have recorded, which is increasing exponentially, he probably has only one session left in him. We don't want to waste it."

"Is he aware of this?"

"That he's nearly finished as a far-seer? Yes. I think he's rather pleased at the prospect of becoming normal."

"Can you tell what the headlines of the newspapers he saw say, at least?"

"The usual stuff, sir. Things going from bad to worse. Nuclear proliferation. Environmental decay. The blow-up getting nearer. We've photographs of them here."

"It reminds me of a science fiction story I once read," I said. "Someone else who could see the future, just like this. The military, for obvious reasons, asked him to draw the most advanced weapon he could see from a century hence. They puzzled over the picture he brought back, turned it over to the best teams of scientists. Someone eventually recognized it as a crossbow."

There was a very mirthless laugh from these, our own best team of scientists. They brought Richard Billings, the far-seer, forward and presented me to him. A very ordinary name, I thought.

He was a somewhat shabby, unkempt-looking man, despite the major's uniform someone had put him into, not unpleasant-looking, but undistinguished and, apart from the pallor they all shared from living underground, out of place in this company of high-domed heads and spectacles. Like many people, he seemed somewhat shy at meeting me. I told him we all appreciated the patriotic thing he was doing. The pallor threw up his blushes and he stammered something.

"I hope I can help, sir" he said. I asked him, as I suppose many had done before, how he thought he did it. "My subconscious—or something—points me at what I see," he said, "but I can hardly remember it. I didn't recognize the newspapers when they showed the photographs of them to me."

"Is it painful?" I asked.

"No, not really, sir."

Dr. Gropius took me to one side.

"The general is right, as far as we know, sir," he said. "We think the next session will be his last."

"And what's he programmed to find?" It was easy to talk of Billings as if he were not there. We thought of him as a weapon, not a man.

"The most advanced artifact existing a hundred years from now."
He smiled wryly. "I hope it won't be the crossbow."

We sat back. Billings, the opti-encephalograph clamped to his
head, his arms and legs restrained, slumped forward in his couch.
There was a faint humming as the current built up. Then a picture
appeared on the screen in front of us.

There was a flat, reddish plain. In the center was a white column,
with what appeared to be some sort of decoration at the top. The
microphones recorded a whistling wind. There were what might have
been low buildings or paving nearby, but scale and size were
impossible to tell.

"A column." I thought of "Ozymandias"—"'Look on my works,
ye mighty, and despair.'" I quoted. "Is it a ruin?" As the scene grew
darker, I recognized the Pleiades in the sky. I could identify the scene
as the Northern Hemisphere, anyway.

"Doric," said someone. "Or Corinthian, maybe . . . Yes, 'round the
decay of that colossal wreck, boundless and bare/ the lone and level
sands stretch far away.'" The picture flickered. There was what seemed
a long pause, and it returned.

"That's the longest interrupting yet," said Dr Gropius, "And the
quickest to manifest itself. It's breaking up fast."

Nothing seemed to be moving in the picture, save that it was
sunset, and as night deepened more stars were beginning to appear.
There was bright Venus, and Orion's Belt.

"It can't have moved since classical times," said someone. "Maybe
it's all that remains of the Roman ruins of Leptis Magna, or
somewhere else in North Africa."

"Or what the Romans called Arabia Felix."

"If that is the most advanced surviving artifact, all the cities must
be gone, all machinery . . ."

"All life . . ." said somebody else.

I have said it was impossible to tell the scale. Now the picture was
becoming fuzzy. I noticed tiny things, possibly insects, were moving
at the base of the column. As I watched, they moved into or under the
low structure near it.

"Well, there's life, anyway," I said.

"A complete waste," said the general. "We could look at this till
Doomsday, and it wouldn't tell us anything useful."

"Except that Doomsday is coming," said Gropius. "And this is all that's left. The last trace of Man. We must have destroyed the Earth big time."

"It remains top secret, with your permission, sir," the general said. "No need for people to know what's coming."

The shuddering patterns of interference were coming more quickly and frequently to the picture now, and the distortions becoming more gross. Then the picture dwindled to a pinpoint of light and died. Our glimpse into the future had ended. We looked at each other wordlessly. There was nothing to say.

But there had just been time to see the white column, on a soundless beam of light, lift from the ground, turn towards the Pleiades, and vanish in a flash.

🐾   🐾   🐾

DEADLY KNOWLEDGE

A story of the Man-Kzin Wars

by Hal Colebatch

DEADLY KNOWLEDGE
A Story of the Man-Kzin Wars

Occupied Wunderland, 2419

"THE MONKEY IS TELLING THE TRUTH," the telepath reported. "It does not know why the other monkeys died."

I knew enough of the Heroes' Tongue to follow what it said. I had not tried to resist it or make its task more difficult, so we were both feeling in better shape than would otherwise be the case. And I had told the truth. The telepath was bewildered, and so was I.

Slave Supervisor nodded, a mannerism he must have unconsciously picked up from humans. Anyway, it seemed I was off the hook.

"Resume your duties," he growled at me.

I made a prostration of obedience—not gratitude, kzin would not appreciate that—and gathered my books and left. The telepath followed me. I gave silent thanks that Krar-Skrei and his pride had not been present. To Krar-Skrei, a dead monkey was a good thing on principle.

An apparently motiveless murder and a suicide. The kzin would not have cared, except we three had been tasked with teaching a class of kzin about human culture, on Chuut-Riit's orders. I could guess why, after killing von Kleist, Thompson had opened his own veins—the kzin punishment for destroying the Patriarch's property and spoiling Chuut-Riit's schemes would have been a great deal worse than a largely painless death in a hot bath. It was an end that befitted a classical scholar devoted to Petronius, who had died similarly on Nero's orders. But why had he killed von Kleist in the first place?

We still had wills, or some of us did, part of the fast-vanishing remnants of legality. Thompson, we discovered, had left everything to his wife, to whom, for all his faults, I knew him to be devoted. Had there been a love triangle there?

Another document had been left by Thompson, apparently meant to be attached to his will like a codicil, and made apparently just before he committed suicide. In it he claimed von Kleist had been a member of the Resistance. This stopped kzin reprisals against Thompson's family—he was written off as a monkey who, by killing a feral monkey, had tried to do his duty to the Patriarchy, even if in a typically monkey-daffy way. Yet as far as I could tell, it was untrue. To a human it made no sense. Anyway, we lived and worked too closely together to have secrets of that magnitude from one another. More, it would have been impossible. The Resistance in Neu Munchen had finished long ago. The humans still carrying on were holed up in the wild country, apart from occasional furtive trips to the city to pick up what supplies they could.

Well, I was too busy staying alive myself to worry overmuch. Suicides, and, for that matter, murders, on occupied Wunderland were by no means uncommon. As I returned to my quarters that night, it seemed to me, not for the first time, that suicide made a good deal of sense for us all. Even if I had had two good arms, I would not have dared even think about escaping to join the Resistance: my mind might easily be swept by a telepath again, perhaps a more thorough and more viciously hostile one.

There had not been much left of the Munchen University. The kzin had forbidden human research into any branches of science that might have military application, and as for the fine arts—well, what was the point of a BA now? The University had some endowment lands, and the collaborationist government allowed it to collect a little, diminishing, rent from these, I presumed to help prop up an appearance of normality, though some of the collabos might have their own games and rationalizations. That kept some of us alive, until the tenants died or walked off, or the kzin took over rent-collecting for themselves. Some of us, yes. There were few humans more helpless on Wunderland—on *Ka'ashi*, rather, than an academic whose department fell apart. Most of the University's remaining productive farmland was worked by robots who didn't care who their masters were.

We had almost nothing to do, apart from competing with the hedge-teachers who gained a pittance from teaching children the basics of reading and writing. We spent our days in the common room, drinking foul *ersatz* coffee, and wondering how long our lucky position as unassigned slaves would endure. To venture out of doors meant the risk of being robbed as the last of law and order gradually broke down, or worse, being conscripted by the kzin for slave-labor. The braver members of the faculty who had joined the Resistance were gone and mostly dead.

We all knew what *might* happen. Shortly after the cease-fire we had been summoned to watch the University's vice-chancellor and his family die in one of the Public Hunts, the first we had seen. Captain von Rathenau of the collabo police force had set it up. The vice-chancellor and his family had not made good sport, however—they had been too old, too young, too out of shape, or too paralyzed with fear to run, let alone fight. So as not to disappoint the kzin youngsters who had turned up for the hunt, von Rathenau, under Krar-Skrei's orders, had then drafted a number of the human spectators to replace them.

The vice-chancellor had not even died for a great cause, just for misdirecting the collabo government, possibly unintentionally, in the hunt for Nils and Leonie Rykermann. The collabos had learned of the Rykermanns' work in organizing the Resistance, and Krar-Skrei, the area governor, had put a price on their heads. The Rykermanns, when they heard about this, had insolently retaliated by putting a price on Krar-Skrei's head—a supply of the geriatric drugs which had suddenly become worth far more than gold, and double that for von Rathenau, who was a more possible target. Krar-Skrei was a terrifying piece of work, even as kzin nobles went.

Our position was similar to that of the purveyors of luxuries in any depression in Earth's history, only immeasurably worse than most. We offered classes to children of the officials of the collabo

Government, with an almost total lack of success. Apart from the basics of reading, writing and counting, what was the point of learning anything? And how could we discipline or examine them? If the child of a collabo official wanted a degree, he or she got one without more ado.

This more-or-less wretched existence had been interrupted by a visit from the collabo security forces. They rounded us up and began checking off our specialties against lists they carried.

Finally they selected three of us: von Kleist, Thompson and me. I did not like either of the others much. Too cowardly or insufficiently patriotic to join the Resistance themselves, I had the feeling that they despised those quaint enough to do so (at least I had an excuse). But when our names were first called, there was little room to think of anything save to not let oneself be overmastered by terror. Something told me to put on a good front.

We were taken to one of the empty buildings and told to wait. The waiting was not pleasant. There was no point in running or speculating on the future. Finally a collabo security guard returned, accompanied by a kzin whose title, we were told, was Slave Supervisor, prefixed by some distinguishing number, and a telepath. The telepath ran over our minds quickly, not very thoroughly, as far as I could tell, merely establishing that there were no feral monkeys among us. Then we were taken into another room. There were a couple of dozen kzin reclining on *footches*. By this time I was on the verge of fouling myself with terror, and nearly fainted, but it passed, and I began to notice things.

A large number of these kzin looked like cripples, with missing limbs or eyes. Also, to judge from the white fur, a number were old. A couple were overweight, and some were small and scrawny. Three were completely black-furred, the color of their priesthood. Not many, apart from a few who were clearly disabled veterans, had impressive collections of ears on their ear-rings. Most of them, in short, did not look like fighting kzin. Also most of them, as far as I could tell, had a sour look, although that was difficult to tell. And they were carrying, incongruously, what I realized were electronic notebooks. The telepath joined us. Even for a telepath, he looked in bad shape, violet-eyed, hunched and bent, and generally very near the end of the road.

Then the collabo security man explained.

Chuut-Riit, he said, had ordered the study of humans. Some humans had been turned over to a specially designated kzin unit for medical experiments. However, we were more fortunate. Our job would be to teach these kzin about human society. Von Kleist would teach literature, Thompson would teach history, and I would teach politics. That explained the curious composition of this group. They were the kzin equivalent of academics or intellectuals, or poor fighters, and, apart from the priests, whose position was anomalous, and the honorably crippled, lowly and despised in their own society. Even so, to us they were threatening enough. Still, the class was orderly. Kzin were bad administrators. But they enforced their orders with ruthless discipline.

Von Kleist was a haughty aristocrat, with the asymmetrical beard and mobile ears of a true *Herrenmann*. He left no one in any doubt that he considered himself several cuts above other members of the faculty and considered teaching at a university to be beneath him. Thompson was a little cock-sparrow of a man, also with a gift for rubbing people up the wrong way. I wondered how long their very limited diplomatic skills would keep them alive among the kzin. Both of them, I felt, regarded the war as vulgar, and human patriotism as the greatest vulgarity of all. Well, their meals were still being delivered three times a day, and they had not *become* meals yet.

The teaching, conducted in the slaves' patois, was not terribly difficult, but hideously stressful. The kzinti had been ordered to learn, and they learned. After a few days, when my terror had subsided somewhat, I even found it interesting to explain voting and parties and majorities. Inevitably, our teaching overlapped somewhat (another possible pitfall—don't bore them!). Otherwise, I knew I was fairly safe, so long as I did not insult them, and there was no call to do that. The main thing was not to imply that monkey social organization was in any way superior to that of the Heroes. A major difficulty was that I dared not give them tests, which they might possibly fail. I became adept, I think, at the use of various psychological tricks for having the cleverer ones discipline the stupid and lazy. If I dared not sneer at their work, another kzin might, and the resultant death-duel did not displease me. I could not be blamed for it.

I kept in mind H. G. Wells's ancient story *The First Men on the Moon*, in which the foolish scientist, Cavor, marooned on Earth's

Moon, was killed by the inhabitants after telling them too much about human society. We got some help: Morris, a shy little man, was drafted to assist us. He had had some family on Wunderl—on *Ka'ashi*—but had none now, and the experience had broken his spirit. Someone told me he had suffered from hysterical blindness for many months afterwards. Anyway, he fetched and carried for us, did our research, cowered at the sight of even an old or crippled kzin, and generally made no trouble.

I found a digest of Nietzsche's aphorisms, presumably brought from Earth by one of the nineteen *Herrenmanner* families, and destroyed it. "The weak and the botched must perish . . . I tell you that a good war hallows every cause." I thought they had rather too much of that doctrine already. Markham, the guerrilla leader was, I knew, devoted to Nietzsche.

At least my conscience was clear. I could not see how teaching them the basics of human civics could harm the human war effort. As time went on, the idea even came to me that I might be importing some civilized values into their minds—but perhaps that was self-deception.

I taught them the theories of Adam Smith, and, straying out of my area somewhat dangerously, of James Watt and the generations-long endeavors which had led to the harnessing of steam, and then of electricity. I found that some of them, including the telepath, had a surprising interest in religion and its role in the history of science. I quoted to them an epigram I remembered from Einstein: "Science without religion is lame, religion without science is blind." I told them of the troubles Columbus had had in gaining finance for his voyages, and the parallel troubles that had nearly destroyed the early American space program. Some of my students, it seemed to me, were coming to comment upon human institutions with less that total disgust. This, I thought, was not uncommon among certain people who studied any subject. Students of some of the vilest societies on Earth, assigned to study them only for the purpose of defeating them, had come to admire them. This also made me feel better about what I was doing. Further, I was learning about them. There was little they bothered to hide from a monkey.

Although literature was not my subject, I learned a little about their own. They had some works I would call "thrillers," but reading or viewing them was considered somewhat shameful, like watching pornography. Their respectable literature dealt with Lord Chmeee and other ancient Heroes, and was embellished with as many stylistic conventions as a Japanese Noh drama or an American Western. When the conventions were not observed, they often had difficulty in telling fact from fiction (I had to be very careful not to humiliate them here). I did not envy my colleagues, scrabbling in their little free time in the archives of the University for books and fragments which had been brought from Earth and forgotten in the excitement of settling a new planet in order to put inoffensive courses together.

I did not see as much of the other three humans as you might expect. By the end of the day we were all too mentally exhausted to socialize. Two or three of my kzin students, mainly the telepath, who, I gathered, was regarded as having become almost useless for real work (which was reassuring) took to seeking me out after hours with questions. Though my free time was limited and precious, I came to find this flattering. I talked some geriatric treatments out of the collabo Government, not exactly telling them, or myself, that I was civilizing the kzin (those telepath sweeps! Always a haunting dread!), but allowing them to draw that conclusion for themselves. The ubiquitous threat of telepaths was subtly changing the ways all humans thought and communicated. Fortunately for us, telepaths were rare, and were assigned to military duties nearly all the time. Even luckier, our telepath, who, I guessed, was assigned to the class to keep a more-or-less watching brief over us all, human and kzin, was of relatively mild nature. When I saw him he did not inject himself with the *sthondat*-lymph drug which heightened his powers, and I did not feel the headache which would have indicated that he was reading my mind. The telepath and I played chess occasionally. Most kzin adore chess, regarding it along with blow-dryers, talcum power and toilet paper as the finest fruit of human civilization. I had an ulterior motive in this: there was no point in the telepath playing chess if he read my mind: that would have made it no game. So I was, I felt, subtly conditioning him to interact with me but to leave my mind alone. Even so, I dared not insult him by *letting* him win. He played like a typical kzin—fast and aggressive. He generally lost the first few games in short order, coming dangerously close to losing his temper—he could crush a solid metal chessman in his claws in a rage—but would then improve.

I caught no trace of him probing my mind; it was just the way he worked. Of course, no other kzin would play with him. It was also a chance to pick up scraps of gossip from him—the kzin, or Telepath at least, cared little about military security. I gathered some details of the humans who were still fighting in the great caves, in Grossgeister Swamp, in the eastern hills and on the other, sparsely settled land masses. Battles were going on in space, and Sol System was still putting up fleets.

I noticed Thompson seemed to have formed a queer association with the telepath, rather as I had done. A case of uttermost underlings coming together. All of us, in our different ways, were protected a little by our value to Chuut-Riit from the casual savagery of kzin society. Much to my surprise, the telepath asked me to read aloud to him. I gathered it helped him relax, or gave him some relief from the mental noise that constantly surrounded him. I had heard rumors of telepaths with prohuman leanings, and perhaps that was what saved me at the time of the meat incident.

I dropped some meat, the food of another kzin (I had had a shock when I recognized the human bones). I was terrified the owner of the meat would attack me. Telepath, to my surprise, stopped him, as slavering, claws extended, he gathered himself to spring.

"Do not harm the Patriarch's property!" Telepath said, and there had been something like a command in his voice.

The angry kzin, one who plainly had been drafted into the class to rid some fighting unit of his stupidity, growled and snarled. Even he, however, could realize that damaging the Patriarch's property and Chuut-Riit's was not a wise move. He snarled some threats about me losing my other arm, and resumed his seat. I gave the telepath some books, and tried to broadcast feelings of friendship to him—with how much success I did not know. But from that time there seemed, though I dared not have presumed upon it, to be some sort of unspoken understanding between the telepath and myself. He was, I guessed, like many telepaths, a secret intellectual, desperately lonely, and as frightened as I was, secretly not only terrified of the strutting Heroes, but also despising them.

Gradually, I began to realize the politics of the situation. I knew Chuut-Riit's interest in humans was not universally approved of among senior kzinti. Some considered it disgusting, virtually a perversion. Others thought it a waste of time. Instead of building up the elite corps that Chuut-Riit had envisioned, many commanders had used the unit as a dumping-ground to get rid of unwanted personnel. Apart from those who were simply old or physically disabled, some of these were misfits because they were stupid, and some were misfits because they were intelligent.

I was, however, beginning to worry about graduating the class. I could not fail any, but if I passed them all as qualified "human experts," the more stupid ones might well let me down in the field. Certainly the consequences would be unpleasant for them, but they would be a great deal more unpleasant for me. I realized that all I could do was try to teach well, keep the content of my classes innocuous, and emphasize my position as the property of the Patriarch. Also, another worry came to me: the obviously bright ones would resent being marked no higher than the obvious thick-heads.

One day, the telepath approached me.

"This *Moby Dick* that Kleist-human speaks of?"

"Yes, Dominant One, have you completed it?"

"We are not far advanced with it yet. But I have a question . . . What became of the cetaceans?"

"The whales? Their killing was stopped by law eventually, Dominant One. It was feared that they would become extinct, and better sources of oil were found . . . *petroleum:* 'Rock-oil.'"

"Yes, you have Cetacean allies now."

"Yes, the dolphins. We brought them to *Ka'ashi.*"

"But Moby Dick was not your ally."

"No, Dominant One. A different species. Larger and more fearsome. Ahab believed he had to be destroyed, partly in vengeance for having taken his leg, partly because" (Careful, now!) "he was an enemy of Man."

"I see." Yes, I thought, *a Kzin would see that.* "I meant to speak to Thompson-human about it, but I sensed he did not wish to discuss the matter. I could have pressed him, of course."

Of course.

"But I did not wish to. Such things are painful to me." No kzin normally admitted pain in any circumstances, least of all to a human, but telepaths were different. It was, I thought, a sign of the delicate empathy between us. It also, I thought, tended to confirm my guess that this one was reaching the end of the line.

"It shows Ahab's obsession," I said. I did not know the deeper literary criticism of *Moby Dick*; in fact, I had forgotten most of the story, but a kzin would not need to know it either. "He must kill the whale at all costs." Something made me add, "Humans are like that, Dominant One." No fearsome headache. He was not trying to read my mind. Then he said, "Like our Morris-monkey."

Morris? Had he read Morris's mind? But if he had discovered anything there, why had he not reported it? I found it difficult to imagine. Morris was the quietest and most self-effacing of us all. And that phrase, "*our* Morris-Monkey," was odd.

Seeing that he had no more questions, I made the prostration and he left, with me wondering what had sparked his curiosity. It was then that, returning to our quarters, I found von Kleist and Thompson dead, von Kleist with his throat cut, Thompson with the veins of his wrists opened in a bath of bloodstained water. I called security. As I said, the telepath cleared me. Not merely because of that frail empathy between us downtrodden beings either. I truly did not know any more. The fact that I had been with him was, of course, an additional alibi.

No motive for the murder-suicide. Thompson, as far as we knew, was happily married—as happily, that is, as anyone could be in those ghastly days—with three children. He seemed to have a great deal to live for. But madness was thick in the air of occupied Wunderland.

The telepath did ask me about it several times, not probing my mind, or not much. I gathered the kzin were as puzzled about the murder-suicide as I was. "Why," Telepath asked, "did the Professor Thompson not simply denouncee the Professor von Kleist if he knew him to be in contact with the feral monkeys?"

"Perhaps, Dominant One, he wished to spare him disciplining." The cruellest and most vengeful human that ever lived might wish to spare another kzin torture. "But I do not understand." It was true, and he knew it. I didn't understand.

"Slave Supervisor wishes to know," he said. I detected fear buried in his voice.

An answer even smacking distantly of smart-aleckry, such as "I wish to know too" was not advisable. "I will inform you, at once, Dominant One, should I learn anything," I told him.

Suddenly a great howling filled the air. Meteor strikes had increased dramatically since the kzin invasion. Before that, Wunderland had had a meteor-guard service. This had held off the kzin force for some time while our hastily convened defense council tried to think of something to do. Now it was gone and we had meteors to add to everything else. The only defense the kzin permitted us was a system of sirens.

I knew nothing about the ramscoop raid then, only saw a glaring light in the sky, from which streamed molten matter, travelling hellishly fast, and on a nearly constant bearing. Telepath didn't need to read my mind. We ran. I was a poor runner. My arm unbalanced me. Telepath grabbed my other arm and pulled me. We reached a shelter—an abandoned storage tank—just before impact, climbed a short ladder and fell in just as the blast-wave hit us. The tank rang like a bell as something fell on it. The blast lifted it off its mountings.

A white streak—a Beam's Beast that had been in the tank—leaped through the air and fastened its jaws on Telepath's shoulder. I was badly shaken up, but still had my flashlight—we, or those of us trusted by the kzin, carried them with Beam's Beasts, Advokats and Zeitungers specifically in mind. After all, it suited them also if we killed the dangerous vermin, and you would have to be lucky and very, very quick to do a kzin much harm with one of the small devices. At the time I was not thinking of Telepath. It was purely a reflex action: if you saw a Beam's Beast, you fired. It was a difficult shot, but the close range compensated for that. I burned its head free of its body, and, using the flashlight as a lever pried the locked jaws apart. The skin was broken, but Telepath's fur seemed to have protected him from worst of the venom. I opened the lid of the tank and slammed it shut again. We were in the middle of a puddle of fire. Many kzin, I knew, if they were frightened of anything, were frightened of fire—I suppose because their fur was iflammable. We sat together in the tank for what seemed a long time, as the air grew hotter and fouler. At last the sound of the flames died.

"I can't move my arm," he said after a time.

There was only one thing for it. It was a highly distasteful idea, but it was a chance to win some brownie points with my masters. Anyway, I owed him. After explaining what I was going to do, I sucked some of the venom out of the wound.

"If you had had a cut on your mouth, you would be dead too by now," Telepath said when I had finished and was spitting and retching, with a finger down my throat.

"That did occur to me," I said when I could. Somehow I knew it was safe now to say something mildly sarcastic to him. We seemed to have moved away from "Dominant One."

"Did it? You saved my life? A monkey saved a kzin?"

"You saved mine," I told him. "I would never have reached this place without you."

He took a spray from his belt, and looked as if he was preparing to apply it. Then he returned it, unused.

"It would dishonorable to read your mind in this situation," he said. "I must assume you are telling me the truth."

I climbed out of the tank, but the rusty ladder would not bear telepath's weight. With my arm there was not much I could do to help him, and in that confined space he could not leap. There was fire and death in the streets all around us. Fortunately, as we later learned, the missiles used in the Ramscoop Raid had been inert dumb bombs, their destructive force coming only from their colossal kinetic energy. There was no radioactivity. Eventually I found an old-fashioned fire engine, one of the museum pieces the kzin allowed us to use. The firemen were unimpressed when I told them I wanted to rescue a kzin, but of course they were part of the collabo government themselves. I could see a couple debating whether to quietly kill me and say nothing about it. I pointed out that they could expect a reward, and that swayed them. I also lied to the effect that the kzin command knew where I was. I don't think they were greedy men—on occupied Wunderland, a small reward from the kzin might well be the difference between life and death for oneself and one's family.

The "meteor" had struck well beyond the outer fringes of Munchen. A direct hit would have levelled the city. We got Telepath out, though his arm was still stiff. Since it did not interfere with his mind-reading abilities, I doubted the kzin authorities would care about that much. We somehow agreed without words to say nothing of who had saved whom.

Somewhat to my surprise, Krar-Skrei supervised some of the rescue operations. Although he looked askance at Chuut-Riit's whole human project and regarded humans as vermin, they were vermin who belonged to the Patriarch, and he did his duty to them as effectively as he might. I saw the burning ruins of a schoolroom cleared, and a badly injured kzin who had been inside taken away.

I also saw Krar-Skrei supervising the lifting of a fallen beam, which had blocked the entrance to a meteor-shelter. The firemen descended into it. I stood, with Telepath beside me, feeling shocked and useless. Telepath caught my arm, thankfully remembering to retract his claws, and pointed.

"The Morris-human," he said.

It was Morris, all right, heading for the unattended fire engine. Telepath was getting out his injector now. Why? Something in Morris's walk? Something Telepath picked up even with his unheightened powers?

It happened very quickly. Morris flung the fire engine into gear and drove it forward over Krar-Skrei and von Rathenau, killing them both instantly, if the bump it made going over them was anything to go by. Morris was screaming something, and I picked up the last words ". . . but I'll slay him yet!" Half a dozen guns turned on the fire engine from a group of kzinti beside a burning wall, and melted it to slag almost instantaneously.

Lucky Telepath. The burning wall collapsed on them. He turned and stared at me. There was no one else in sight alive. I knew what he was thinking, and he knew I knew: The human firemen were all working down in the shelter. I was the only witness to his negligence. He began to raise one arm. I reached, as furtively as I could, for my flashlight, a pea-shooter wielded by a cripple against a saber-tooth. Then he lowered his arm. "A bad accident," he said.

I agreed. "Not even the usual suspects to round up," he continued. I started laughing hysterically.

I am no telepath, but even I picked up the wave of Telepath's relief and joy. Krar-Skrei was dead.

Since the course was nearly completed, the first class of Chuut-Riit's human experts was pronounced graduated, and its members posted to the fleet and elsewhere. That solved a problem for me. I presented them all with diplomas, written on parchment made of the finest human skin, each illustrated by a picture of a Hero standing rampant atop a pile of slain simians.

I felt as if my teaching had been a furlough in the cool First Circle of Hell, but that I could not take any more teaching, and contemplated escaping into the eastern mountains before the next class, which would presumably also include a telepath with a watching brief. Perhaps the Resistance would have me in spite of my arm. They must be running very short of personnel. Perhaps I could even survive on my own. If not, so be it.

But that was to be the only one of Chuut-Riit's human classes. In quick succession, Chuut-Riit was killed as a result of techno-sabotage, civil war broke out between the followers of Traat-Admiral and Ktrodni-Stkaa, and the UNSN Hyperdrive Armada arrived. The sky was suddenly filled with fighters, and humans in battle-armor descending with lift-belts.

Escaping to the wild was not necessary. The kzin lost interest in me and I was able to keep alive, cowering with a few other academics in a sub-basement while the battle raged above us. Since then I have seen some rediscovered film of the fall of Berlin in 1945 (our civics classes had become more realistic by then). It was like that, only worse. Once a lost kzin kitten blundered down among us, and, moved by some impulse I still do not understand, I took him up into the street and found a kzin warrior and handed him over—the only really brave thing I have ever done. The kitten, I remember, had a curious red patch on the fur of its chest, and specially elaborate ear-tattoos, and the kzin who received it prostrated himself before it, before snatching it up and vanishing with it into the smoke.

The fighting moved on. I talked my way past the vengeful humans, and fortunately, when he was recovered, my old colleague Nils Rykermann spoke up for me. There was no telepath this time to defend me, and I had some hairy moments—my former head of department was beheaded, and his deputy taken to Munchen Zoo and fed to the kzinretti—but once again my arm served as an excuse, and perhaps I was lucky in the composition of the panel I faced. I found the firemen who had helped Telepath and me, and expended my credit, such as it was, pleading for them, pointing to the lives they had saved in the Ramscoop Raid.

Had von Kleist and Thompson survived, the Resistance would have made short work of them, I mused—dirty *KzinDiener*. At least I, heart in my mouth, had occasionally towards the end left food parcels where the Resistance *might* find them. It wasn't much, but it had, just, passed under the telepath's radar, and some humans remembered it.

Liberated Wunderland, 2420

THERE WAS PLENTY for all of us to do in the months that followed. The kzin who remained on Wunderland were no longer our dreaded conquerors. Many of those who remained had formed some sort of relationship with humans. There was modern medicine available again, and my arm was repaired.

I was walking back to my apartment one evening when a voice hailed me out of the shadows of an alley: "Professor!"

Not a voice produced from a human voice-box. I spun round. A dark shape, too big for a man, but small for a kzin. Well, we were officially at peace on Wunderland now, and I knew it was no use running from a kzin—many had tried. I waited until it emerged into the bright light of the main street.

It was tTelepath. He looked bad, but telepaths usually did. He stumbled as he walked, and almost fell at my feet.

Did I owe him anything? Thinking it over, I decided that perhaps I did. He could have made my life a lot more uncomfortable, and a lot shorter, if he had tried. I remembered the incident of the meat, the time in the tank, and the risk he rook letting me live at the end. And, well, even in this case, I felt as a teacher I owed a former student something. I called up an aircar and, lifting him with considerable difficulty (lifting a normal male kzin would have been out of the question, but my repaired arm with its metal bones was now stronger than a natural one), carried him home.

I had thought he was starving, but he appeared no more emaciated than before. A large bowl of hot milk and a couple of raw chops and sausages did seem to do him good.

"Remember the meat?" he asked me. Like all telepaths, his command of the language was perfect, though his accent was strange. What was wrong with him, I learned as he talked, was that he was suffering from a near-terminal case of uselessness. He was shunned by other kzin, humans fled from him. ARM had assessed him, like all telepaths they had captured, and found him so nearly burnt-out as not to be worth recruiting. He was in a kind of passive state, which was a recognized clinical symptom indicating that the end was near. Like practically all telepaths, the drug had left him a wreck, and he had not been physically able to handle the effects of sudden, brutal, total withdrawal, though mentally he seemed clear enough.

I called Leonie Rykermann, who had been a student at the University at the time of the invasion. Kept young with unlimited geriatric drugs, she and her husband, Nils, had been among the most respected of the Resistance leaders, and were now political powers. Further, like a surprising number of other Resistance leaders, she got on well with kzin and was running an orphanage for some of the many parentless kzin kittens, as well as human children, on the planet. She came and spoke to the telepath for a time. I gathered she could find him a job at the orphanage, where he might feel useful.

As they were preparing to leave, he asked me: "Do you remember the poem, 'Spanish Waters,' that Herr von Kleist used to say for us?" I didn't, but I remembered von Kleist had been interested in sea stories. He piped up:

> *I'm the last alive that knows it, all the rest have gone their ways.*
> *Killed, or died, or come to anchor in the old Mulatas Cays*
> *And I go singing, fiddling, old and starved and in despair,*
> *And I know where all that gold is hid, if only I were there . . .*

"But," he went on, "I don't know of much gold."

Liberated Wunderland, 2425

FIVE YEARS OR MORE PASSED before I saw him again. The UNSN had taken the telepaths in hand and were well on the way to developing nondestructive drugs for them. Apparently the kzin Patriarchy had always known that the *sthondat* lymph-derived drug burned out the telepaths' brains, leaving them not merely mindless, but, unless someone mercifully euthanized them, in a state of endless, screaming horror. Under the Patriarch, they were generally euthanized, not from mercy, but merely to stop the noise and because they were now useless (we heard that better drugs were produced in small quantities on Kzin and reserved for the Patriarch's own telepaths, the highest masters of the art, who were treated as nobles in their own right). The Patriarchy needed the telepaths, but feared them for many reasons. The solution they had arrived at resulted in short, down-trodden neurotic lives for them.

Even with the incongruous wide-brimmed hat and sunglasses, giving him an appearance something like a tiger that had eaten an old-time gangster, he was looking a great deal better. In fact, apart from his small size, he looked like a healthy kzin. Indeed, I did not recognize him at first. He was leading a well-grown kit with buttons on its claws. One of the orphans, I guessed. I remarked that I was pleased to see him looking so well.

"It is the new drugs, the human drugs," he said. "I am under a life-debt to you and your kind, Professor."

"If that is so, I am under one to you," I told him. "Let us say the scales balance."

"Have you got a few moments?" he asked me. "There is something I would share with you."

The *Lindenbaum* café was not far away. It had *footch* couches for kzin now. I wondered what the prewar students would have made of it. Not a good idea to think that way. It raised too many ghosts.

"As a matter of fact, it was to see you that I came here," he said. "You remember Herr von Kleist?"

"Yes." I nearly said "Of course," but one who is powerfully conditioned never says anything that might be interpreted as rudeness to a kzin, even a small and apparently friendly one. Feeble telepath or not, he could have dismantled a tiger without undue trouble.

"And Herr Thompson?"

"Yes, indeed."

"Would you be interested in knowing why they died? And Herr Morris?"

"Certainly. I have often wondered."

"Herr Thompson, before he died, prepared a package," he said. "It was star-locked."

That meant it could only be opened when the stars had moved to a certain position in the sky. Generally an attempt to force it resulted in the destruction of its contents. The kzinti had got the technology, like many others, from one of the scientific races they had conquered in the past. They had invented very little of their own.

"He gave it to you?"

"No indeed, to another monk . . . human. He, in turn, fled Munchen to join the Resistance and left it with a third human, what you call an 'attorney.' I remember you explaining those terms to us."

"Yes."

"I could follow all this easily enough. I had read Herr Thompson's mind, and from that I read the minds of the other human and the attorney."

"Did you tell the Patriarch's authorities?"

"No."

"May I ask why?" I would not have dared put such a question, save that I felt he was inviting it.

"What have they ever done for me, except make me a wreck and rob me of my strength and pride? But I bided my time. When the Ramscoop Raid came, the attorney's offices were in one of many buildings reduced to rubble. I let Herr Morris wreak part of my vengeance for me. He did more than I expected. Much later, after I was released from the assessment camp, after I had seen you, I found the package—I had read the attorney's mind and knew where it was stored. He was dead and had no further use for it. I took it and kept it.

"I did not know how long it would be before the star-lock allowed the package to be opened—centuries, perhaps. At last I had an idea, a very simple one, which the ingenious beings who invented the star-lock could not have anticipated, though perhaps Herr Thompson should have. I took it to the planetarium."

"As simple as that!"

"As simple as that. I opened it. It contained, as I had suspected, a message, which I read. By then, the kzin were overthrown on this planet. I kept it for some time, unsure what to do with it. Recently I decided to give it to you . . .

"Thank you."

"I had thought it might contain a treasure, or the guide to one. I warn you, it does not."

There must be something about humans and locked boxes. I felt an absurd sense of disappointment.

He was wearing a garment over his fur like a vest with pockets—purely utility. From one of these he produced some sheets of paper.

"This is what it contained," he said

I read:

There is not much time to explain. I wish it to be known, by my descendants at least, that I am not a maniacal killer. And I am not a traitor. I have killed von Kleist for the benefit of the human race. Now I must kill myself, to avoid the Telepath's probing and Kzin torture, both of which would reveal the truth and make what I have done pointless. By the time this is opened it should not matter. Things will have been settled one way or another. I hope it will allow my name to be restored.

I tried to subvert the Kzin with stories of human prowess.

I begged von Kleist to see reason, but he dug in his heels through sheer stubbornness. He was determined to put Moby Dick *on the kzin reading list. An academic dedicated to his studies.*

He claimed, when I pressed him, it would give them a better understanding of human courage and determination. I told him that many of them might have trouble telling fact from fiction, but it made no impression. He called it a great classic.

Yes, a great classic that might destroy us all. For what is its message, to a kzin reader? That the whale wins in the end, in spite of all Ahab's effort and sacrifice. THAT HUMANS CAN BE DEFEATED, THAT HUMAN BRAVERY AND DETERMINATION ARE NOT ENOUGH FOR SUCCESS, that we are but monkeys that batter our lives away in a futile quest for vengeance upon a brainless fish. And the fish wins. Its message of human despair and nihilism would work its way through the kzin fleet. It would hearten the enemy.

That is what, even now, the von Kleists will never understand. For them, ideas and consequences exist in different universes. The power of words to create or destroy. I suggested Churchill's wartime speeches. He said they were not literature, which it was his job to teach. He would have spread poison through the Patriarch's weapons, made the death of every human who had died fighting the kzin seem as meaningless as Ahab's, for the sake of teaching literature. If they understood it was fiction, that would be worse, for the very knowledge that a human would write such a fiction would increase their contempt for the human race, and their confidence in themselves.

My motive has been to help the human race survive. Care for my family.

I dialed my flashlight to high power and focused it on the paper. As it crumbled to ashes I asked: "Do you know what happened to his family?"

"No," he said. We both knew there was a good chance they were dead. But I could advertise for them.

"So what are you doing now?"

"I am still at the orphanage. I teach the orphans reading and writing. What you and the other professors taught me."

"Not *Moby Dick*, I trust."

"No, that would contain quite the wrong lesson. My favorite is called *The Magic Pudding*: 'We much prefer to chew/the steak and kidney stew. . .' Giving you this has rid me of a burden. There was another page, giving details of where he had hidden a cache of diamonds, industrial diamonds, that he had salvaged from a bombed factory at the time of the first kzin landings. Leonie will be able to use them, for the orphanage is always short of funds. There are young kzin in it who might have grown up like me. Farewell, Professor. Drink blood and tear cattle into gobbets!"

He left. Seeing me alone, the human waiter sought my order. I drank a glass of wine to Thompson's memory.

🐾 🐾 🐾

LIONS ON THE BEACH

by Alex Hernandez

🐾 LIONS ON THE BEACH 🐾

"He only dreamed of places now and the lions on the beach.
They played like young cats in the dusk
and he loved them as he loved the boy."
—Ernest Hemingway,
The Old Man and the Sea

"THERE ARE MONSTERS beneath the surface," Daneel Guthlac said to the kit standing next to him at the edge of a cliff overlooking the roiling Kcheemic Ocean. Gliding toothy pteranobats, which infested many of the marine cliffs of Sheathclaws, skimmed over the water with long snouts in frothy waves, ready to snap up their prey. Occasionally, a large creature would burst out of the sea and catch one of the flyers. "When I said we were going to bag the biggest, meanest beast in all of Sheathclaws, I meant it."

"What do you mean?" The kitten's fur flattened, his naked tail curved between his legs in the presence of the infinite, crashing water. Ashamed of his display of fear, he forced his tail to relax.

"See that town down there?" Dan pointed toward a collection of houses at the bottom of the cliff, where surf met rock in battle. The houses were painted bright orange to fill some deep-seated psychological need and stood on stilts to defend against sudden storm surges. "These kzinti have learned to live off the sea."

"I told all my créche mates I would bring back a wombadon! When I come back with fish, they're going to tear me apart!"

Dan scratched the kit's scruffy neck and felt the welts of his mate's teeth beneath the fur. Schro was about the size of an average adult human, which meant he was small for his age, an inheritance of his biological Sire, and the older kzin kittens got, the crueler and more aggressive they became. On any other kzin world, the puny kit would've been killed. On Sheathclaws, he was merely the target of vicious bullying. Dan sent him a telepathic flash of his own days in the créche: a small monkey surrounded by violent, broad-pawed kittens. The human boy quickly learned to toughen up and use all his cunning to survive. "Trust me, son. When we return to Shrawl'ta, those little bastards will fear and respect you."

Schro's ears receded incredulously. He didn't know which he feared more: the terrible sea, or his peers.

Dan and Schro crunched down the slope onto the rocky shore. Tall kzinti with saffron pelts watched their descent with reserved interest. Only a ragged kzintosh, whose fur had grown out patchy after severe burns had stripped him of most of his flesh, left one of the square, long-legged buildings and headed their way. The local leader.

"Chief Programmer?" Dan called from a safe distance.

The kzin slowed his advance and approached less urgently. He was massive, three heads taller than Dan, with fierce and undefeated eyes. "I haven't been Chief Programmer in a long time, human." He glowered at the odd pair, an unruly man with long, sandy hair and close-cropped beard, and a soft runt of a kitten. "Daneel Guthlac?"

"Correct, and this is my son, Schro."

The old Hero breathed in the kit. Dan sensed that he found the scent familiar and unpleasant. Dan instinctively touched his sidearm, but the kzin decided it was only the stink of monkey clinging to the kit's spotted fur. "I call myself Fraaf'kur now, and this is my territory, Krazári."

Sea-lion? Dan got a blaze of immense pride attached to the kzintosh's current name and opted not to correct his assumptions of what a sea lion actually was. Instead he asked, "Krazári means something like Ocean Master in the Heroes' Tongue, right?"

"Yes, those two words had been mutually exclusive until kzinti settled on Shasht, my home planet."

"And now you have an entirely new ocean to tame here on Sheathclaws. I envy you."

The kzin's ragged fur puffed up pompously, but he said nothing, unsure if the human was genuinely envious or only mocking him.

"Fraaf'kur," Dan stifled a smile, "we want to book passage on your boat. We heard you were the only kzintosh in all of Raoneer that could take us fishing."

"My get could also take you and your adopted kit out on the sea," he emphasized the word "adopted" with a hint of disgust. "The longnecks are plentiful this season and make impressive trophies."

"I was thinking we could go a little higher on the food chain." Dan flashed him a wicked smile that made Fraaf'kur's ears flatten. Dan wanted the Hero to understand that behind the blunt, ape grin was a kzintosh's soul waiting to pounce. "Ketosaurs hunt longnecks. If one is plentiful, the other couldn't be too far behind."

Schro's eyes widened at the mention of the sea monster. Dan could tell the kit was wondering if his father was mad enough to try to catch one of those. The kit searched their telepathic rapport and learned that, in fact, he was. It filled him with confidence.

"I could take you to them and show you how to hunt them, but they are much too large. We'd never get one back here to eat or mount. It would be a wasted kill."

"A simple engineering problem I think I can fix."

Fraaf'kur made a low clicking sound with his throat, but Dan could sense the grudging respect the kzin was developing for this bold human. Dan also knew Schro was picking it up with his heightened *ziirgrah* and that pleased him more than impressing this old dock cat.

"Very well. We will make preparations in my cabin."

"Does my son have permission to explore Krazári? He's never seen a kzin fishing town before."

"Yes, but don't stray too far; pteranobats have carried off and devoured a few of my get in the past."

"Stay close and stay sharp," Dan instructed his son.

The kit dashed away and disappeared between house stilts.

Dan followed Fraaf'kur into the house he'd come out of. It was nice. It looked like the seaside cabins of Harp, but designed with kzin comfort in mind. The swan-like skeleton of a longneck hung from the ceiling. When the door shut, the kzin turned to Dan and asked, "Are you really here for the ketosaurus or for the humans skulking around on the island a few kilometers off the coast from here?"

"The fishing trip is real. The créche is not an easy place for a small kit with a monkey father. Having the skull of a ketosaurus for show-and-tell will boost his chances of survival. That said, our good friend the Apex did suggest I check out the island while I'm here, and you don't turn down the Apex."

"How did you end up with the kit?" the kzin asked finally.

"I was married and divorced with no human kits of my own. She cited my obsessive work on the *Righteous Manslaughter*'s hyperdrive as the cause for leaving me. All of a sudden, I found myself alone and with nothing to show for all my hard work . . . I had killed his Sire in combat, and since my family has a history of rearing kzin kits, I took him as my own."

Fraaf'kur sniffed the air as if he found the whole matter distasteful.

"How did you end up out here?" Dan asked. "I thought the Apex had set you up in Shrawl'ta when he saved you and what was left of your shipmates from the *Manslaughter*."

The kzin silently worked the controls of an old holoset for a while, then said, "I tried to live there. When the Apex offered me two females of my own and prestigious work in his Hall, I was glad for it, but as I learned more of Sheathclaws—its founding by a treacherous telepath and its *laissez-faire* attitude toward *kz'eerekti*, I was revolted with the entire system and with myself for being a part of it. I came here and tried to recreate my life on Shasht before the war.

"My get may be proud of their one drop of Shadow's blood, and they may mewl to the Maned God, but *I've* instilled in them a love of the sea and they chose to settle here in Krazári. I'm proud to say they've made names for themselves out in these waters. Our pride trades seafood to Shrawl'ta."

A staticky hologram of the coast sprang from the holoset, and Fraaf'kur stopped talking. Dan could see a clump of rock out in the middle of the ocean, as if a piece of the same cliff he had descended had been torn off and tossed into the sea. Another image replaced the aerial view, this one a close-up of the isle itself. It was bare of everything except a few humans and a flock of pteranobats. "These are the images I've taken of the island. For the most part, they ignore my boat. The humans are clearly from the nation of Angel's Tome."

Of course, they are, Dan thought, *most humans on Sheathclaws resided on the human-controlled part of the continent, Angel's Tome.* "From the city-state of Hem," Dan added out loud, recognizing their white uniforms. "Hem's got the largest concentration of Rejoiners and they hate me for not delivering your old warship to them so they can end Sheathclaws' long seclusion and become part of the growing network of human worlds in Known Space." He continued to watch the shifting images. *Something was off.*

"So you think they're building a launch site?" The kzin asked, scratching the back of his neck, his old wartime training creeping back.

"No, I see no sign of construction. Wait. Are all these images from the same day?"

"No, different days, almost a week in between, why?"

"No one has moved. The lighting changes, the sun rises and falls, the tides come in and withdraw, the pteranobats circle around, but the people never move. You didn't find this odd?"

Fraaf'kur snorted. "I'm not well versed in primate behavior. You lot always seem to be standing around talking your nonsense."

"No, this is very strange. We need to find out what's going on out there."

"How do you intend to find out?"

"I'm going to need you to purposefully run aground on that island. Then, I'm going to walk up to them and ask for help."

"You want me to ground my *Nautical Devastation*?"

"For the Apex, of course. How soon can we go?"

"One of these days, you won't be able to hide behind your friend, the Apex," Fraaf'kur rumbled irritably. "We can leave now if you're ready. You can attempt to take a ketosaurus, and then I can get you to that island."

"I just need some equipment from my gravcar and we can go."

Nautical Devastation, the huge catamaran with a copper-colored sail, had been designed by Chief Programmer to navigate the tumultuous coastlines around Raoneer. Despite the old Hero's qualms about Sheathclaws, the incongruent blend of advanced kzin technology being applied to such an ancient human vessel was in itself a product of Sheathclaws' mixed culture. The double-hulled boat pitched and yawed rhythmically in heaving waves enlarged by the planet's weaker gravity. Dan wondered if kzin ever got seasick.

"We're nearing the beasts' territory!" shouted Fraaf'kur. "We'll cut through it on the way to the island. Our opponent hunts by sound, so I'm transmitting the cries of a wounded longneck into the water."

Dan nodded, but watched his son. The kit had been crackling with nervous energy ever since they'd cast out. He was a thin, orange smear against the vast ocean; his juvenile spots on the verge of elongating into the stripes of an adult. In a year or two, Schro would no longer be a kit, *his* kit—*kzin grow up so fast*—and there was so much he wanted to tell him: about his past, his genetic Sire, about his potential, but he feared losing him. *Better to wait until he's older, more sure of himself.* Now, he wanted to simply appreciate these moments with his savage little son.

Too bad the mysterious island nagged at him, with its immobile humans standing among the surf and rocks as the scenery changed around them. Dan could now see the outline of the island on the horizon, and all his instincts told him to run.

"I can't see or smell anything. I can't hunt out here!" The kit slammed into Dan, knocking the thoughts out of his mind.

"Relax, Schro, I know you feel vulnerable, surrounded by endless blue, your sharp sense of smell blunted by the salt in the air—"

"I'm not scared!"

"I know you are," Dan kneaded the plush fur on his son's shoulder. He could feel his fear like whiplashes across his mind. "Lying about it only makes you careless. I'm telling you it's okay. Recognize that you're out of your element, understand that you're only a small morsel of food in this new ecosystem, and be on guard. You have a more powerful sense that surpasses the merely visual and olfactory. Use your *ziirgrah*. Sweep the waves with it. Be vigilant."

The kitten dug his claws into the catamaran hull and focused his empathic awareness on the tall and languid waves. Dan did the same, adding to the kit's range and sharing his perception. It felt like psychic sonar. He was vaguely aware that Chief Programmer—Fraaf'kur—watched them suspiciously from the helm. Dan ignored this and paid attention to his son.

Schro slowly crawled to the bow of the boat, careful not to lose his purchase on the undulating deck. "There's something out there, father;

fish and longnecks and something else, something I've sensed before but different. It's stalking an elderly longneck, keeping to the deeper, colder waters."

"Fraaf'kur, take us further out in that direction," Dan shouted, pointing to where his son had indicated. He, too, had caught a mental glimpse of the monster waiting in the depths and, for the first time, doubted his plan with the massive gravbelt would actually work.

"Daneel, the only way to kill this thing is to penetrate its head with *chugra*. Its back is heavily armored with scales, and hitting it in a flipper will only enrage it. The *chugra* launcher is kept in the storage compartment in the other hull." The old dock cat adjusted the sail and hurled his ship toward the hiding beast, the fire of the hunt burning within him.

"This isn't my kill, it's Schro's! Kit, go get the harpoon."

"How will I kill it?" The juvenile hesitated, but, runt or no, he was a full-blooded kzin and the hunt was beginning to possess him.

"Stun it with your *ziirgrah*—confuse it—yours is more powerful than most kzinti. Then, when it's dazed, fire the harpoon into its skull."

"More powerful? How do you know? Are you sure I can stun something as cunning as a ketosaurus on the hunt?"

"Yes, I can feel your ability through our link," Dan lied. "You could potentially rival even the founder of Sheathclaws, the rogue telepath Shadow, himself."

Encouraged, Schro bounded across the trampoline that connected the twin hulls and found the heavy harpoon gun. It was longer than the length of his entire body. Kzin kittens were incredibly strong by human-child standards, but Schro wrestled awkwardly with the immense weapon, and the constant shift of the floor beneath him didn't help.

"Careful with that! If you drop it into the sea, I'll toss you in after it!" roared Fraaf'kur.

Dan shot him a livid, protective glare, but the kzin only flapped his ears contemptuously, his mane thrashing in the frosty wind. Dan turned away from the mangy captain and met his son, fighting every fiber in his being to help him carry the heavy gun. "We're getting closer to it, can you feel it?"

"Yes, and it knows we're coming. It's not afraid of us, but it's really annoyed we're spooking the longnecks."

"Very good. You said it felt familiar yet different, how so?"

"I don't know . . . its mind feels like the alliogs that roam the steppes of Raoneer, only less jumpy, more confident and patient, like it could kill anything."

"Good. I'm glad you picked up on that. The ketosaurus is a therapsid-like creature, distantly related to the alliog. It grew massive when it returned to life in the sea."

"No more lessons! I want to see it."

Dan laughed at that, but then the water turned black below the *Nautical Devastation* and the ship's name suddenly felt like a hollow threat. "Hold on, son!" A row of dark green scales, longer than their boat, sawed through the water then disappeared into the blue.

"Everyone, dig in with your claws!" Fraaf'kur growled as he pressed close to the deck. "The only way to get at it is to let it chomp down on the boat and then spear it between the eyes! Are you ready?"

"What?" Schro clutched the harpoon gun tightly. It was all he could do not to wet himself.

"Can the ship take a hit like that?"

"This is a kzin craft, monkey! The *Nautical Devastation* is built for war!"

A gigantic flipper rose into the air and slapped the water with such thunderous force that the catamaran rocked and spun like so much flotsam in the sea. To his credit, Schro tried to aim his harpoon at the creature, but Dan grabbed him and hunkered down close to the bucking bow. "We can do this, kit! This is why we're here," he whispered through gritted teeth. "But we have to do it right."

With one paw, Fraaf'kur got control of the flapping sail while desperately working the tiller with the other, and, after a long, queasy while, the *Nautical Devastation* straightened out. Just ahead, a range of olive-colored scutes rose from the water like a sudden rock formation; two of the outcroppings were large, yellow eyes and two were flaring nostrils, each an eruption of mist. Dan and Schro both knew that the ketosaurus now perceived them as a slow and stupid longneck.

"It looks like a crocodile-humpback-whale hybrid," Dan said, and instantly regretted not having better researched their prey—now their predator—before leaving Shrawl'ta.

Schro got up and tried to target the leviathan again.

Then a voice, like that of the Maned God himself, boomed within Dan's skull. *Daneel Guthlac, you are a strange and interesting creature.*

Schro stopped and looked down at him, astonished, "The sea monster can talk! It's telepathic!"

"You heard that?" For a moment, and despite the clarity of the words—no, not words, but complete thoughts forming in his mind like ice crystals—Dan wondered if he imagined it.

"I didn't hear anything," Fraaf'kur snarled from his post. "These beasts are not telepathic! I've waged war on them before; they're worthy and dangerous opponents, but that is all. "

Confused—terrified—Dan scanned the ketosaurus with his weak telepathy. He knew the cetaceans of Earth were intelligent, but this . . . the creature was unremarkable. The warrior was right; there was nothing there except simple, primal urges.

I am both attracted and repulsed by you. I don't know how to proceed, the great voice proclaimed—or was it a second, distinct voice?—and the monster slid its gargantuan bulk beneath the waves.

There was an obvious disconnect between the dumb marine animal and the alien intellect speaking through and around them. "Schro, quickly link with me and sweep the area with your *ziirgrah*! I don't think that was the ketosaurus."

"A full-blown kzin telepath?" the Hero screamed, traumatic memories of the murderous telepath aboard his old spacecraft seizing him.

"Steady yourself, Fraaf'kur. That didn't feel like a kzin mind or a human one."

All of a sudden, the monster crashed into the catamaran with an explosive breach that launched the whole rig meters into the air. Without claws to maintain his hold, Dan was thrown off the boat. The acute agony of hitting the freezing Kcheemic Ocean was like going for a spacewalk in your underwear. Incandescent white blinded him. He was dying; he knew, he had almost died once before when the drug-crazed telepath aboard the *Righteous Manslaughter* had viciously mangled his mind. Hell, psychologically—*spiritually*—he had died. It was a miracle he had hung on long enough to fire a single laser beam and fry the telepath's deadly, preternatural brain.

We wish to learn from you, Daneel Guthlac. Your patchwork psyche is fascinating to us, but you are an uncontrollable variable. Your own thoughts reveal you to be dangerous.

Fear and urgency cleared his mind, and in one perfect zen moment, he *knew* the alien minds were coming from the island. The ketosaurus was only a weapon. Then, encroaching hypothermia forced him back to his immediate situation, and he tried to swim back to the boat in an achingly slow and desperate doggie-paddle.

After what felt like an eternity, something sharp, like knives, sank into his left arm and hauled him out of the water, where the wind-chill made him shake wildly. Dan was distantly aware of Schro licking his face and the same knives slapping a thermal patch on his back. Warmth slowly crept into his bones, and with it came rational thought.

"What happened?" Dan asked feebly. He realized he was draped over the side of the starboard hull on his belly and facing the sail, which lay in the water.

"The heavily reinforced port hull held, but the *Nautical Devastation* still capsized dishonorably," was all Dan understood of Fraaf'kur's howling. The rest was cursing in the bloodcurdling dialect of Shasht.

"The boat's on its side . . . Schro, are you okay?" He could sense his son's terror and fury; the kit's dormant telepathic power had sharpened like a spike by the unexpected attack.

"Yes, I still have my harpoon!" He had held onto it with his prehensile tail. "Are *you* all right, father? I thought you were dead!"

"I'm just cold—and surprised the thing didn't go for me when I was in the water."

"You're nothing to it. The ketosaurus is treating us like a wounded longneck. Soon it's going to strike the mast."

As if on cue, the leviathan slammed its jaws shut on the mast and thrashed violently, testing the boat's tolerances to the brink. Dan held on with all his might, and through the ferocious quake, Schro's piercing cry got his attention. The kit had climbed down the now vertical trampoline and impaled the ketosaurus with two harpoons; one psychic, which bewildered its rudimentary mind, and the other, the steel projectile embedded within the creature's left eye and driven through his brain. The jerking crescendoed into death throes, and then everything stilled.

Long moments passed. The three worn sailors just watched their monstrous kill bob in the water as if waiting for it to spring to life and pummel them once more.

An hour passed. It was clear that the sea monster was never going to move again, so Fraaf'kur carefully pried back a large scale on the ketosaurus' side and tore off chunks of its flesh. He ceremoniously offered the first bite to the proud and still-shaky Schro, and they ate their terrible sashimi perched on the starboard hull as it jutted out of the water. The stony island loomed large in the horizon. It was close, about a kilometer away.

Dan had tried contacting his gravcar, but his wristcomp was damaged from the salt water. "We need to get to the island somehow. The telepathic voices are coming from there."

"I can swim it, but then what? Without protective fur, you'll freeze to death in minutes, and Schro here can't swim. We need to right the ship. You're an engineer, human, got any ideas?"

"I have an idea," Schro volunteered to their surprise. "The industrial gravbelt, we can use it to lift the ship out of the water, enough to get it straight."

That would work. "What about the trophy? We brought that to tow the ketosaurus back. What about your créche mates?

The kit—no, he was no longer a kit, he was an adolescent kzin now, a *kzinchao*—radiated confidence. "I don't need to prove I killed the top predator on the planet. It's enough that *I* know I killed it."

Fraaf'kur slapped Schro's back. "Not a bad idea, runt! We stowed it in the port hull. I can dive down and retrieve it." Without another word the Hero plunged into the ocean, and, with expansive paw strokes and a rhythmic swish of his powerful tail, Fraaf'kur disappeared beneath the surface. Dan was instantly reminded of how cold the water really was.

"I didn't know kzinti could swim," Schro said, using his *ziirgrah* on Fraaf'kur. "He's actually enjoying it."

"Where he's from, Kzinti have learned to swim, and on Sheathclaws, the lighter gravity and saltier oceans help buoy a kzin's heavier frame," Dan said, but he could tell something was wrong. Schro had crossed the link they had easily shared since he was a newborn kit and was now rummaging in Dan's mind, which shouldn't have been possible without the *sthondat* drug that boosted a talented kzin's natural *ziirgrah* into true telepathy.

"What are you doing?" For the first time ever, Dan shut his mind to his son.

"What is a Schrodinger's cat, father? Why did you name me after it?"

Dan signed heavily. He was unbearably thirsty and didn't want to talk; he especially didn't want to have this conversation here, now. "I had been unsuccessfully working on the captured *Righteous Manslaughter*'s hyperdrive for years before you came along. Honestly, I had quantum mechanics on the brain when I named you. It was only a créche name, so I figured, what the hell, you would earn your own Name in time."

"Are you sure that's it? I get the sense it means something like being both alive and dead at the same time. The feeling is very strong."

To Dan's infinite relief, Fraaf'kur's orange head popped out of the water. His fur was slicked back and he did indeed look like a marine mammal, like an actual sea lion. "I got it! Someone help me hoist it up." He panted hungrily as he hefted the sealed crate.

In silence they affixed the gravbelt to the catamaran, where the mast intersected with the hull connectors. Dan activated the powerful motor and dialed up the artificial gravity field until it encompassed the entire ship, while Fraaf'kur poured his weight onto the starboard hull so that the sail swung up, perpendicular to the water, and the port hull surfaced.

"The rudder is completely gone and the sail is torn, but not tattered. If you increase the gravity motor's strength and lift us up off the surface, only a few centimeters, just enough to remove the friction of cutting through the water, I can use the sail to steer."

Dan complied and they were off. The airborne ride was rougher than being on the raging sea as they were now susceptible to the rapid, intense winds that hit them at odd angles. Nobody spoke. Fraaf'kur fought with the disobedient catamaran, his hunter's concentration totally absorbed.

Schro sulked by himself in the bow of the port hull; something clearly bothered him, something he had seen in Dan's mind. For the first time, Dan noticed the kit looked half-formed somehow, as if the Maned God ran out of kzin stuff and added a bit of human to finish the job. His body language and mannerisms were all too primate. Dan had always been accused of being too kzin, but Schro wasn't kzin enough. It's what his créche mates picked up and instantly pounced on—his humanity. Dan couldn't help but feel responsible for that, so he sat on the trampoline and focused on increasing or decreasing the output of the motor to the tempo of the surging waves.

The *Nautical Devastation* skidded onto the rocky shoal of the desolate island. Dan noticed a big, unmarked gravtruck abandoned on the shore, now a roost for several pteranobats; the leathery fliers eyed them as potential carrion. They disembarked quietly as if to avoid disturbing the death-like serenity of the beach. The only sound was the chill wind and pervasive screeching of immature pteranobats up in the guano-coated hills.

"Well, you wanted me to run us aground," Fraaf'kur rumbled bitterly, breaking the eerie ambiance. "Now you go talk to your people." He motioned with a jab of his muzzle toward the humans.

To Dan's disbelief, none of the Rejoiners, who were only a few meters away, reacted to their arrival. They just stood there transfixed, clustering around the few shrubs that grew on the stony ground, like living statuary adorning some gorgon's lawn. There was no sign of the crystalline, glacial presence that had assailed him out on the sea.

Schro loped off toward a group of humans. He sniffed at them and the air around them. "They've been here for weeks, and they've relieved themselves in their clothing. This doesn't feel right."

Dan approached more cautiously and waved a hand in front of a gaunt young woman's face. Her eyes were open and raw, as if she hadn't blinked in ages. "They're alive, barely. I can sense that congregating around these bushes is of utter importance to them, certainly more so than eating or sleeping." The small plants were strange themselves; he only spotted three of them, anchored to large rocks. Their general shape was conical, and they were covered in auburn, hair-like fibers, quite unlike the standard lavender-to-purple flora of Sheathclaws. "Perhaps these plants have got them ensnared with some hypnotic pheromone?"

"No." Fraaf'kur sniffed one of the shrubs, his nostrils fluffing the lank hairs of the thistle. "This thing is not vegetable, it smells of animal!" Abruptly, he jumped two meters back and away from it as if it were a land mine, his tail lashing nervously. "I know what these things are," he roared, pointing at the three tapering shrubs—or what appeared to be shrubs. "*Tzookmas!*"

"What the hell is a *tzookma*, Fraaf'kur?"

"We need to get out of here! Now!"

But he didn't move. He was caught just like the poor Rejoiners who had come to this dreadful island, seeking to secretly build a powerful transmitter to contact Earth, or some other human planet. *How did he know that?*

All of a sudden, a medium-sized pteranobat swooped in close to the fuzzy cone and was instantly snapped up with a quick whip of a tongue and swallowed into the gaping mouth concealed by the rust-colored hair.

Schro scrambled away.

Dan pulled out his sidearm and immediately fired at the thing—nothing happened; like the wrsitcomp, the weapon had been rendered inoperable by salt water. Dan tossed the useless beam gun aside and slowly moved toward the immobile kzintosh. "What are we dealing with here, Fraaf'kur?"

"They're called grogs in your human tongue. Intelligent, stationary creatures, like cognizant trees or oysters, with vast telepathic ability, able to hijack the brains of any living thing!"

"Can you move?" Dan asked, now terrified, already aware of the answer.

"No!" yowled Fraaf'kur.

Despite his intense fear, or precisely because of it, Schro poised himself to assault the shrub—the grog. "I can still move!" All kzinti, even prepubescent ones, generally had only one response to danger: attack blindly until it or you were dead. Schro was no different.

Dan immediately grabbed the young kzinchao by the scruff of the neck and yanked him back with all his strength, receiving a few gashes in the process. "Pull back, Schro! Don't antagonize them. They've spoken to us before; maybe we can talk to them now."

You think of yourself as more enlightened than the kzin, but you attempted to fire upon us first. Negotiation was a last resort for you, too, Daneel Guthlac; or is the kzin architecture within your psyche affecting your behavior? You are quite the puzzle.

"What are you talking about?" But he knew, the alien was growing an idea in his mind as sharp and shimmering as a diamond. There were traces of *Manslaughter*'s telepath embedded within him, like psychic shrapnel. Their two consciousnesses—their two souls—had been in mortal combat when he killed the psychotic kzin . . .

"My biological sire is the evil telepath aboard the *Righteous Manslaughter*?" Schro hissed as he finally connected the pieces. "I'm a genetic copy of one who killed most of the crew, and attacked you and the Apex when you tried to rescue them?"

Dan felt sick waves of disgust and betrayal roll off his son. *Damnit, the grog was broadcasting widely.* This was the moment Dan had worried about since the kit first asked why he had a human father.

"A clone of the hated telepath!" Fraaf'kur roared. "I knew your stink was familiar! I will have your scrawny pelt, you little monster!"

Schrodinger's cat was a cruel joke of a name, Schro purred to himself. Then, suddenly, he screamed and leapt at Dan, savagely shredding his flesh with his black claws. He sank his teeth into Dan's shoulder and mauled brutally, tearing soft muscle and tendon. Dan felt like the *Nautical Devastation* in the maw of the ketosaurus. Then everything turned bright red when a sharp canine tooth scraped his bone. He screamed and squirmed. For a brief second, Schro was indeed both alive and dead, simultaneously Dan's little kit and bloodthirsty telepath, existing in that terrible moment before the wave function collapses.

Dan did not fight back. He was spent, and he refused to harm his son. He loved him—and not in the harsh way a kzintosh sire cared for his kits, but in the unconditional, sacrificial way humans love their children. He tried to hug Schro with his one good arm.

Stop, projected one of the grogs. A mob of weak, emaciated humans pulled Schro off him. Dan just lay there on the cold sand and stones, listening to the surf and the two kzinti's snarling curses. The sun, 46 Leonis Minoris, was a bleary red eye in the sky, passing judgment. The physical pain was excruciating, but the hurt and emptiness in his core were utterly unbearable.

The ghost of *Manslaughter*'s telepath oozed into the void.

"You can't control us can you?" asked Schro, peering at the inert alien, with feral curiosity.

No. We don't know why. We believe your shared mental architecture and distinct but overlapping minds are creating a feedback loop we can't manage. This is very attractive to us, as it is how we exist with each other, but we fear you, especially the two of you, because we can't control you.

"Kill it! Kill the feeble humans holding you back and kill the *ch'rowling* thing," Fraaf'kur pleaded with Schro. He was more afraid of the *tzookmas* than the clone of the telepath who had killed his crewmates and maimed and marooned him on this miserable planet. "These things are rumored to be devolved descendents of the Slaver race! We're all defenseless against them!"

Our great mnemonic archives have no memory of this Slaver race. As far as we know, we have always been as we are. We dominated this planet and its simpler organisms for billions of years. We carpeted entire continents in vast reefs, all telepathically linked, but then something happened, our population crashed—either because of disease or unexpected climate change—we were on the decline long before your people arrived.

Dan tried to sit up at this. The small action hurt immensely, but he wanted to face the faceless threat. Blood poured from his arm in buckets, and he knew that if he survived, he would spend at least a month hooked up to an autodoc—the idea of needles horrified him irrationally. When he was finally able to look up from his own gore, he saw the enslaved humans restraining his vicious son. "You say you fear us, but you wield unimaginable power against us . . . What do you want?"

We hold these beings because we wish to learn from them. We soak up their knowledge, their memories, their experiences. This being, Fraaf'kur, has current information of other worlds, of beings like us; perhaps a related species or a subspecies. We value this more than you can know.

We've known our world's position is close the Kzin Empire for millennia, and this planet, with its wide rangelands and big game, is very alluring to them, so we've always telepathically guided them away from here. But when your grandmother, Selina Guthlac, and the fugitive kzin telepath, Shadow, set down on this planet, their interspecies telepathic rapport intrigued us. There was only a clutch of us left then, and so we allowed them to stay and we observed them from afar.

And we've been watching this uncontrolled experiment in telepath breeding ever since. We theorize that, given a few eons of progress, you

*could develop into beings like ourselves. Your friend here accuses us of
being devolved Slavers? We could very well be highly evolved kzinti.*

Dan was struck dumb. He could sense that this had piqued Schro's
interest as well. The grog farthest from them snapped up a passing
pteranobat as if this bombshell hadn't been dropped. Dan stared at
the reddish fur of the grogs, the vestigial paws hidden beneath the
hair, their appetite . . . and he was suddenly glad Fraaf'kur couldn't
"hear" their psychic communication or he would have had an
aneurism right then and there. Dan looked at his son, who had
stopped struggling. The mindless humans backed off.

"Why interfere with us now?" Dan asked the impassive, pointed
mass of hair.

*We did not interfere with you. It was the humans from Hem, the
ones who risk our security and yours with their need to contact the
greater universe, who interfered with us. We were content to study you
from a safe distance. You believe we have trapped them, but with
proximity came a finer focus, and we were the ones who became
spellbound by the most intimate details of their minds.*

*Even as we disagree with their rash actions—and especially now,
with new information of these grogs from the planet Down gleaned from
Fraaf'kur's memories—we understand their need to reach out to others
like themselves. The three of us have become something like the
Rejoiners.*

Dan was starting to black out. Violet spots danced in his vision. He
forced himself to concentrate. "So then what do you want? You could
have easily turned us away and had us forget all of this. Why all the
theatrics with the ketosaurus? I'm sorry; you might be too alien for
me, because I don't understand your motivation." He closed his eyes
and let the foreign fractal thoughts form in his mind.

*We could have turned all the others away and, in fact, we will. Even
your friend here, Fraaf'kur, will have no memory of any of this. We
have already implanted the urge in some of his nearby offspring to come
here and fetch their father, but as we said, we cannot manipulate you
and your child—*

"I am not his child!"

You are, Schro. More than you know, for he is all that is left of
Righteous Manslaughter's *telepath. Daneel Guthlac carries the part of
him that has found peace here on Sheathclaws. That part, although*

subtle, is incredibly strong and drove him to create you. Manslaughter's telepath did heinous things, but he was not evil. His mind was simply infected with rage, hate and addiction. You are healthy and happy. You are his redemption.

Schro grunted defiantly, but it was all bravado now. His *ziirgrah* was too sensitive, and he knew the truth, whether he wanted to or not.

Dan opened up to him, and the grogs, and bared the monster he had unwittingly hidden just under the surface. The astral remnant of *Manslaughter's* telepath—really, just a collection of primal needs and sensations—flowed up from the recesses of Dan's subconscious. It examined the kit with spectral tendrils and recognized its own reflection in the unpolluted pool of Schro's mind. Content with what it saw, it sunk back down into the dark cerebral abyss from which it came.

You think we used the ketosaurus as a weapon, we did not. We wanted you here, Daneel Guthlac and Schro. We moved through the elementary network of latent kzin telepaths on this planet and rooted the idea to send you here in the Apex's mind. We used the ketosaurus as a tool to bring out your true potential.

The young kzin said nothing. He turned and stalked away toward the interior of the island.

"Schro!"

You asked us what we want, Daneel Guthlac. We want what you have. Offspring. A second chance. We are all that you see; three adult females moored on this barren island. We are old. Our sessile lifestyle gives us slow metabolisms and long lifespans, but we will most likely not live long enough to see you complete your work on the hyperdrive, and so our new dream to meet the other grogs of the universe will rest in our daughters.

"I don't have that anymore."

Give him time. We're having a parallel conversation with him at the moment and we believe he can be reached. You have raised him well.

"You want us to clone you? You need to give us something for me to even begin to trust you. Free these people. Send them home now."

Without another word the group of humans marched back to

their waiting gravtruck. Dan couldn't see them go, but he heard their boots tromping on sediment and then, after a moment, the whirl of the gravity motor.

"If I help you with this, what do we get in return?"

The easy, obvious answer is that with greater numbers we will be able to better protect this world from a kzin invasion force. The Patriarchy will never know this colony exists.

The more complex and interesting answer is that one day we hope kzinti and humans will participate in the reconstruction of our glorious thoughtscapes.

The image of a cathedral-like structure, made entirely of stained glass and coral, was superimposed on the hostile reality of the island within Dan's mind, and he intimately understood that the torpid physical existence of the grogs was only a mere shadow of their rich and vibrant psychological lives.

And with that beautiful image crystallized in his mind, Dan passed out.

Daneel Guthlac awoke to a loud bang, like bone smashing into metal.

He sat in the passenger seat of his gravcar, connected to a portable autodoc. The interior of the car was pleasantly warm, but a dull, throbbing ache stabbed him in the shoulder. His son was in the driver's seat. Disoriented, Dan looked out the window, but all he could see were heavy rain clouds coasting by. "What happened?"

"I returned with Fraaf'kur to Krazári. He's got a great story about how we ambushed the Rejoiners, and after a heated battle where you, our trusty human mascot, were severely injured, we sent them packing before they could get started on their transmitter."

It took Dan a while to process that and remember the events of the last few hours . . . days? "Why is it that I always end up severely injured when I try to save Sheathclaws?"

"Because humans are delicately built . . . Anyways, once there, I got your car and went back for you."

"Thanks and—how do you even know how to fly this thing?"

"Autopilot." He waved his paws in the air. "I just like moving the wheel. It makes me feel better." His ears fluttered, but his demeanor was somewhat distant.

Then Dan realized that he couldn't feel their psychic link any longer and he missed it terribly. It was like having a stranger sitting next to him with the voice and scent of his son. "Hey, are we okay?"

"No." His son looked at him for a long second, then returned to his senseless driving. "Not yet, anyway. I understand what you did and why you did it, but it still feels shameful to be a copy of someone so disgusting."

"Try having him burrowing in your head."

They said nothing for a while. Dan heard that odd organic bang again.

"You know, I was thinking about what the grogs were saying, that there's a feedback loop between us, you've got a little bit of *Manslaughter*'s telepath in your soul, and I'm, genetically, *Manslaughter*'s telepath with a little bit of you in mine. I think we need to live in our own heads for a while."

"Fair enough." Dan wanted to dig his fingers in that orange coat and give him a rough shake, but didn't. "Where are we going now?"

"Back to Shrawl'ta. I also gathered the genetic samples of the three grogs. I'm thinking three exact clones and three produced by fusing the same sex gametes of two different ones. That should give us six baby female grogs in total. They said they'll make sure the biotech people don't ask too many questions."

"That worries me. Who's to stop them from subtly herding the unsuspecting people of Sheathclaws like cattle once we increase their numbers? We're allied now, but what happens once our goals change, or conflict?"

"They won't. Their reach will become greater and greater as their numbers increase, but they won't control us because they value our minds, our ideas and concepts. They need us to be free to create in order to enjoy us. That said, they might steer someone particularly interesting to their island and immerse themselves in their mind for a while, but they've agreed to not let any visitors waste away. Ultimately, according to Fraaf'kur's memories, the humans of the planet Down have learned to work with their local grogs, and we will as well."

"You sound like you know what you're talking about."

"I do. The grogs gave me the information I needed for this specific task. I'm going to finish the year at the créche—actually looking forward to confronting the little sons of *prreti* that made my life so miserable—then I'm going back to the island with the cloned grog spawn."

"By yourself?" This was too much for Dan; his head spun from the injuries and the pain killers.

"Yes, that is the arrangement I made with them. I will learn how to make the most of my *ziirgrah* without the need for the *sthondat* stimulant, and perhaps teach the little clones a thing or two about making a Name for oneself."

This opened up a lingering wound. "Listen, Schro, about your Name—"

"Don't worry about it, father. The grogs have given me a new kzinchao Name. I am now Trainer-of-Telepaths."

"That's a good Name." Dan closed his eyes and said, "You know, I hoped I would get at least a year with my little kit, but you've matured into a fine kzintosh . . . You kzin grow up too damned fast." He wanted to drift off to sleep. The autodoc was demanding he rest, but the banging outside the gravcar persisted. "What is that noise?"

"That's the skull of the ketosaurus. After I got you on the autodoc, I went back and beheaded the beast."

Dan half-opened his eyes and looked at his son, "I thought you said you didn't need it?"

Trainer-of-Telepaths' ears twitched roguishly. "I said I was a little bit human, but not *so* human that I would abandon such a spectacular and hard-earned trophy."

Dan grabbed a handful of fur and gave him a shove. "There's hope for you yet."

🐾 🐾 🐾